Mrs.
Desperate Doings

A WWII tale of daring to save a tiger and expose a thief.

An Elaine Faber Mystery

Send, Enjoy Elaine Faber 2022

Elk Grove Publications

Mrs. Odboddy's Desperate Doings

Published by Elk Grove Publications

© 2022 by Elaine Faber

ISBN-13:978-1-940781-29-7

This novel is a work of fiction. Though based on actual WWII historical events, involvement of the novel's characters are purely fiction and the product of the author's imagination. Any resemblance to actual events, locales, organizations,or persons, living or dead, is entirely coincidental and beyond the intent of either the author or publisher.

Cover photos Shutterstock.com: *Can we talk?* © Everett Collection, ID:227271556; *cat stuck in a tree* © jimboscar, ID: 1705151317

Sumatran tiger in zoo © Jan Zwierzyna, Shutterstock ID: 2131292837
Scene break tiger tracks © Julie D. Williams

Cover layout and book formatting: JulieDeWilliams@gmail.com
Printed in the United States of America

Acknowledgments

A book doesn't get written without the help of numerous people along the way, and this book is no exception.

My husband, Leland Faber often provided Information regarding WWII technology regarding automobile, household details or weapons. I now know the inside-out workings of a Model A's starter, radiator, inner-tube tires, clutch, emergency brakes and floor gear shift. Lee is always a willing listener when I'm seeking the right word or phrase and able to provide a detailed description of a technically challenging detail.

Ongoing critique members included Dee Aspin, Erin Veliquette, Susan Wright, Ellen Cardwell, Margaret Duarte, Dee Bright, June Gillam, Michelle Hamilton, Judy Pierce, and others. Their insightful suggestions provided many improvements in the story.

Beta readers included Ruth Powers, Londa Faber, Judy Pierce, and Lois Parrish. Again, I value their corrections and suggestions.

Julie Williams again provided expert formatting, editing, and cover design for Mrs. Odboddy's Desperate Doings, as well as for all my other novels.

A heartfelt thank you to everyone who helped create another hilarious Mrs. Odboddy mystery adventure.

Glossary of Characters
in Order of Their Appearance

Agnes Agatha Odboddy – Intrepid hometown patriot and justice warrior

Godfrey Baumgarten – Former CIA agent and Agnes's main squeeze

Barnaby and Benjamin Merryweather – Courageous volunteer firemen and shoe repair experts

Katherine Odboddy – Agnes's beloved granddaughter and sidekick

Maddie – Katherine's much-loved foster child

Vincent Buckwalder – CIA agent and Katherine's current boyfriend

Ling-Ling – Siamese 'boss' of the Odboddy household

Myrtle and Mr. Higgenbottom – Agnes's best friend and her compliant husband

Charles Blackwell – Black, disabled, homeless veteran who apparently 'likes' big cats

Chief Waddlemucker – Newbury's audacious Chief of Police

Officer Dimwiddie – Newbury's 'top-cop' and Waddlemucker's plucky assistant

Doctor Schatzsman – Well-known physician with questionable integrity

Horatio Pustlebuster – All-around despicable Newbury's city council president

Col. Farthingworth – Commendable ranking officer at nearby Boyles Springs Military Base

Pastor Lickleiter – Spiritual leader at The First Church of the Evening Star and Everlasting Light

Jackson Jackson – Self-appointed helper to 'Newbury's widda' women' and city hall elevator man

Chapter One

The faint cry of feline distress filtered through the apple tree as Agnes slung her leg over a limb and reached to grip a higher branch. "Hang on, Ling-Ling. Mama's coming."

"Meow!" The cat's shrill yowl suggested displeasure that Agnes should question her agenda to reach the top of the tree.

"Agnes! Come down this instant." Godfrey, Agnes's boyfriend, put his hand over his eyes to block the sun and peered into the branches. "What in tarnation do you think you're doing?"

Agnes yanked her skirt down over her rump in an attempt to cover her chubby thigh and flannel stockings. "It doesn't take a rocket scientist to see that I'm trying to rescue Ling-Ling," she called. "She's been up here for hours and won't come down. If you'd come when I called you over an hour ago—"

"I came as soon as I could, Lambkins, after I called the fire department. They're bringing a ladder. Now, come down before you fall and break your noggin. Barnaby will get the cat. Rescuing cats is the fire department's specialty." He turned toward the sound of a siren shrieking in the distance. With almost nonexistent emergencies in the little town of Newbury, rescuing a cat was a chance for the volunteer fire department to blow the horns and drive the truck.

"Don't worry. I've almost got her." Agnes loosened her grip on the branch to reach for the Siamese cat as she climbed higher. "Just a little more. Come to mama, baby." Wasn't that just like a cat? "You rascal. I have half a mind to leave you here, and let you starve. Come here before I..." *Crack!* Agnes gasped as the branch under her foot gave way. "Saints preserve—"

Godfrey sprang toward the tree as Agnes flung out her arms and grasped at branches to break her fall. Pieces of twigs and leaves pummeled Godfrey's head. As she plummeted toward the ground, images and questions flashed through her mind. Godfrey's image intermingled with her little ward, Maddie and her granddaughter, Katherine. Would Shere Khan, the displaced carnival's tiger find a home without her help? *It's true. Your life flashes before your eyes right before you die.*

Agnes hit the ground with a thud. Her head flung back and thwacked against the apple tree. Then everything went dark.

"Mrs. Odboddy. Can you hear me?" The voice calling her name seemed to come from far away.

"*Ow.*" Her cheek smarted. Had someone slapped her? Another slap? Nearly dead, and now being attacked? What was the world coming to when an old woman couldn't fall from an apple tree and die in peace? Agnes opened her eyes as Ling-Ling leaped from branch to branch and dropped lightly beside her hip. "*Meow!*"

Agnes's head lolled back against the tree. *Now she comes down, after I risked my life to ...* Her dizziness cleared and Godfrey's face and two others faces hovered over her. *Fireman? Why?*

A soft hand touched her face and she turned toward Katherine, kneeling beside her. "Grandma. Are you all right?" Katherine looked up at the men in heavy overcoats hovering nearby. "Is she okay? Did she break anything?"

"Hard to say, ma'am." Barnaby Merryweather, the gray-headed volunteer fireman, kneeled and touched the lump on the back of Agnes's head. "She has some scratches and a sizable bump on the back of her head. Better have her doctor check her over to be sure. She took a pretty good whack. Agnes? Do you know what day it is? Who's the President?"

"*Ow!*" Agnes swatted at the fireman's hand. "Of course I know what day it is. April 26, 1944, and Franklin D. Roosevelt is the President. Now, help me into the house." Her hand dropped onto Ling-Ling's back as she nuzzled under her arm. "I see the wretched cat managed to rescue herself."

"If you'd asked my opinion before you risked your fool life, Grandma, I could have told you she'd come down when she was darned good and ready."

"I called Godfrey. When he didn't come, I thought I could get her down, myself."

"And, look how well that turned out," Katherine patted her grandmother's cheek. "You could've killed yourself."

"It takes more than a bump to kill an old bird like me." Agnes touched the lump on her head and twisted her neck from side to side. "*Ow.*"

"Give me a hand, Barnaby," Godfrey said. One could always count on Barnaby Merryweather, a volunteer fireman for the past twenty years, always the first on the scene in any emergency, whether a kitchen fire or a cat up a tree. Godfrey put his arm under Agnes's shoulder. "Can you stand, sweetkins?"

"I think so. Let's give it a try. You're right. I should have called the fire department in the first place."

Barnaby and Godfrey lifted Agnes, helped her across the yard and into the house where they lowered her onto the sofa. Barnaby's son, Benjamin, also a volunteer fireman, followed Katherine inside.

"Now I mean it, Agnes. Your doctor needs to check that bump," Barnaby said. "It looks like it's swelling up more."

"Agnes knows what's best for her, Dad. Maybe she doesn't want to see the doctor." Benjamin said. "It's not your decision, old man."

Barnaby scowled. "Thanks, Son! Where did you get your medical degree?"

"Just sayin' she knows how she feels better'n you," Benjamin snapped.

Barnaby, a long-term citizen of Newbury, opened the Merryweather Shoe Repair in 1932. He recently handed the business over to Benjamin. Word was, they argued about replacing the heel on a shoe almost as much as how to run the volunteer fire department.

Agnes rolled her eyes at the two Merryweather men. "Stop bickering. I'll contact the doctor later, if my head still hurts."

Barnaby stood and pulled the straps on his hat. "Guess we're not needed here. Next time your cat goes for a climb, Agnes, stay out of the tree!" He turned and stomped out the front door.

Benjamin followed his father to the porch. "You don't need to be rude, Dad."

"Oh dry up!" Barnaby hollered as Benjamin pulled the door closed behind him.

Agnes glanced between Katherine and Godfrey. "Why were they here in the first place? I didn't call them."

Godfrey ducked his head. "I told you before, plum blossom. We needed their ladder to rescue the cat. Then, by gum, you fell smack at my feet. I really do think we should call the doctor. You never know about a head injury."

"*Humph!* Head injury, my Aunt Fanny. It's just a little bump. Katherine? Can you fix me a cup of tea and bring me a headache powder?" Agnes stared at Katherine. Her mouth pulled into a frown. "Why on earth are you wearing that ridiculous hat?"

Katherine's hands went to her head. "Hat? I'm not wearing a hat." She glanced at Godfrey, then back to Agnes.

"My dear!" Godfrey patted Agnes's hand. "I really think you should lie down. I'll get you an ice pack for your head." He hurried toward the kitchen, paused at the door, and looked back. "I'm calling the doctor."

"Whatever for? I told you I'll be fine… Katherine, would you be a dear and bring me a headache powder? My head hurts like the dickens." Agnes swiped angrily at tears on her cheeks.

"Agnes, my sweet," Godfrey said, his cheeks as pale as cottage cheese. "You already asked… Never mind. I'll get you that cup of tea."

Katherine hovered over the doctor, wringing her hands. What on earth possessed a seventy-year-old woman to climb the darn apple tree in the first place? She should have known if a cat can climb up a tree, when it's good and ready, it can climb back down.

Dr. Willard Schatzsman dropped his stethoscope into his bag. "I'd say what we have is a classic case of a concussion, Katherine. I'd really like to put Agnes in the hospital overnight. But, since I know she'd sooner die than cooperate with medical advice, and you'll be with her all night, she can remain at home."

Ling-Ling jumped onto the sofa and snuggled next to Agnes's hip.

The doctor snapped the clasp on his medical bag. "She'll need to be awakened every two hours throughout the night. Ask her questions and make sure she's not suffering any cognitive deficit. Her hallucinating earlier worries me."

Agnes sat up from the sofa and scowled at the doctor. "What do you mean? I'm not hallucinating."

"I'll watch her like a hawk, Dr. Schatzsman," Katherine said. "I'll sit up all night if I have to."

Godfrey pulled the blanket over Agnes's legs and tucked it around her hips. "I'll stay and sleep on the couch, Katherine, if you want me to spell you during the night."

"Go home, Godfrey, and stop fussing, both of you. I'm fine." Agnes stroked Ling-Ling's back. "I'm just tired. Why don't you all leave me alone and let me rest. Ling-Ling can take care of me. She'll come and wake you if I need anything."

Dr. Schatzsman and Katherine exchanged frowns. "Well now, Agnes, I expect Katherine can take better care of you than Ling-Ling, so let's have her in charge for the time being." He stood and picked up his bag. "Call if you have any concerns, Katherine. Any concerns at all. I'll speak to you tomorrow."

Katherine walked the doctor to the door. "Thanks, Doctor. I'll keep a close eye on her." She closed it behind him. "Would you like me to make you a sandwich, Grandma?"

Agnes didn't answer. She stroked Ling-Ling's tan ear, then laid her cheek against the cat's head and began to croon a lullaby.

Katherine dashed into the kitchen. "Godfrey? Will you come in here and help me, please?" What would she do if Grandma was permanently impaired? She set the tea kettle on the stove, held a lighted match to the burner, and turned on the gas. Flames danced around the jets, sending up a red and yellow blaze. Katherine turned the knob to lower the blaze beneath the tea kettle.

Godfrey entered the kitchen, his eyebrows raised. "What do you need?"

Katherine gulped down the lump in her throat, put her finger to her lips, and whispered. "What do you think? She's obviously not herself. I'm scared. What if—"

"I've seen a few concussions in my day. Don't worry. This isn't unusual. She'll be fine, but she needs to be closely watched throughout the night."

"I can do that."

Godfrey patted Katherine's hand. "Set your clock for 2:00 A.M. and I'll get up at 4:00 A.M. That should be enough. By morning, I expect she'll be back to normal."

The tea kettle whistled. Katherine filled the tea ball with loose tea leaves and poured boiling water into a turquoise Fiesta mug. She swirled the tea ball several times, added sugar and handed the cup to Godfrey. "This is her favorite cup that came free in the Duz detergent. Take this to her while I make a peanut butter and jelly sandwich. Sugar may help."

Godfrey carried the mug into the living room. "Here you go, my pet. I've brought you a nice cup of tea. Now sit up straight and I'll put a pillow behind your back."

Katherine took bread from the bread box and peanut butter and strawberry jam from the icebox. She remembered the late summer days they boiled jars, stirred sugar into a big pot of bubbling strawberries, filled the containers with the concoction and poured hot wax on top to seal the jars. Little Maddie wrote *Strawberry Jam – 1943* on a label and attached it on the front.

Katherine stood by the sink and gazed out the kitchen window. They still needed to pick the last remaining pumpkins in the victory garden. Maddie would be so disappointed if Grandma's injury foiled their plans to bake pumpkin pies this weekend.

She glanced at the clock. "Oh my stars! Maddie!" She was supposed to pick her up at school. "Godfrey…? Will you stay with Grandma while I run and pick up—" She hurried into the living room. Grandma had nodded off. Godfrey lay slouched into the chair by the fireplace, head lolled to the side, fast asleep.

Katherine grabbed her jacket off the coat rack and yanked open the front door. "Isn't that just like a man? Fat lot of help you'll be at four o'clock in the morning."

Chapter Two

cuckoo ... cuckoo ... cuckoo ... Agnes opened her eyes. 3:00 A.M. Hadn't Katherine awakened her an hour ago, shaking her shoulder, asking ridiculous questions. 'Do you know your cat's name and who was England's prime minister?' Of course, she knew Ling-Ling's name. Everyone knew that Winston Churchill was England's Prime Minister.

The full moon lit up her room almost as bright as day. She gazed around. A teacup on the dresser. Her red flannel bathrobe flung over the bedpost. A vase of flowering weeds Maddie had picked and stuck in a glass, 'to brighten your room,' she'd said. Precious child.

It was nearly nine months since they'd brought Maddie back from Washington, D.C., a ward of the court, with Katherine now officially her foster mother. Maddie added all the joys and difficulties expected from a nine-year-old child, with perhaps a slight emphasis on *difficulties*.

Agnes sat up and pulled the coverlet closer. Her fingers traced the lump on the back of her head. Still there. Her head throbbed like the dickens. When had Katherine brought the last headache powder and a glass of water? It must have been at 2:00 A.M. Agnes glanced again at the clock beside her bed. *3:03 A.M.* Much too soon for more medicine.

Maybe a breath of fresh air would help. She tossed back the blankets and stood, then slipped into her red flannel robe and tiptoed barefoot down the hall past Katherine and Maddie's shared bedroom. No need to wake Katherine. *She'll worry if she knows I'm up.* All the fretting from Godfrey and Katherine yesterday afternoon and last evening had nearly driven her nuts. 'Put this pillow behind your back, Agnes. How do you feel, my dear? Does your head still hurt, Lamp Chop?'

'Drink this tea, Grandma. Can I get you anything, Grandma? Let me tuck you in, Grandma.' You'd think she was an invalid from all the fussing. Agnes stopped short at the entrance to the living room.

Godfrey lay on the sofa, one arm flung over his head, his foot sticking out from under the afghan. His snores were louder than the backfire from Chief Waddlemucker's 1938 Hudson.

Agnes tip-toed past the sofa, opened the front door, and crept onto the porch. She stood on the top step and sucked in a deep breath of cool night air. With the huge full moon overhead, it looked more like twilight.

A flag fluttered from the flagpole in front of the house across the street. Mrs. Williams had replaced the blue-starred flag, which represented a family member in the military, with the gold-starred flag, which represented yet another young man lost to the terrible 'tiger of war.'

Agnes stepped off the porch and walked toward her 1930 Model A, parked in the driveway. She traced her initials on the dusty fender— AAO. If she had thought to bring her keys, she could have taken a drive. It was a beautiful night and the fresh air somewhat eased the pain in her head.

Not wanting to go back into the house and risk awakening Godfrey, though the likelihood was about as real as waking a hibernating grizzly bear, she started down the sidewalk. The concrete chilled her bare feet. Perhaps she'd take a wee walk around the block.

Agnes passed Mavis's house next door. A light shined behind her front bedroom window shade. Probably a night light. Mavis didn't like sleeping in a dark bedroom any more than Maddie. Maddie had become more confident than when they first brought her home. Her grades improved and she had fewer nightmares, but she still insisted on a nightlight. It was a small concession in exchange for a full night's sleep.

Agnes turned at the corner and started down Cherry Blossom Way. She knew a lady who lived on this block. What was her name? Alice Something. She worked with Agnes's team of volunteers every other Tuesday at the hospital, rolling bandages for the troops.

Agnes trudged past the houses and scanned each one. Which house was Alice's? The blue one with the white trim, or the white one with the blue trim? She giggled, wondering if the two neighbors purposely combined their house-paint budgets and exchanged their left-over paint.

She stopped short when several houses ahead, a man emerged from the side yard, carrying a large painting. Dressed from head to toe in dark clothing, he moved stealthily toward a car parked at the curb and shoved the painting into the trunk.

Agnes ducked behind a hedge, adrenaline pumping through her chest. She drew her bathrobe closer to her neck and peered around the bush. Surely, a law-abiding citizen didn't move in the middle of the night. More likely, it was a thief liberating anything else of value while the homeowners were asleep or away on vacation.

All thoughts of Maddie, Alice, and Mrs. Williams disappeared, replaced with righteous indignation and a determination to root out conspiracies, Nazi spies, and underworld characters of ill repute. As a hometown patriot and self-appointed scourge to the underworld, it was not only her responsibility as a lawful Newbury citizen to report evil-doers, but her God-given duty to expose such shenanigans.

So, exactly what kind of skullduggery was this miscreant up to? Agnes leaned around the bush to take another peek. The man struggled toward his car with another large painting. He shoved it into the trunk with the first painting, gently lowered the lid, and moved toward the driver's side door. As he eased open the door, he turned and peered down the street directly toward the bush where Agnes was crouched. Could he see her red flannel bathrobe? Agnes jumped back, her bare foot coming down onto a stone. *"Ouch!"* Perhaps the thief heard her yelp, because he leaped into his car, started the engine, and tore down the street as though General Patton's *Hell on Wheels* battalion was on his tail. The moonlight fell across the driver's face.

"Oh my stars! Dr. Schatzsman. I'd know that face anywhere." Wasn't he one of the first people she'd seen after she fell from the tree yesterday? It's not as if anyone else in town had a grey-striped beard like that. Even wearing dark clothing, his slight frame and beard were recognizable in the moonlight from two houses away. And, she recognized his dark Ford coup. She couldn't let this happen to her neighbor. "I've got to get home and call Chief Waddlemucker." Agnes stood and hurried back around the corner toward her house. She burst through the front door and shook Godfrey's shoulder. "Wake up. Call Chief Waddlemucker. There's been a burglary."

Godfrey jerked upright, attempted to throw back his blanket, caught his foot in the hem, and tumbled off the sofa. He landed on the floor with the blanket over his head. "What? What…"

"Stop clowning around, Godfrey. I don't have time… Oh, never mind. I'll call him myself." Agnes hurried into the kitchen and flipped on the light.

Katherine emerged from the hallway, tightening the belt on her bathrobe. "What on earth is going on in here? Grandmother! What are you doing out of bed?" She glanced into the living room. "Godfrey. What's going on?"

Awakened by the noise, Maddie began to call Katherine's name. Katherine threw up her hands, turned back toward the bedroom. "I…I have to go…" She raced down the hall. "There, there, Maddie, it's all right. I'm coming…"

Agnes ducked her head into the living room. "Put your pants on, Godfrey and come in here. As long as the whole dang house is awake, you might as well set the tea kettle to boil while I call the chief." She picked the receiver off the wall phone and started to dial.

Godfrey hopped into the kitchen with one leg in his trousers, the other hairy bare leg attempting to find its way into his pants leg, caught around his ankle. He held the pants up with one hand while he plucked the telephone from Agnes's hand. "Wait a minute, Snookums. Let's talk about—"

Agnes slapped at Godfrey's hand. "Dad blast it! Give me back that phone. I need to report a burglary."

Having mollified Maddie, Katherine dashed back into the kitchen and grabbed Agnes's hand. She pointed her finger at her face. "Grandmother, sit down and don't move." She shoved her into a kitchen chair. "Godfrey, put your pants on. Then I want to know what all the shouting is about. Why you are out of your bed at..." Katherine rubbed her eyes and peered at the chicken clock over the stove... "at 3:40 A.M."

Agnes glared at Katherine's stern face. "I went outside for a breath of air. But listen. I was taking a little walk and saw Dr. Schatzsman robbing a house around the corner—"

"Oh, Grandma, for pity sake. Stop! You've been saying crazy things all day. Now, listen to yourself." Katherine's face paled. "I didn't mean that. I'm sorry. You're not yourself, Grandma. You've hurt your head and that's making you think..." She glanced at Godfrey and spread her hands. "Help me out, would you?"

Godfrey crouched by Agnes's knees and took her hand. "Sweet cheeks. You shouldn't have gone outside in the cold. You just imagined Dr. Schatzsman out there, because you saw him right after you hit your head. You're still seeing things that aren't real. Now, let Katherine put you back to bed. In the morning, you'll realize it was only a dream."

Agnes shook her head. "It wasn't a dream. I saw him put two big paintings into his trunk. When he saw me, he skittered out of there like Lucifer with a ticket punched for Hades." She crossed her arms over the bosom of her red flannel bathrobe. "I know what I saw."

The kettle whistled. Katherine poured boiling water into three mugs, set one in front of Agnes, and dropped in the tea ball. "Okay. Then, at the very least, drink this. It will help clear your head."

"My head doesn't need clearing, thank you very much. Since it appears that anything I say is construed as either a lie or nonsense, I'll take my tea and my invalid-self back to bed." With a toss of her head, Agnes stomped down the hall toward her room.

Chapter Three

"Every zoo wants to get rid of their tigers, not take another one." Mildred

Agnes pulled the covers over her head when Katherine opened her bedroom door. "Are you ever getting up today? It's 9:45."

"Leave me alone," Agnes mumbled under the blanket.

"I know you're mad, Grandma, because you think we disrespected you last night. We were only trying to do what was best for you. Who loves you more than me and Godfrey? Anyway, Mildred's here. She heard about your fall. She even brought you some daisies."

What a relief. For the past hour, Agnes listened wistfully to the chatter coming from the kitchen, but was too stubborn to give up her snit. Katherine, Godfrey and Maddie were yucking it up, while the smell of waffles, maple syrup, and freshly ground coffee nearly drove her to distraction.

She pulled the covers over her head each time Katherine asked her to join them. Would she swallow her pride and join the family? Not on your tintype. She'd rather starve than apologize for her tantrum. So she'd stayed in bed, hungry, desperately wanting a bath, pouting, and feeling terribly sorry for herself.

Thank goodness, Mildred came. It gave her an opportunity to join the family without losing face or needing to apologize. Stubbornness prevented her from following her own best advice. 'Get mad—get over it.' Why rehash who was right? Forget the 'I said, and then you said.' In a household with two strong-willed women, there were bound to be disagreements and tiffs. Where Katherine got such a bull-headed attitude was anybody's guess.

Agnes tossed back the covers. "Tell Mildred to have a cup of coffee. I'll be right out." She moved across the room, surprised that her back and neck were still stiff and tender, even though the pain in her head was less.

Agnes pulled a pair of bloomers and a brassiere from her dresser drawer. She'd have to wait until later for a bath. She attached her brassiere and wiggled into her All-In-One corset, a snug rubberized affair that smoothed out the bulges around her middle. Straps on the bottom clipped onto the tops of her stockings—her best ones with only two *patriotic holes.* All patriotic housewives willingly wore stockings with holes so silk could be used to make parachutes.

Younger ladies often drew lines up the back of their bare legs to look like stocking seams. A respectable gentleman would never look closely enough at her legs to determine whether she was or wasn't wearing stockings.

Agnes dropped an old nylon slip over her head, and stepped into a housedress, then hurried to the bathroom, washed her face, and brushed her teeth. Pulling her hair into a bun, Agnes attached the two silver chopsticks she always wore, in remembrance of her late husband, Douglas.

In 1918, already middle-aged, Douglas accepted a noncombatant position and was sent to England to teach coding. He died during an air raid, never knowing that Agnes had an affair with Godfrey while Douglas was overseas. Overcome with shame for her wretched behavior, Agnes vowed to never see Godfrey again, and to wear the silver chopsticks every day as a penance. Twenty-four years later, she relented, and Godfrey once again entered her life last year.

Godfrey jumped up and pulled out a chair when Agnes entered the kitchen. "My queen. Won't you join us?"

Agnes nodded and sat. "Morning, Mildred."

Katherine poured coffee into a mug and set it on the table. "Coffee, Grandma? Would you like a waffle? We have apple butter and syrup."

"Yes, please." Agnes sipped her coffee. *Ah!* Ambrosia from Heaven! She was as patriotic as the next person, and graciously accepted rationing for the sake of the troops, but it not only required a ration ticket, but was restricted to one pound every six weeks per adult. It was almost more than she could bear. "What brings you here this morning, Mildred? I assume you heard I have no ill effect from my fall. So, I must assume you have news about our letter writing campaign on behalf of the tiger."

"I did want to be sure you were OK. As for the tiger, the ladies at The First Church of the Evening Star and Everlasting Light have been working hard, Agnes. To date, we've sent thirty-two letters to zoos all across the United States, and so far the only results are either negative or a request for us to let them know if we find a place for Shere Khan, to see if there's room for one of their own. Seems every zoo in the country wants to get rid of their big cats, not take on another one. Trying to find a reasonable home for that displaced carnival tiger has become more of a trial that you let on several months ago. I fear the ladies are tiring of the project."

Katherine set a waffle in front of Agnes. "Maddie? Hand Grandma the maple syrup."

"You can't really blame the zoos, ladies," Godfrey said. "Rationing has restricted their ability to provide meat for the big cats. I've heard they're either sending them away or disposing…"

Maddie put her hand to her mouth. "Oh!"

Godfrey must have realized how distressing it was for Maddie to hear such news. He glanced between Agnes and Katherine. His face flushed, as he fumbled with his napkin. "I mean…*er.* Is there another waffle, Katherine?"

"Maddie, if you're finished eating, take Ling-Ling to your room and read her a book. We need to have a grown-up talk," Agnes said.

"Okay, Grandma." Maddie stood and set her breakfast dishes in the sink. She carried Ling-Ling down the hall. "I'll read to you from my jungle book."

When Maddie's bedroom door clicked shut, Agnes glowered at Godfrey. "Thanks a lot, knucklehead. While you were at it, why didn't you share that the tigers were being euthanized and get it over with." Her glare would have melted the nose off a snowman.

"Gee-willikers, babe, it just popped out. I'm sorry. I didn't think—"

"Exactly the problem, Godfrey. You didn't think." Agnes turned to Mildred. "So, are there any zoos we haven't contacted yet?"

"All the letters have been sent, but eight still haven't responded," Mildred said.

Agnes tossed her napkin onto the table. "I don't know what to do. "How long will your brother let us keep the tiger's caravan at his farm if I run out of money to feed him?"

"The tiger's caravan isn't hurting anything," Mildred said. "My brother won't turn him away. Especially since the young man from the carnival stayed on to take care of Shere Khan. Wendell's helping out around the farm in exchange for room and board."

"How come that kid isn't in the military? He looks fit enough to me," Godfrey said.

"He has a hearing loss that kept him from active duty. I hear that he's a volunteer with the militia here in town." Katherine topped off Agnes's coffee. "He's classified 4F."

"*Humph!* More likely he suffers from swimmer's ear. But, at least he's able to clean the cage and feed the tiger. Unfortunately, my funds are getting low," Agnes said. "When the money runs out, how will I pay for the tiger's meat? We have to find a permanent home and soon. Maybe I should send another letter to the State Capitol and see if they've given me a complete list of every zoo around the country." Tears sparkled in Agnes's eyes. "If we can't find him a home in time, he'll have to be destroyed. I can't accept that. Not to mention what it would do to Maddie."

Most people would never have considered such a project. Leave it to Agnes to accept the nearly insurmountable task of locating a temporary home, convincing a young man to take care of the tiger without pay, taking on the financial burden of feeding him and then tracking down a zoo willing to take him in.

"It's a credit to the ladies of The First Church of the Evening Star and Everlasting Light's Social Society to agree to write the letters in the first place. I feel like I've let them down if our efforts come to naught. I can't bring myself to even think about…" Agnes shook her head. "I was so sure we could do this. Maybe I was too hasty."

"Don't think like that, Grandma. Any day now, we'll find a zoo willing to take Shere Khan. We have to keep looking. Maybe a little praying for a good outcome wouldn't hurt."

Mildred nodded. "That's true. I'll check with the ladies again and make sure that everyone has written to the zoos on their list. Maybe we should send a second letter to the zoos that haven't replied." She snapped her fingers. "With the war on, maybe the letters went astray. Anyway, putting all this aside, exactly what happened last night, Agnes? Godfrey tells me that you were having hallucinations. He said you thought you saw old Dr. Schatzsman robbing a house down the street. Really, Agnes, you must know that concussions can make you think all sorts of crazy things. I hope by this morning you realize—"

Agnes pushed back her chair, stood, and put her hand to her forehead. "You know what? My headache is back. Thank you for your concern, Mildred, but if you don't mind, I really must excuse myself and get some rest." She felt three pairs of eyes peering at her back as she turned and trudged down the hall.

Chapter Four

"I'm suspected of being a homicidal maniac, armed with scissors." Agnes

Agnes paced her bedroom, the problems she faced with Shere Khan weighed heavily on her mind. No matter how much she might regret her commitment to save the tiger, she made promises she felt unwilling to break, and yet unable to keep. She paced the other direction. Surely, by contacting every zoo in the country, a safe place could be found for the tiger.

Agnes fanned her face. It was so stuffy in her small bedroom. She went to the door and peeked out. Mildred and Godfrey must be gone by now. She tiptoed down the hall and into the living room where Katherine sat, reading a magazine. "Hi, Grandma. I'm reading the most interesting story in the Saturday Evening Post. It's called *I Escaped from the Island of Terror*. It's about a guy—"

"Sounds great. Save it for me. I'm going for a little walk. The fresh air might help my headache."

"Another... *Um*... Do you want me to go with you? I wouldn't want you—"

"No need. I'm fine. I've got some decisions to make. I won't be gone long." Agnes opened the front door and stepped out. At least this time, she was wearing shoes.

What should she do about Dr. Schatzsman? Should she call Chief Waddlemuker and report what she saw, or was Katherine right, that her concussion had made her imagine it? One way or another, she needed proof. She certainly couldn't ruin the doctor's reputation by falsely accusing him of larceny. She had plenty of experience with that, having recently been accused and exonerated of a crime she didn't commit. Come to think about it, Alice what's-her-name, lived on Cherry Blossom Way, almost next door to the house she'd seen burgled. Maybe Alice knew something about a recent burglary. What she needed was an excuse to visit Alice and ask questions without directly involving the doctor.

Agnes walked past the yellow rose bushes that separated her yard from her next door neighbor. She bent a rose stem, attempting to pluck it from the bush. *"Ow!"* What she needed was a pair of scissors. She sucked her pricked finger as she returned to the house and opened the front door.

Katherine lowered her magazine. "Did you forget something?"

Agnes grabbed a pair of scissors from her sewing basket and called over her shoulder as she hurried out the door. "I'm cutting some roses for my friend around the corner."

With a bouquet of roses in one hand and the scissors in the other, she tromped down the street to Cherry Blossom Way, eyeing the houses on each side of the street. Now, which of the two blue and white houses was Alice's? She turned at the sound of squeaking brakes. A Newbury police car pulled to the curb behind her.

Chief Waddlemucker stepped out of his 1938 Hudson and eased the door shut. "Morning, Agnes." He took a step toward her, his hand resting on his holster. "Mind telling me your intentions for those scissors?"

Agnes glanced down at the scissors. "Is there a new law against walking while carrying scissors?"

The chief shrugged. "I just spoke to Godfrey at the gas station. He says you fell and suffered a concussion and that you were acting a little wonky. Now, here you are marching down the street with a pair of scissors. You can see why I might be concerned."

What exactly was he implying? That she was Looney Tunes, on her way to commit murder? Wait till she got her hands on Godfrey.

"If you must know, I was taking some flowers to my friend. Do you have a problem with that? She lives right down the street in that blue house…or maybe it's the white house…one of them." She nodded toward the two houses. "So, if you don't mind, I'll be on my way."

How embarrassing. Perspiration trickled between the mounds of her bosom. She tossed her head and marched up the sidewalk to the blue house, next door to the one that was burgled. She stepped onto the porch, rang the bell, and glanced over her shoulder. *Please, please be Alice's house.*

The chief returned to his car and pulled it to the end of the driveway where he sat behind the wheel, staring at her. She and the chief never could see eye to eye, but nothing like this had ever come between them. Suspected to be a homicidal maniac armed with scissors, in broad daylight, no less.

After waiting several minutes, and no answer at the door, Agnes laid the roses on the doormat and stepped off the porch. She flounced past the chief's car with her nose in the air, and headed for home. She would have to wait until the following Tuesday to question Alice at the hospital where they rolled bandages for the troops. How was she supposed to prove Dr. Schatzsman's guilt or innocence if she was thwarted at every turn?

Agnes retraced her steps along Cherry Blossom Way while Chief Waddlemucker's car inched down the street, about half a block behind her. By the time she reached her driveway, the back of her dress was dark with perspiration, more likely from frustration and embarrassment than from the effort of walking two blocks.

She stopped short when Godfrey's car stopped in front of her mailbox. Wouldn't she give him 'what for'? Blabbing to the chief like that. She hoped Godfrey hadn't mentioned her witnessing the doctor removing paintings from the house around the corner.

"Angel face! How are you feeling this morning?" Godfrey hurried up the sidewalk holding up a candy bar. "Sweets for my sweet!"

Agnes laid the scissors on the porch rail and snatched the candy bar. "Thanks for nothing. I've never been so embarrassed in my life."

"What's wrong? Why would a candy bar embarrass you? I thought you liked Mars bars." Godfrey pulled on the collar of his plaid shirt and unbuttoned the top button, revealing short grey hairs on his chest. His eyebrows pulled together. "I thought you liked chocolate."

Agnes brushed past him and stepped onto the porch. "Of course, I like chocolate. What I don't like is to be grilled on a public street by the Chief of Police for no reason whatsoever. What did you tell him?"

"Chief Waddlemucker? *Er … ah …* I may have said you fell out of an apple tree and had a concussion."

"What else?" Agnes tapped her foot on the top porch step.

"Maybe I said you were hallucinating and talking to the cat?" Godfrey's face flushed.

"Apparently you gave him the impression I was off my rocker…" She glanced down at the scissors on the porch rail. Her cheeks warmed. It really wasn't so far-fetched that the chief would be concerned, seeing her striding down the street with roses in one hand and scissors in the other, especially after being told she was hallucinating. "Oh, phooey!" Now she'd have to apologize for her rudeness. She wondered if the Odboddy method—*get mad—get over it*—would work in this instance. "Well, what's done is done. Come on in the house. We have some coffee left from breakfast. I'll fix you a cup."

"That would be love…" As Godfrey stepped onto the porch, the toe of his shoe caught on the top step. He threw out his hands to catch his balance as he pitched forward.

"Good gravy!" Agnes reached back to steady him, but her hand whacked into his arm and threw him even more off center. Godfrey tumbled onto his hip, his left foot under him. *"Ow!"* His right foot hit a flower pot, sending it crashing against the porch pillar.

The front door opened and Katherine poked her head out. "What's going on out here?" Her hand flew to her mouth and her eyes widened at the sight of Godfrey sprawled on the porch floor. "Godfrey? Are you okay?"

"He tripped and fell," Agnes said, kneeling to take Godfrey's arm. "It's my fault." She and Katherine helped him sit up and brushed dust from his shirt. "Are you hurt? Can you get up?"

Godfrey shrugged. He unwound his leg from under him and turned his foot to the side. *"Ow!* I think it's sprained." He tried to stand. "Nope! Can't do it. I'm going to need help."

Katherine and Agnes helped him to a standing position. He hopped into the house on his good leg and tumbled onto the sofa. Katherine lifted his foot onto the coffee table and slid a pillow under it. "There. Keep your foot elevated. You're going to need an ice pack."

"He was distracted because I was yelling at him. I'm so sorry, Godfrey."

Godfrey leaned back onto the sofa pillows. "Now, Agnes, that's not so. I wasn't paying attention. Like when you fell out of the tree. Sometimes bad stuff just happens. That's why they're called accidents."

Katherine eyed the swelling and purplish tinge around Godfrey's ankle. "I'll call Dr. Schatzsman. Your ankle could be broken."

"I'll make an ice pack. That should keep the swelling down." Agnes followed Katherine into the kitchen, opened the icebox and used an ice pick to chip at the block of ice until she had a few pieces wrapped in a tea towel. It seemed inevitable that she could always turn the simplest situation into a disaster with the worst possible outcome. Poor Godfrey. When would she learn to hold her tongue?

Chapter Five

D r. Schatzsman dropped the roll of adhesive tape into his black bag and snapped the lid. "This ace wrap should help keep the swelling down. Keep your foot elevated as much as possible for the next few days. I've got a pair of crutches in the car you can borrow."

Agnes fluffed the pillow under Godfrey's foot. Now was her chance to ask a few pointed questions. Could she catch the doctor off guard? "You do have time for a quick cup of coffee, don't you, Dr. Schatzsman? I'm sure you must be exhausted after being at the hospital all night seeing patients." An innocent smile flickered across her face.

The doctor looked up. "Coffee? I suppose I have a minute. But, I wasn't up all night. Why would you think that?"

"Oh, I just assumed so. You look so tired this morning. So, you were home all evening? You weren't visiting patients down the street in the middle of the night?"

The doctor raised his eyebrow. "No, actually I was...*um*...at a city council meeting and got home about 10:00 P.M., then straight to bed. What strange notions you have." The doctor's ears appeared to tinge a shade of pink.

"Grandma!" From Katherine's stern expression, she knew why Agnes asked such a question. "Why don't you go and get that coffee for the doctor? Now!"

Aha! He was guilty. No doubt about it! His evasive answers proved he was at the house around the corner last night, but it wasn't enough to convince Chief Waddlemucker. She'd still need proof. Agnes brought in the coffee mug and set it on the coffee table. "Here you go."

"So, Agnes," the doctor's face was a mask of controlled emotions. "How's your headache? Did you get some sleep last night? I hope you didn't toss and turn or have bad dreams. Sometimes a concussion can do that. Nightmares, even. Makes you think you see things that aren't real." His eyes narrowed as he peered at her over the edge of his cup.

Hairs rose on the back of Agnes's neck. Perhaps he recognized her last night, after all. How could she dispel his suspicions? "Oh, I feel ever so much better today." She flashed him a radiant smile. "Really, I do! Slept like a baby all night and just the slightest headache this morning. *Sorry, Lord. It was only a little white lie, and it was necessary.* She glanced at Godfrey and then at Katherine. Hopefully they wouldn't mention her 3:00 A.M. jaunt, or that she had accused the doctor of thievery, now sitting three feet from her knees. "Katherine? Perhaps Dr. Schatzsman wants milk or sugar in his coffee. Would you mind fetching that?" Maybe a quick subject change would disarm the situation.

Katherine jumped up. "I'll get right on that." She hastened into the kitchen, as if eager to escape the cat and mouse game Agnes was playing in the living room.

The doctor set his cup on the coffee table. His taut lips suggested he wasn't buying the load of donkey donuts she was unloading. It was his move. "Now Agnes, I'm very worried about you. A concussion is nothing to take lightly." He leaned forward and unsnapped the clasp on his black bag. "I want you to take these pills." He opened a bottle and poured out a handful onto the coffee table. "Here are some free samples. Take one in the morning and one at bedtime. They could prevent serious consequences that can follow a concussion."

Agnes blinked rapidly as she stared at the pills he laid on the table. "What kind of consequences?"

Dr. Schatzsman smiled. "I'm referring to medical conditions with big names you wouldn't understand. As your doctor," he peered over the top of his glasses, "you'll have to trust me. We wouldn't want any life-threatening consequences, now would we?"

Her fingers tingled as she touched the bump on the back of her head. She took a hankie from her bosom and dabbed her forehead. "I'll go and find something to put these in," she said, as she scooped the pills off the table.

The doctor stood and took his coat from the coat rack. "If you'll come out to the car, Katherine, I'll get those crutches for Godfrey." He turned back. "You'll need to stay off that foot. If your ankle isn't better by next week, we'll do an x-ray. Have Katherine drive you home.

"Good day, Agnes. So glad you're feeling better after your fall. If you heed my warnings and don't do anything stupid, there's a good chance of full recovery. Otherwise…well…" He opened the door and Katherine followed him onto the front porch.

A chill careened up Agnes's spine. What did he mean by 'doing something stupid'? It sounded like a thinly veiled warning not to talk about last night. Was his concern genuine, and the pills meant to prevent a serious medical condition? She had to believe the latter, since he'd signed a *hypocritical oath*, after all. He wouldn't purposely give her anything harmful. Right?

Chapter Six

"Lord, You won't be surprised to hear that I'm in another jam." Agnes

gnes hurried to the ringing phone. Was it Katherine? She was supposed to be lunching with Vincent. Since Dr. Don Dew-Right broke their engagement last year, and Vincent, the young man they met in Washington, was doing his best to capture Katherine's heart, who knew what kind of issues she might have? Or maybe it was Godfrey. How was he managing crutches on the stairs to his apartment over the Newbury Theater? Agnes grabbed the receiver off the kitchen wall phone. "Hello? Godfrey? What's wrong?"

"Mrs. Odboddy? It's Wendell Peaberry. I'm calling from the Higgenbottom farm. Mr. Higgenbottom said I should call and tell you that I ... *um ... er ...* What I mean to say is—"

"Mr. Higgenbottom? Mildred's brother? What's this about? Who are you again?"

"You know. I'm Wendell. I worked for the carnival that used to have the tiger. I've been taking care of Shere Khan out at the Higgenbottom farm. Mr. Higgenbottom said I should call and let you know that—"

Agnes's heart lurched. Was Shere Khan sick? Didn't she have enough problems keeping the animal fed, much less a veterinary bill, should he become ill? *Oh, Lord, what now?* She held her breath. "Is Shere Khan all right?"

"Oh! He's fit as a fiddle. Couldn't be happier. I'm really sorry about the short notice, but here's the deal. I was offered a job in Sacramento. I've been working for room and board here on the farm. I can't afford to turn down a paying job. You'll have to get somebody else to come and take care of Shere Khan. Mr. Higgenbottom, he said you could spit tobacco through a knothole before he would go into that cage hisself, so, he said I'd better tell you to come and fetch that critter off the farm or he'd haul the beast right back and drop him in your front yard."

Agnes's heart felt like a strawberry shaped pincushion full of pins. "You can't be serious." She could just imagine the neighbors' reaction when Higgenbottom's tractor pulled the tiger's caravan-trailer around the corner and parked it in her driveway. Not to mention the need to scoop up piles of tiger 'doo-doo' the size of cow pies, all while he gnawed on a ham bone in the corner. She shuddered at the thought. "What am I supposed to do now, Wendell? How can you desert me like this? Can't you stay until I find a replacement? I need more time…"

"I'm really sorry, Mrs. Odboddy. I know it's mean to leave you in the lurch like this, but what about me? I have to be in Sacramento next week or I'll lose the job. I'd stay if I could… But, you gotta understand."

"I do understand, Wendell. Next week, you say?" The knot on the back of her head throbbed.

"*Yeah*. I gotta catch the bus to Sacramento at 10:00 A.M. next Thursday morning. I'll stay until then."

It was clear that he didn't want to leave Shere Khan any more than Agnes wanted him to go, but how could she expect him to turn down a paying job? Wendell's departure added another dimension to the problems she already faced with her commitment to save the tiger.

"Thanks for calling, Wendell. Tell Mr. Higgenbottom not to worry. I'll think of something. Goodbye." Tears pricked her eyes as she hung up the phone. Agnes put her hand to her throbbing forehead. How could this happen? Wasn't it bad enough that she was running out of money for the tiger's food and hadn't found him a permanent home? Now, he had no caregiver. She couldn't afford to hire someone, even if there was an able-bodied man in the county willing to clean the tiger's cage and feed him. The dreaded option of destroying Shere Khan seemed to be back on the table, as the city council recommended. That rapscallion, Horatio Pustlebuster, the city council president, had pushed that agenda ever since the tiger was left homeless several months ago. Only through the intervention of multiple ladies from The First Church of the Evening Star and Everlasting Light, and Mr. Higgenbottom's offer to allow them to park the tiger's caravan at his farm, had the city council's measure been temporarily dropped. But, sure as kittens in spring, if there was an issue with a caregiver, Pustlebuster would use the advantage to bring it up again.

She wrung cold water from a tea towel and pressed it against her head, remembering the day at the county fair when she first observed the almost spiritual connection between Shere Khan and Maddie.

'Shere Khan remembers me from when we were together in Heaven,' Maddie had said. 'He only wants me to pet him, not the other children.' Whether they ever *played together* in Heaven before their time on earth, as Maddie insisted, was a concept Agnes didn't understand. The Bible said, *The lion shall lay down with the lamb, and a little child shall lead them.* Lions and lambs? Why not a tiger? She didn't dispute Maddie's explanation, but it made it harder to imagine destroying the tiger if she couldn't keep him at the Higgenbottom farm.

Her headache eased somewhat, Agnes tossed the wet towel onto the washing machine on the closed-in back porch. Was it time to ask the Almighty for another intervention? Hadn't she gotten into enough trouble with Him in the past, making promises she couldn't keep? She went to her bedroom and pondered her spiritual indebtedness over the last few months. Were there any bargaining chips she had not yet expended? Promising to attend church every Sunday, come rain or shine for three months had gone well. She'd only missed a few Sundays under the most difficult circumstances. Feeling on pretty good terms to ask for another intercession, she knelt by the side of the bed, folded her hands, and bowed her head.

"Lord, it's me, Agnes Agatha Odboddy. Yes, I know you must be pretty disappointed with me most days, but I do my best, Lord, really I do. You won't be surprised to hear that I'm in another jam. It's not about me this time, Lord, it's for Shere Khan. Surely, You approve of my efforts to save him, because it's a worthwhile mission. I know you're busy with the war and all, so I'll get straight to the point. I need a caregiver for the tiger right away, and I need a permanent home for—"

Bing ... Bong ... The doorbell? Agnes's head came up as she turned toward the bedroom door. She bowed her head again. "Someone's at the door, Lord, so I need to go, but I'll be back as soon as I can. I'd appreciate it, Lord, if You could ponder on a solution while I'm gone. *Uh ...* Amen!"

Agnes hurried to the front door and flung it open. She put her fist to her mouth. "Oh, my stars. You! I can't believe it. What are you doing here?" She grabbed the visitor's arm, pulled him into the living room and thrust him onto the sofa. "Did you come on your own or did God send you?"

Her visitor raised his eyebrows and shrugged. "Well, I ... I guess it was my idea."

Now, in the past, due to her inability to keep her mouth shut and her nose out of things that were none of her business, Agnes often found herself in a pickle. As a result, she would get on her knees and bargain with the Lord for deliverance. More often than not, thanks to the benevolence of the Almighty, her conundrum would reach a satisfactory solution. But, never in her history of misadventures had He answered her prayer *before* she even got to the 'Amen,' proving that He'd seen the problem coming and was already several steps ahead in solving it.

There on her sofa sat Charles, the young man from Albuquerque she met last summer, who risked his life and freedom to help her. Thanks to Charles, when she was unexpectedly waylaid, he provided an unconventional method of travel to Little Rock, where she was able to reconnect with Katherine and complete her journey to Washington, D.C., to visit the president.

Now, some months later, imagine her surprise to find Charles at her door. Surely, God sent him to Newbury to help save the tiger.

"Charles Blackwell, as I live and breathe, if you're not the last person on earth I expected to see today, and a most welcome sight for sore eyes. What are you doing here?"

Charles's toothy grin beamed in his black face as he settled back onto the sofa. "Guess I got tired of traveling, and I said to myself, Charles, you've never seen the Pacific Ocean. Didn't Mrs. Odboddy invite you to visit? So I hopped the next freight train headed west, worked my way across the country, and here I am." A wrinkle creased his forehead. "It's okay that I came, isn't it? I won't be a burden. I didn't expect you to support me. I mean to get a job as soon as I can."

"Don't be silly. You're as welcome as the day is long. I owe you much more than a place to hang your hat and a few meals. In fact…" She tapped her finger on her upper lip. If God sent him, surely he would be willing… "Charles, how do you feel about farm work?" Her brain whirled a mile a minute. She could see it all coming together. A smile twitched her lips.

"Like hoeing and weeding and such? Or driving a tractor? As it happens, I've done that quite often. In fact, I've—"

"And, how do you feel about working with animals, like chickens and cows, maybe a few pigs or horses… or other animals?"

"Oh, I love animals. Do you have something in mind?" His smile brightened. "On a farm? Why that would be just—"

"Exactly. As it happens, a friend of mine needs a ranch hand. *Um*…how about cats? You okay with cats? Really big cats?" Ling-Ling chose that moment to wander into the living room, her tail at half-mast. She jumped onto the sofa and sniffed Charles's arm. Apparently satisfied that he was not a door-to-door evangelist or an ax-murderer, she crawled into his lap, circled and lay down. In complete capitulation and demonstration of acceptance, her chest began to warble and she proceeded to wash her left shoulder.

Charles's raised eyebrow lowered as he stroked Ling-Ling's head. "Oh, I'm fine with big cats. Siamese, right? She's a fine big cat. What's her name?"

"*Umm*... Ling-Ling. She's our official greeter. Looks like you've received the Odboddy seal of approval. Katherine and Maddie will be back soon. We're having chicken pot pie tonight for supper. Of course, you'll stay and eat with us. If you'd like, we can bed you down here on the sofa. I'll take you out to the farm tomorrow and you can meet Mr. Higgenbottom and the ti—...*er*...*uh*... the en*tire* family." How *does* one move the conversation from 'working as a farm hand and liking big cats,' to the caregiver for a tiger? Slowly... slowly. Don't rush him.

"Sounds good."

Why was she so nervous? Why else would the good Lord send Charles to her doorstep at that exact moment if he wasn't meant to accept the job of caring for the tiger? "Now, Charles. Here's the deal about the job. There is no pay except room and board and the satisfaction that you're helping with a delicate situation of the most importance."

Up went Charles's eyebrows again. "What exactly do you mean by a *delicate situation*? It's not something illegal, is it? I mean, I'm a disabled veteran and as patriotic as the next guy, but I don't relish the idea of going to prison."

"Illegal? Of course not! But, you agreed that you like really big cats... Let's just say... How do you feel about...*um*...tigers?" Her stomach roiled like a pit full of alligators.

"Tigers? I suppose I can take them or leave them. I've never seen one up close." Charles stared long and hard at Agnes. A muscle twitched along his jaw. His dark eyes snapped. "Precisely, what does my liking tigers have to do with a farm job, Mrs. Odboddy? What on earth are you roping me into?"

Agnes gazed around the living room, not meeting Charles's eyes. She had to tread softly. She didn't want to scare him off now, just as she rounded the corner toward success. She opened her mouth to speak when the front door flung open and Katherine followed Maddie inside.

"We're home. Oh. We have company." Katherine hung her jacket on the coat rack and turned. "Why, I remember you. You're the man who helped Grandma on the train last summer, aren't you? Was it…Charles?"

Charles stood and shook her hand. "That's right. I'm taking you up on your invitation to visit. Agnes was telling me where I might find a job on a farm."

"The Higgenbottom farm?" Katherine turned a skeptical face toward Agnes.

Maddie stepped forward. "That's where Shere Khan lives and—"

"Maddie!" Agnes grasped the child's arm. "Go into the kitchen and get a glass of milk. There are some cookies in the cookie jar." She gave her a gentle push toward the kitchen and turned. "Well, now, Charles, if you'll excuse me, I have a few things I need to tend to. Katherine will bring you a cup of tea." She touched Katherine's shoulder and propelled her toward the kitchen.

"Sounds good. If you don't mind, I might just lie back and close my eyes for a while," Charles said, as the women disappeared into the next room.

While Charles rested, Agnes relayed the news about Wendell's new job and her plan to recruit Charles to take his place as Shere Khan's caregiver. "I haven't exactly told him about the tiger yet, but I'm convinced his being here is a God-thing, so I'm not too worried."

"Are you sure? What if he says 'no'?"

"Why else would he be here within minutes of Wendell's leaving and my asking the Almighty for guidance? Now, all we have to do is keep Maddie quiet until I've sprung it…I mean, convinced him that it's a good idea."

Chapter Seven

After an eloquent speech regarding Shere Khan's virtues, not to mention the privilege of caring for such a noble beast, Agnes finally wore down Charles's defenses. He agreed to go to the Higgenbottom farm, meet Shere Khan, and see what was involved in the care and feeding of a full-grown tiger. He promised to keep an open mind before he decided whether to stay or hop the next freight train out of town.

Sparrows nose-dived overhead, and when Mr. Higgenbottom and Godfrey went to the barn to check out his new tractor, Maddie led Charles firmly by the hand past the Odboddy chickens cackling and scratching beside the barn. She chattered a mile a minute, explaining how Grandma's chickens once lived at her house before coming to the farm, and how each of them was given one of Agnes's lady-friends' names before the hens were found to be roosters. She calmed Charles's concerns regarding taking care of the tiger. "You'll see, Charles," Maddie said. "You'll love him every bit as much as I do, once you get to know him. Why he's so gentle, he wouldn't hurt a fly. He can do tricks, too. Do you want to see him sit on top of a ball? Wendell can make him stand on his back legs and beg. He's a trick-tiger, you see, not like the wild tigers you see in the movies. I'll come every so often and help you take care of him, if you want."

Charles nodded and smiled at Maddie's negotiations. His smile faded when he gazed through the bars at the huge tiger. Shere Khan lay on his side, his gaze fixed on Agnes and Katherine as they approached the cage. His head jerked back when Maddie's voice broke into his reverie. "Shere Khan. It's Maddie. We've come to visit and brought our friend, Charles. Now you be a good boy and say hello." The tiger rose and ambled toward the bars. He shook his head and yawned, showing rows of sharp teeth. An earthy, animal scent rose from the straw covering the floor of his cage. He lay back down and licked his shoulder, reminiscent of Ling-Ling's sign of acceptance. Obviously shaken by the size and appearance of the animal, Charles pulled his hand free of Maddie's and stepped back. What must have been going through his mind? *Me? Get into the cage with that beast? What kind of idiot do they think I am?*

Wendell came from the barn and extended his hand. "I'm Wendell. Nice to meet you. I hear you're considering taking my job." He peered into Charles's face. "You're not scared, are you?"

Charles shook his hand. "Charles Blackwell. I'm not exactly scared. I've never been so close to a tiger before. He's bigger than I thought."

"Well, he's big, for sure, but he's just like a big house cat. Here, let me take him out of the caravan and you'll see for yourself." Wendell pulled a key from his pocket, unlocked the padlocked door, and stepped inside. He snapped a leash onto the tiger's collar. "*Hup*" Shere Khan stood and sauntered out the door behind Wendell, down the steps, and onto the grass. "Meet the folks, Shere Khan. This is Charles." The tiger sniffed Charles's hand, moved toward Maddie, and rubbed his head against her leg. From his greeting, he appeared to remember her from their last visit.

"Be careful, Maddie," Agnes said. "Don't let him get too close."

"It's okay, Grandma," Maddie said, stroking the tiger's head. "See? He loves me. Don't be afraid, Charles. You can pet him."

Shere Khan turned again toward Charles. His eyes locked on the young man's face. It appeared as though he was giving him good measure, but reserving judgment until he knew him better.

Agnes stepped forward and took Maddie's hand "Come now, Maddie. Let's give Shere Khan and Charles some time together. You'll be a distraction if you stay. We'll go over here and watch from that bench while Charles and Shere Khan get acquainted."

"Now, you be good, Shere Khan. I'm watching you," Maddie said.

Wendell attached Shere Khan's leash to a chain attached to a pole in the yard that allowed the tiger to walk around in the grass and stretch his legs but kept him securely attached to the pole. "There you go, old fellow. Have a good roll in the grass."

Wendell proceeded to outline the tiger's routine. He explained in detail the care and feeding of the animal as he raked straw from his caravan and forked it into a wheelbarrow. He described the importance of cleanliness to prevent disease and showed Charles how to wash the water bowls and remove any old bones that could attract insects. Charles hosed down the caravan's interior and replenished it with fresh straw. They wheelbarrowed the soiled straw into the fields and spread it around some of the crops. From the condition of the crops, tiger poo was well-favored by the vegetables.

As the men worked and chatted, Shere Khan crouched in the grass and eyed the chickens scratching in the dirt dangerously close, but barely out of reach of his chain. From time to time he would jump toward one of the hens, but the attack was more of a ruse than in earnest. A little hen danced toward Shere Khan and then fluffed her feathers and scuttled back toward the barn when he appeared to show too much interest in her.

"Did you see that?" Wendell said, pointing to the hen scuttling away. "As gentle as he is, never forget that a stalk and kill instinct still lingers inside his well-fed soul. That's the key. Keep him well-fed, but always use extreme caution while he's eating. Always feed him inside the cage and keep the door locked when he's eating. He's tame as a kitten, remember, but, he's still a wild animal."

Agnes chuckled at Charles's reaction, his eyes wide. Hopefully, Wendell's cautions wouldn't scare him off from accepting the job.

Once they completed cleaning the cage, Wendell left Charles alone with Shere Khan and returned to the barn.

The plan was for Charles to remain at the farm and work with Wendell over the next week. Each day, Wendell would leave Charles with Shere Khan for longer periods of time. By the end of the week when it was time for him to take the bus to Sacramento, hopefully, Shere Khan would accept Charles as his keeper. The last thing they wanted was a depressed or angry tiger missing Wendell and left to deal with an inexperienced caregiver.

Across the yard, Katherine and Mrs. Higgenbottom hung laundry on the clothesline, somewhat hampered by her little dog yapping and hopping around their feet.

The chickens clucked and scratched in the dirt beside the barn. From time to time, two of the roosters would fluff their wings and attempt a show of dominance.

From the bench where Maddie and Agnes sat talking and watching, Agnes pointed to the largest of the roosters. "Is that Mrs. Whistlemeyer or Sofia?" Hadn't Katherine teased about the roosters being named after her lady friends?

Agnes waved at Mr. Higgenbottom and Godfrey as they drove past on a tractor headed toward the pasture, Godfrey's crutches sticking up behind the seat. Somehow, he convinced Mr. Higgenbottom to let him drive the tractor.

"You stay here for a minute, Maddie." Agnes walked toward Charles. She stopped just beyond the length of the tiger's leash and crossed her fingers behind her back. "So, what do you think? Have you made up your mind? Will you stay?"

Charles grinned and gave Shere Khan's head another stroke. "*Yeah.* I'm willing to give it a try. Babysitting a tiger is something a guy should do at least once in his life, right?"

"Good. It shouldn't be for very long. With all our letters out to the zoos, we should hear something soon and…" She turned toward a cloud of dust and the rumble of a large black car barreling down the driveway. It stopped near the house, and a man stepped out from the passenger door. He looked like he might be a traveling salesman, wearing a three piece suit, his red hair parted in the middle and slicked flat on both sides with Brylcreem.

The man scanned the yard. His gaze moved past Charles and the tiger and then he walked toward Mrs. Higgenbottom at the clothesline. After exchanging a few words, she pointed toward Agnes. He pulled a paper from his shirt pocket as he crossed the yard and waved it toward her. "Mrs. Odboddy? I'm told you're the one I should talk to. I'm here, representing the Newbury City Council."

Horatio Pustlebuster! What in tarnation is he doing here? Agnes looked him over from head to foot. Arrogant. Obviously thought he was better than an average citizen.

Perspiration dotted his forehead. Agnes crossed her arms over her bosom and lifted her nose. "What do you want with me? I paid my taxes."

"This isn't about your taxes, ma'am." He nodded toward Charles and the tiger. "This tiger you've adopted has been of much concern to the city council, particularly after it escaped last fall and the sheriff had to organize a county-wide hunt. A tiger running loose in the county is a concern to every civic-minded official."

Agnes glanced at Shere Khan lying in the grass, his leash buried in the long grass and looking as if he was lying, unrestrained. He rolled onto his back with his feet in the air. "That's ridiculous. He's not running loose. He's on a chain and—"

"After some debate, we took a vote and unanimously agreed that the animal cannot continue to remain on this farm unsupervised." Mr. Pustlebuster shoved the paper into Agnes's hand. "This is a seven-day cease and desist notice. The tiger must be removed from the county."

"Wait! He's not unsupervised. He has a twenty-four-hour-a-day keeper." She jerked her head toward the tiger's caravan. "Most of the time, he's in that cage over yonder."

Mr. Pustlebuster's nose lifted as if smelling rotten potatoes. "I've given you fair notice. You have seven days, and after that…" Agnes's fists knotted on her hips. She closed her eyes and rubbed her brow as a sharp pain shot through her forehead. "When did you pass a law telling a private citizen what kind of animal he can or cannot have on his own property?" She stepped sideways to catch her balance as a wave of dizziness threatened. *Lord, help me. I feel like I'm about to faint.* She glanced at Charles, leading Shere Khan back to his cage.

The councilman sniffed and turned toward his car. "The matter is out of my hands."

"What am I supposed to do in seven days that I haven't already done?" Agnes followed him across the yard. "We've written dozens of letters, trying to find a zoo to take him. I can't guarantee I'll find a place in seven days." Her eyebrows knit. "*Huh?* What happens then?"

Mr. Pustlebuster called over his shoulder. His fingers made a gesture across his neck like a knife. "Then the city council will order Chief Waddlemucker to destroy the animal." The driver of the car hopped out and opened the passenger door.

Agnes ran up and grabbed the lapels of Mr. Pustlebuster's coat. "Chief Waddlemucker would never obey such an order. It's inhumane."

The councilman yanked his coat away. His eyelids lowered and his mouth twisted into a sneer. "If the good sheriff refuses to execute the order, the city council will have no choice but to remove him from office." He tossed his head. "One way or another, that dangerous animal will no long threaten the good citizens of Newbury County! Good day." He slipped into the car and slammed the door. The car roared away down the driveway in a cloud of dust.

Agnes swallowed a lump in her throat. "You son of a…," she yelled. "I'll find a place for Shere Khan or my name's not Agnes Agatha Odboddy. So, put that in your pipe and smoke it!" Her words disappeared into the dust settling around the yard.

Chapter Eight

"Is there a heavenly reward for trying to save an innocent animal?" Agnes

gnes stood in front of Shere Khan's cage, her arms spread wide. Chief Waddlemucker and Officer Dimwiddie stood, not twenty feet away, rifles to their shoulders.

"It's not right! You can't do it!" Agnes screamed. "You'll have to shoot me first, Chief. You cannot kill this innocent animal." Perspiration soaked the front of her housedress. Her legs trembled, threatening to give way at any moment. Waves of pain surged through her head. The usual sounds of the barnyard stilled, as though each animal and fowl held its breath, waiting to see the conclusion of the terrible drama. A crushing sense of defeat surged through Agnes's chest, and the tears she'd repeatedly shed for the past seven days, once again tumbled down her cheeks.

How could this happen? Hadn't she done everything possible to change the city council's mind? Hadn't she appealed to the mayor to no avail, and placed ads in the Newbury Gazette, pled her case before the council, and tried to get a stay on Shere Khan's death warrant?

"You better move, Agnes. You know I don't want to do this. They've got me over a barrel. I've got my orders, and there's nothing I can do about it. The animal has to be destroyed." Chief Waddlemucker took a step closer, chambered a round and moved his rifle from side to side as the tiger paced back and forth in his cage. Just as the chief pulled the trigger, in desperation, Agnes jumped in front of the tiger.

An explosion! She screamed and then felt her body tumble down,

down… It was over. All her efforts had failed. Even her last desperate attempt to protect the tiger with her body had failed. *Am I dead?* Was she bound for Heaven or…? Was there a heavenly reward for trying to save the life of an innocent animal? Even if you failed?

"Grandma! Wake up. You're having a nightmare." Katherine's voice broke through her terror. "It's okay. Wake up, now." Light from the bedside lamp washed over Agnes's face. She lay panting, the bodice of her nightgown clammy with perspiration.

"Oh, Katherine. Thank God!" She grasped her granddaughter's shoulders. "I was having a horrible nightmare. It felt so real." She put her hand to forehead. "My head…"

"Let me get you a glass of water and a headache powder. Did you take Dr. Schatzsman's pill last night? He said it was important to take them morning and night."

Agnes nodded. "I took it. I don't like it, but I haven't missed a pill since he gave them to me."

"Good." Katherine hurried toward the kitchen while Agnes steadied her breathing and rubbed her tingling hands. No small wonder she was having nightmares, with the events of yesterday still fresh in her mind. That horrible councilman! He's the one who should be shot.

How could she assure Shere Khan's future? She only had seven days to find him a home, six counting today. What could she do in such a short time? Maybe they could move Shere Khan's caravan to a far corner of the Higgenbottom farm, out of sight from the highway. They'd have to lie to the city council. If they found the tiger, Higgenbottom would likely be fined, at best—at worst, possible charges, like obstructing justice or something. It wasn't likely Mr. Higgenbottom would even agree to such duplicity. His sister, Mildred, convinced him to accept the tiger's caravan in the first place. He wasn't exactly on board with all the chaos that followed.

Katherine returned with the headache powder in a glass of water. "Here. Sit up and drink this. You'll feel better. Let me guess. You were having a nightmare about Shere Khan, weren't you?" She shook her head. "This is really getting out of hand, Grandma. I told you taking on this project would be too much. Now, look. You're having night terrors and headaches."

Agnes drank the water and set the glass on her nightstand. "More likely the headaches are due to my tumble from the apple tree. It wasn't supposed to be like this. I'd hoped our letters to the zoos would locate a nice place for the tiger." She wrung her hands as tears pricked her eyes. "What am I going to do? I can't let them shoot him."

"I don't know. What I do know is, you can't solve it tonight. Why don't you go back to sleep? She glanced at the clock on the night stand. "It's only 2:30 A.M. Things will look better in the morning." She patted Agnes's hand. Agnes lay back on her pillow and Katherine pulled up the sheets and tucked the blanket around her. She switched off the bedside lamp. "Now stop worrying, and try to go to sleep. Call me if you need me, okay? Good night."

Agnes closed her eyes. Maybe tomorrow there would be a reply from one of their inquiry letters. Having solved the problem of a caregiver for Shere Khan, now there was a worse problem. If she couldn't change the city council's decision, there were few options. Maybe appealing to the city at large wasn't a bad idea. A newspaper ad, like in her dream. And, another quick prayer for good measure… She'd put the new issue in God's hands.

The sunlight from the window shined across Agnes's face. As she came to full wakefulness, she heard sounds from the kitchen. Muffled by her closed bedroom door, Maddie's laugh and a mumble from Katherine became clearer. She glanced at the clock. *Seven o'clock already*. She had slept a long time.

Katherine would be getting Maddie ready for the school bus. Ling-Ling would be slurping up the rest of the milk from Maddie's cereal bowl. Katherine would be rinsing out her coffee mug and making a peanut butter and honey sandwich for Maddie's lunch.

Agnes stretched and put her hand to her head. The headache wasn't so bad this morning. The sun was shining and today was going to be a good day. She could feel it in her bones. There could be a reply from a zoo about Shere Khan. She could go down to the hospital and see if *Alice what's-her-name* from Cherry Blossom Way was there. It would be a chance to question Alice about whether her neighbor's house was burgled or if it was a hallucination, as Katherine insisted.

She decided to think about something other than Shere Khan's predicament. Hadn't she already turned that matter over to the Almighty? Why should she worry now that He was in charge? Hadn't He provided Charles when she needed a new caregiver? Hadn't He created the whole world in seven days? Surely, He could find a new home for Shere Khan in the same amount of time. She smiled, determined to share her thoughts with Katherine and Maddie.

Agnes headed to the bathroom. A little box that sat on the shelf over the sink held Dr. Schatzsman's pills. She hated taking medicine. Good food, exercise, and clean living had always been enough to guarantee good health. But, it was important to follow doctor's orders, especially when your life was at stake. Best take the doctor's pill before she forgot. She ran a glass of water and swallowed the morning pill. Bathed, dressed and coiffed, with the silver chopsticks through her bun, she joined Maddie and Katherine. "Good morning, girls. You shouldn't have let me oversleep, Katherine."

"You needed your rest." Katherine glanced at the chicken clock over the stove. "I fed Ling-Ling. Maddie's about ready to leave for school." She handed Maddie her metal Mickey Mouse lunch box. "I put in some extra cookies to share with a friend. Hurry! The bus was due any minute." Katherine kissed the top of Maddie's head and scooted her toward the living room.

"Bye, Grandma." Maddie blew Agnes a kiss and went out the front door.

Katherine poured a mug of coffee and set it on the table in front of Agnes. "You look well. I assume you got to sleep. You gave me quite a scare last night." She gestured toward the box of Wheaties. "Do you want some cereal? Or toast?" She gestured with the toasted bread she prepared for herself.

"I think I'll just have toast this morning. I'm not very hungry," Agnes said, taking the toast from Katherine's outstretched hand.

"Wait! That was supposed to be my—" Too late.

Agnes carried the toast and her coffee to the front porch. Ling-Ling followed her out the door. Yellow roses along the fence between her and Mavis's house were in full bloom. Spring was definitely in the air, adding to the sense of tranquility in Agnes's heart, a welcome relief from last night's terrifying nightmare. She pushed away the memory of panic and terror. *Must have been something I ate.*

Katherine stepped onto the porch. "Well, I'm off to work. I'll see you tonight." She hurried down the sidewalk to her car, waved and drove off to the beauty shop where she'd be on her feet all day, washing and applying finger waves to Newbury ladies.

Agnes turned to Ling-Ling, curling around her ankles. "Katherine works so hard, bless her heart. I should fix something nice for supper tonight. Maybe I'll put on a pot of beans and bake some cornbread."

The paperboy cycled past and waved. "Morning, Mrs. Odboddy." He pitched her newspaper over the fence onto the lawn and rode off down the street. Thank God, he was too young to be drafted. At least this was one boy who would escape the horrors of war. She glanced toward Mrs. Williams's house across the street. The cherry tree in her front yard was covered with a perfusion of pink blooms, in defiance to the gold star flag on her front porch, representing the son sacrificed to this senseless war.

"I'll cut some roses and take them over to her this afternoon," Agnes mused. She picked up the *Newbury Gazette*, under new management since last fall, and sat in the porch rocker to read the news. Ling-Ling jumped into her lap, curled around and lay down. "Good gravy!" Agnes shook the newspaper. "Did you see this?"

Purrt! Ling-Ling lifted her head, and with ears flattened, she glared at Agnes as if to say, *Must you make such a racket? Can't you see I was getting ready for a nap?*

"Sorry, Ling-Ling. Didn't mean to disturb you, my dear, but listen." She read aloud from page one. "Mr. and Mrs. Ledbetter just returned from attending their daughter, Melinda's, wedding in Sacramento. The bride's mother wore a snappy navy blue two-piece suit with white epaulettes at the neck and sleeves and a carnation corsage. She carried a navy blue purse with matching shoes and… Oh, you don't care what she wore, do you? Here's where it gets interesting." She folded the newspaper. "Upon returning to their home at 2557 Cherry Blossom Way, Mr. Ledbetter discovered two expensive paintings, a Salvador Dali, and a Picasso, purchased on their European tour in 1937, missing from their home!" Agnes lowered the newspaper and stroked the cat's back. "Sure as a striped skunk, that's the house where Dr. Schatzsman carried out those two paintings the other night." She jumped up, spilling Ling-Ling onto the floor.

Yow! Ling-Ling streaked off the front porch in protest.

"So, Godfrey is full of prunes. I wasn't hallucinating. I have to report this to Chief Waddlemucker." Agnes hurried into the kitchen and dialed Godfrey's number.

"Hello?"

"Hi, it's me. How are you doing? Are you getting along okay on those crutches?"

"Slows me down some, but I'm managing," Godfrey said. "How about you? How are you feeling this morning?"

"That's not what I called about. I'm going to see Chief Waddlemucker in a little while. I could stop by and fix you something to eat." Agnes smirked, knowing how Godfrey would react to her announcement of another police station visit. She couldn't wait to hear him stammer and back-pedal when he learned about the newspaper article verifying her suspicions of Dr. Schatzsman.

"Why are you going to the police station? You know the chief has to follow a direct order from the city council if you don't move the tiger."

Oh. Darn. There is that... An image of Shere Khan's big yellow eyes loomed in her mind.

Agnes was so pleased with putting Godfrey in his place after accusing her of imagining Dr. Schatzsman's escapades, she momentarily forgot Chief Waddlemucker's role in Shere Khan's imminent future.

"Oh, you're right. I wasn't thinking about Shere Khan at the moment. As it happens, I was reading the paper and saw an article about Mr. and Mrs. Ledbetter's house being robbed of some valuable paintings while they were on vacation. Remember? I told you I saw Dr. Schatzsman on Cherry Blossom Way? Well, guess where the Ledbetter's live. Go ahead, smarty-pants. Guess."

"*Uh.* I guess you're going to tell me they live on Cherry Blossom Way. So, next, you're going to tell me that you plan to tell Chief Waddlemucker all about your midnight escapade the other night."

"Well? Don't you think I should report what I know about a burglary? You said I shouldn't say anything before, and I agreed because of my concussion, but now I have proof."

"No, you don't. Your testimony wouldn't stand up in court. It would be your word against a well-known doctor. He'd deny the charge and say you were hallucinating after your fall. Even if someone believed that you saw the burglar, identifying the doctor would be questioned because you just saw him that day and, admittedly, right after your concussion."

Agnes's confidence waned. Maybe he was right. "I can see your point. It probably won't make any difference, but, *dag-nabbit*, I have to report what I saw."

"Then, if you insist on talking to the chief, I'll come with you. I can corroborate that you told us the same story when you came back that night."

"I suppose it wouldn't hurt. I'll pick you up in an hour."

"On the way back, could we stop at the grocery store and pick up a few things? I'm pretty tired of eating pork and beans and peanut butter sandwiches."

"Why didn't you say something? Katherine or I would have gone to the store for you."

"Oh, it's not the shopping that's the problem. It's carrying the groceries up the stairs on my crutches."

Chapter Nine

"Go ahead. Give it to me with both barrels." Chief Waddlemucker

Agnes drove Old Betsy across town. With all the windows down, she could catch the spring breezes and the scent of the flowering trees and flowers. She approached the Crest Theater where Godfrey lived in the upstairs apartment. The huge marquee in neon lights over the front entrance spelled out the recently released film, Frankenstein Meets the Wolf Man. She climbed the outside staircase and knocked on Godfrey's door.

"Come on in. It's open," Godfrey called from inside.

"Are you ready?" Agnes opened the door.

"Let's go." Godfrey clumped toward her on his crutches. Agnes helped him down the stairs and into the car. "Can you bear any weight on that foot yet? Maybe you need to get an x-ray." She got him settled in the front seat and walked around the car. Once inside, she turned the key, shoved in the clutch, and pushed the starter.

"It's better. I think I'm about ready to move up to a cane. Crutches are so inconvenient on the stairs. Not to mention, a little bit dangerous."

"I can imagine."

Several minutes later, she pulled into a parking space at the Newbury Police Department. "Well, here goes nothing. Though, I don't know what good it will do. The chief never listens to a dad-burn thing I have to say. This time probably won't be any different."

"I warned you. Don't be surprised—"

"Heard it. Let's go!"

Jackson Jackson waved from the elevator when they came through the entryway door. "Why, Mrs. Odboddy," he called. "Aren't you a breath a' fresh air, comin' in here this mornin' all bright and chipper. And, you've brought yer' ol' frien' Mistah Godfrey. Is you come to see the chief again?" His grin brightened his dark face in an expression of pure joy at the sight of old friends.

"I've got something important to discuss with the chief." They stepped into the elevator, Jackson pushed the button, and the doors slid shut. "Is he in a good mood today?"

"Why, let me think," Jackson tapped his finger on his forehead. "As I recollect, he did smile at me this mornin' when he come in, so I guess he's in a fair mood, considerin'."

Agnes's eyes narrowed, "Considering what, exactly?"

"Considerin' he were up late las' night, afightin' with the city council over that tiger a' yours. And, Chief Waddlemucker, he 'bout to have a corrumnary over they sayin' he gotta shoot that poor critter if he ain't gone by next weekend."

Agnes grabbed Godfrey's arm. Her stomach lurched. "Oh, Jackson, no! You can't be serious."

"Chief, he say, he'll retar' before he obey such a' order. He most beside hisself with worry, 'cause he need his job, what with his wife and chile, but he say he won't obleege them in such a unhuman demand and kill an innocent beast."

"Were you at the city council meeting?" Godfrey grabbed the metal railing circling the elevator to steady his balance. "We didn't know it was open to the public."

"No, suh. I wasn't in attendance. It were jes' me overhearin' the chief and the councilmen talkin'. After the meetin', I traveled the chief and that Mistah Pustelbustah' feller down the elevator. They jus' flingin' argumentations back and forth, like I tole ya, as we was goin' down."

The elevator doors opened. "Guess you knows where his office is. You been here enough times. I hopes you find some place for that tiger-cat real soon. I shore don't wanta see him get kilt, just 'cause he a tiger." He shook his head. "That ain't right."

"No, it's not. Don't worry. They'll have to go through me first. The only way Shere Khan gets shot is over my dead body." The terror of last night's nightmare flashed through her mind. Her throat constricted. She swallowed a lump and grabbed Godfrey's arm again, as a wave of dizziness passed over her. Her knees felt weak. "I'm ready. Let's go." They walked down the hall toward Chief Waddlemucker's office. Was he inside considering how to keep his family fed without a job, or resigning himself to slaughter an innocent animal at the order of men with no conscience?

Godfrey held the door and followed Agnes into the police department. The clink-clink of several typewriters stopped, and the officers looked up. Officer Dimwiddie leaned on the counter, fanning through the pages of a telephone book. He laid it aside as Agnes approached the counter. Godfrey dropped into a chair beside the door, near enough to hear the conversation and come to her defense if need be.

"Morning, Mrs. Odboddy," Officer Dimwiddie said. "You here to see the chief? Is he expecting you?"

Agnes lifted her nose. Her stomach clenched. She shook her head to dispel the nightmare's images of Officer Dimwiddie pointing a rifle at Shere Khan. "I don't have an appointment. Since when does a responsible citizen need an appointment to report a crime? Is he in or not?" She knotted her fists to keep them from shaking.

Officer Dimwiddie flinched. "*Um … er …* right! I'll tell him you're here. Have a seat. I won't be a moment." He crossed the office and knocked on the chief's door.

"Enter!" A muffled voice replied from inside.

Dimwiddie opened the door and stuck his head in. "Mrs. Odboddy and friend. Do you have time to see them?"

The chief's audible sigh reached the listeners in the outer room and then a moment of silence. "Send them in."

Officer Dimwiddie waved to Agnes. "He'll see you now."

Agnes helped Godfrey to his feet and into the chief's office. Godfrey leaned his crutches against one of the chairs facing the chief's desk. He sat. Surprisingly, the chief's office was neat and clean, bookshelves dusted and a nice fern waved gently on the open windowsill behind his desk. Mrs. Waddlemucker must have visited recently because it was doubtful the chief would have dusted and brought a fern from home. "Have a seat. What's on your mind?" Chief Waddlemucker glanced at his wristwatch. "I have a meeting in fifteen minutes."

Agnes's mouth dropped open as she noticed the chief's disheveled hair, his necktie askew, and his armpits circled with perspiration. His normally robust, ruddy, complexion looked wan and pasty. Was the chief's appearance the result of his run-in with Pustlebuster? Were things really as bad as Jackson suggested on the way up in the elevator?

Agnes set her purse on the chair, clasped her hands behind her back and paced back toward the door. Her heart raced. Not only did she hold Shere Khan's life in her hands, but now the chief's future, as well. The all too familiar light-headed sensation she experienced too often since her fall swished through her head. If she didn't sit, she was going to fall down. She hurried to the chair beside Godfrey and plopped down, her hand to her forehead.

"Angel-face. Are you all right?" Godfrey grasped her arm and gazed around the office. "Can we get some water, Chief?"

Chief Waddlemucker pushed a button and spoke into a black box on his desk. "Bring us a couple glasses of water, would you, Dimwiddie?" He stood and came around the end of his desk, pulling his handkerchief from his pocket. "Here, Agnes. Take this."

"Thanks." She dabbed her forehead. "I'm okay. Just got a bit topsy-turvy for a minute. I guess all this tiger drama is getting to me," she said, twisting the chief's handkerchief. Should she ask him about the council's edict? She bit her lip. More likely, repeating the question would embarrass Chief Waddlemucker and get Jackson into trouble for gossiping.

"So, what brings you here today?" The chief leaned back against the edge of his desk. "I suppose you want to yell at me about the city council's demands." He sighed. "Go ahead. Give it to me with both barrels. I'm getting used to it." Dots of perspiration broke out on his forehead.

The sound of horns and raucous noises from the street billowed through the open window. Agnes's gaze moved from the open window to the door as Officer Dimwiddie entered. A gust of wind caught the door and slammed it shut with a bang behind his back.

Agnes jerked. Her ears rang. Her vision wavered. Like her dream, instead of a rifle pointed at her, Officer Dimwiddie's tray held a glimmering object. Sunlight from the window bounced off the silver tray, casting a flash of light into Agnes's eyes. Panic careened through her chest. *It's a pistol!* She screamed and collapsed on the floor, fists over her ears, her legs drawn up in the fetal position. She whimpered, "Stop! Don't let him kill me... Oh, Lord, no!"

Shocked by her bizarre outburst, the chief and Godfrey froze. Then, Godfrey dropped to his knees and pulled Agnes into his arms. "There, there, none of this. I'm here. What is it, dear heart? What's wrong?" He pulled her head to his chest, rocked her and rubbed her back as she sobbed.

"Dimwiddie," the chief said, "Give me that water." He leaned over Agnes. "Here, drink this." He put the glass to her lips.

Agnes swallowed a sob and sipped the water. She stopped whimpering, and glanced, wide-eyed, at the two men hovering over her. "What? What happened?" She pulled free from Godfrey's arms and gazed from one face to the other. Then, realizing she was on the floor, she put her hand to her mouth. "Oh, Lord, what have I done?" She struggled to her knees and climbed back into her chair. "I...I...can't imagine what came over me." Her hands trembled. "I saw Officer Dimwiddie there and...and...I thought he had a...a never mind what I thought. I'm sorry." Her cheeks burned with humiliation. She'd just acted like a horse's ass?

"It's all right, lambkins," Godfrey said, sitting back in his chair. "It's not your fault. You're still recovering from a concussion. These things happen. Isn't that right, Chief?" Nodding, Godfrey glared at Chief Waddlemucker, as though defying him to disagree.

"*Um*... oh, right. Why, I remember back in '16 during the battle of Verdun, one of my comrades suffered a concussion. He kept seeing white rabbits in our bunks for several weeks. Eventually, he was fine, but we had a jolly time at his expense, teasing the poor lad. *Heh*... *heh*..."

Agnes crossed her arms over her chest, her cheeks still tingling. "I can assure you, I am not seeing white rabbits, Chief. I...I... Can we change the subject, please?" She sipped more water and set the glass on the desk.

"Of course. *Um*... what did you come to see me about, Agnes?"

Agnes opened her mouth to report her suspicions about Dr. Schatzsman's burglary at the Ledbetter's home. In light of her embarrassing display, discussion of her concussion and possible hallucinations, there was no point recounting her recent midnight trek and accusing the prestigious doctor, now. She couldn't even mention her concerns about the city council's decree, now that Jackson made her aware of the chief's role in the controversy. She shook her head and then stood. "Come, Godfrey. I've changed my mind. Folks have enough on their mind today. I don't need to add my concerns to the chief's agenda."

Godfrey sighed. "Yes, my queen. Anything you say." He stood. "Good day, Chief Waddlemucker. Thank you for your time." He pulled the crutches under his arm and hobbled to the door.

"Any time, Agnes," the chief called as she exited into the outer office.

Unable to meet Officer Dimwiddie's gaze, Agnes left the office with her head down. Prickles ran up and down her back, knowing that office staff was staring as they opened the outer door into the hallway.

Chapter Ten

"What you had was a flashback." Godfrey

O you want me to drive, Snookums?" Godfrey said, as they left the chief's office and approached Agnes's car.

"Don't be ridiculous. How can you drive with your right foot bandaged? I'll drive."

"But, dumpling, you just had…a…spell, or something in there. I'm not sure you're up to it. You should let me—"

"And, risk letting you wreck Ol' Betsy? Not on your tintype." Agnes yanked open the driver's door and slid in. "Get in."

Godfrey shrugged. "As you like." He got into the car and slammed the door. "Weren't we going to do a little grocery shopping on the way home? I have a list here, somewhere." He dug in his various pockets and pulled a scrap of yellow paper from his jacket. "Here it is. Eggs, bread, cheese, lettuce, canned peas…potatoes, maybe some soda crackers. I can live without the soda crackers."

Agnes chuckled. "Not a problem." She drove for a block and turned toward Godfrey. "If walking into the store is too much for you, give me the list. You can wait in the car while I get your stuff."

"I'm fine. It's only a few things."

Agnes drove in silence thinking about her episode in the chief's office. She shifted gears at a stop sign and glanced at Godfrey. "You're unusually quiet. Are you mad at me for embarrassing you in there?"

Godfrey shrugged. "Actually, I'm worried about you. You haven't been yourself since your fall. You should be resting more instead of running around town. Are you taking the medicine the doctor gave you?"

Wasn't he a sweetheart to be worried? "Of course. I'm not a dunce. As for running around town, I thought I was helping you with your errands."

"I appreciate you driving me, but then you had, *umm* ... your spell or whatever you call it. What exactly happened, anyway? Maybe you should see Dr. Schatzsman again."

Agnes turned into the Wilkey's Market parking lot and pulled on the brake. "Quite honestly, I don't know what happened. I had a nightmare last night. Maybe it was something to do with that."

"Do you want to tell me about it?"

"I suppose. If you think it will help. It all seemed so real. The chief and Officer Dimwiddie were ... were ... going to shoot Shere Khan, because of the city council's edict." Agnes lowered her head. "I was in front of the tiger's cage, trying to stop them and then they ... fired. I thought they killed me. Then Katherine woke me and I was in a cold sweat."

Godfrey patted her hand. "It's okay, dumpling. You don't need to say anymore. What you had was a flashback. I've had the same thing a few times. It's because of your head injury. It's pretty common when someone suffers head trauma. When the door banged shut and you saw Officer Dimwiddie, it must have brought back the night terror and triggered a panic attack. When your concussion heals, it will probably never happen again. You should tell Dr. Schatzsman—"

"No. I'll take his medicine, but I don't want to see him. He's a thief, and I don't want anything to do with him."

"There you go again, Agnes. I've told you—"

"And, I've told you. I know what I saw, and you aren't going to convince me otherwise." She nodded toward the front door of the grocery store where paper signs in the window advertised an availability of meat and sale items. *Coffee $0.24 a pound – eggs $0.43 dozen – Round Steak $0.41 a pound – Potatoes $0.18 ten pounds*

"Are we going in, or sit here and gab all afternoon?" Godfrey hobbled on his crutches to the front entry. Agnes held the door for him and followed him into the store. "Morning, Mrs. Wilkey. I've brought you a customer." She beamed at the woman and gazed around the store. It held all a customer could want. Vegetables lined the left wall, and a small counter against the right wall held the available meat. Rows of canned goods ran down the center of the store. A few sundries, mostly cleaning supplies, or day-old food and vegetables somewhat past their prime, were displayed closest to Mrs. Wilkey's small counter next to the cash register. "Good morning."

Godfrey pulled the grocery list from his pocket. Agnes took Godfrey's list. "Sit down over there and chat with Mrs. Wilkey. I'll get your things."

"Yes, my queen." Godfrey sighed and sat on a box of canned peas near the counter. "I'll be so glad to get rid of these crutches. I feel so helpless."

Agnes pushed the wire shopping cart down the aisle. Within minutes, all the items on the list were in her basket and she returned to the counter "Here you go, Godfrey. Everything you needed. Do you have the right ration coupons?"

As Godfrey completed his transactions, Agnes picked up a copy of the *Newbury Gazette* and glanced at the headlines. Another local boy—killed in action. Another submarine—sunk with dozens on board. Another report of an enemy destroyer—sunk. Tit for tat. Death and destruction. Some of ours, and some of theirs. Didn't German families grieve for their lost loved ones as much as American families? She shook her head. Where was the sense in it?

Agnes shifted the paper to peruse the story below the fold. Another home burglary, right here in Newbury. Jewelry and artwork snatched from the mayor's house while they were out of town for the weekend. A shiver crept up her neck. Was Dr. Schatzsman at work again? Somebody had to do something. Her cheeks warmed. She wasn't able to tell Chief Waddlemucker about her suspicions this morning. *Maybe we should go back...*

Agnes opened the newspaper to page two. Maybe she could find something more positive on the society page. An article about a combat artist, Edward Reep, caught her eye. *War Artist to Visit Newbury*. She scanned the article.

Edward Reep, renowned war artist and photographer was coming to Newbury! The winner of multiple awards and numerous national art show competitions in 1941 and 1942, his war paintings gained in value. They were being snapped up by art dealers and art collectors alike. The article described a recent award for two, eight-foot square, and one, eight by twenty-four foot murals at the Soldier's Club in Monterey, California.

It was to be a one-man show, right there in Newbury and Mr. Reep would donate a portion of the proceeds to assist the local Newbury Veterans Hall. He was seeking a suitable location and sponsors. Any local citizens interested in working on this project were to call the *Newbury Gazette*.

Imagine! An artist! Right there in Newbury. Agnes lowered the newspaper. Her lips curved in a smile as an idea formed. Maybe she should volunteer to help. It would take her mind off Shere Khan. Within a few days, the matter would be resolved, one way or another. The skin on her arms prickled. It would be good to have something else to look forward to after... She shook her head.

Mrs. Wilkey tapped the counter. "Now that you've read that newspaper, do you plan to pay for it?"

Agnes shoved the folded newspaper into her purse. "Godfrey? Pay for the newspaper." She picked up his bags of groceries and pushed open the door, leaving him to fish another quarter from his pocket. "Thanks, Mrs. Wilkey," she called over her shoulder.

Godfrey shuffled after her. "Where's the fire, punkin-heimer?"

Agnes held the car door open for Godfrey. "Do you want to come to dinner? I'm making a pot of chili beans and cornbread. Katherine can stop by on the way home and pick you up, or you can come with me now."

"I should get back to my apartment and put away the groceries. If Katherine doesn't mind, have her pick me up later."

Chapter Eleven

"With the faith of a mustard seed, we can move mountains." Agnes

With Katherine's boyfriend, Vincent, and Godfrey joining them for dinner, it was a chance the four of them could come up with a plan regarding the looming deadline concerning Shere Khan. Agnes's heart ached. Only a miracle could save the tiger now.

All afternoon, between stirring the chili beans and putting a batch of cornbread in the oven, Agnes sat at the kitchen table, listing obstacles and brain-storming possible solutions for a permanent housing plan. By the time Katherine and the men arrived, Agnes devised a Last Resort—No Holds Barred plan in case the four of them couldn't find a better solution. After dinner, they retired to the living room with glasses of lemonade to discuss the problem.

"We've had no luck with our letters to the zoos, and Grandma's appeal to the city councilman fell on deaf ears," Katherine said. "We're out of ideas, not to mention, nearly out of money. I hate to say it…" Katherine lowered her head and put her finger to her mouth, lest Maddie should overhear her. "I fear we may have to accept the inevitable."

Agnes jutted her chin and crossed her arms. "I'll not hear of it! There must be something we can do. How about a fundraiser at the church? Maybe the ladies would—"

"Grandma. You're being unrealistic," Katherine said. "This isn't the church ladies' problem. They've already helped with the letter writing. You can't expect them to help pay for his food, too. Besides, where would we keep him? He can't stay at the Higgenbottom farm past Saturday. You have to face it, Grandma. Nothing's working. You've done your best."

Godfrey patted Agnes's hand. "It's a darn shame, that's what it is. That tiger's not hurting anybody out there. What's got the city council so riled up, anyway?"

"It's that Pustlebuster character," Agnes said. "I'll bet my Sunday bib and tucker, he's doing it for the attention." She clenched her fists. "I could just kill him! What about a newspaper ad? We could make an appeal directly to the public. Maybe—"

Katherine set her lemonade on the table. "There's not enough time to get an ad in the paper. It's Thursday. The city council's deadline is Saturday. I hate to say it, but we've done everything possible. Maybe it's time to give up and let him go."

"What about Maddie?" Agnes lowered her voice. "Are you going to lie to her and tell her he moved away? Or went with another carnival?" Katherine shrugged and picked at her fingernail.

"Suppose we could move him from the Higgenbottom farm somewhere the council wouldn't know about?" Vincent said.

Katherine shook her head. "That's just pushing the can down the road. Grandma's out of money. Who's going to take care of him? Charles can't work for free for long. The only logical answer was a zoo, and no zoo has responded."

"I'll get a job." Agnes stood and paced the living room. "Charles will stay for a while. But ... where could we move the tiger's caravan? It has to be somewhere that provides a place for Charles. He might agree to work for free, but he still has to eat. How..." She put her hands over her eyes. "Isn't it a good thing we're trying to do? Why is it so ... so hard?"

Katherine went to her grandmother and wrapped her arms around her. Agnes leaned into her shoulder and wept. "I've pra...prayed for an...an...answer...for Shere Khan. Why doesn't He show me what to do? I can't let them shoo...shoot him. I just can't." Agnes's tears soaked the collar on Katherine's dress.

Katherine rubbed Agnes's back. "Sometimes the answer to prayer is 'No', Grandma. He's not obliged to say yes every time, just because we ask."

"But, the Bible says with the faith of a mustard seed, we can move mountains. I don't want to move a mountain, just a tiger. That's not unreasonable, is it?" Agnes gazed from Vincent to Godfrey.

Vincent looked down at his feet.

Godfrey's hand dashed across his eyes. "Must have something in my eye," he mumbled.

"I heard you crying, Grandma. What's wrong?" Maddie stood in the doorway, holding her ceramic tiger. "Is it about Shere Khan?"

"Maddie! Now, there's nothing for you to worry about." Agnes dabbed her eyes with a handkerchief and hurried across the room. "Charles is taking care of Shere Khan, remember? Why don't you go into the garden and see if you can find any ripe tomatoes on the vines. I'm sure I saw a little green tomato the other day. If you find some, bring them inside."

Maddie nibbled on her thumbnail. "Okay. But, when you go to Mr. Higgenbottom's farm to see Shere Khan, I get to come, okay?"

"Of course. Now run along, dear." Katherine waved her away. "We need to have some big people talk. We'll have chocolate pudding later for dessert."

"Okay." Maddie left the room. The screen door slammed as she went onto the screened-in porch and down the steps into the victory garden.

Vincent snapped his fingers. "I may have an idea, but…I don't want to get your hopes up. I have to check out a few things first. I'll let you know if anything comes of it."

No amount of persuasion could get Vincent to share his plan, despite multiple questions. Later that evening, after dessert, Vincent offered to drive Godfrey home.

"I'm going to bed early too, Grandma. I have a headache." Katherine said.

Katherine's headache may have been an excuse to avoid any further conversation with Agnes about the tiger, but the pain in the back of Agnes's head was real. As soon as Katherine's bedroom door closed, Ling-Ling followed Agnes into the bathroom. As she stared at the little mirror over the sink, the cat sat on the bathmat and proceeded to wash the back of her ears. Agnes peered at the tranquil cat's reflection in the mirror. "Desperate times calls for desperate measures," she said. Ling-Ling paused in her ablution and looked up. Her expression seemed to say, *why do humans get their panties in a bunch? Accept whatever comes. You can't change it.*

Unlike Ling-Ling's serene acceptance of Shere Khan's fate, Agnes felt the plight of the tiger deeply. Tears sparkled in her eyes as she came to a decision. Since no one else would step up and solve the problem, she would take matters into her own hands. Sometimes, when the cause was just, one had to make personal sacrifices to set things right, even at the peril of one's own life. "I need a good night's sleep tonight," she whispered to Ling-Ling. "Tomorrow is the last chance I'll have to do what must be done to save Shere Khan." She took two of Dr. Schatzsman's pills from the medicine cabinet, filled a glass with water, and swallowed the pills. "If one pill will keep me from having a brain bleed, then I'll take two tonight to be on the safe side."

Chapter Twelve

riday AM: Tears filled Agnes's eyes as she stood on the front porch and waved to Maddie and Katherine. "Good bye. Good bye. Have a good day. I love you!" Ready to put her Last Resort plan into motion, after today, things would never be the same. She had counted the cost, made her decision, and was ready to face the consequences.

No sooner had Katherine's car disappeared around the corner than Agnes returned to her bedroom, pulled a shoebox off the closet top shelf, and laid it on her bed. She opened the shoebox, removed her WWI service pistol and retrieved the bullets from inside a sock in her underwear drawer. Agnes loaded the pistol and shoved it into her purse.

A little visit to the Newbury City Council office was in order. That hateful Mr. Horatio Pustlebuster would be there. He was responsible for the city council's decision to remove Shere Khan from the Higgenbottom farm. He was the one who demanded Chief Waddlemucker shoot the tiger if he wasn't moved by the weekend…which was tomorrow! Without Pustlebuster's influence, the council would have listened to reason, and the tiger's caravan could have stayed at the farm. Given a little more time, the ladies at The First Church of the Evening Star and Everlasting Light would have found a permanent home for the tiger. Perhaps a few less city council members would result in a few more constructive decisions.

Putting aside the inevitable consequences of her drastic decision, she drove in a daze across town and parked in front of the city hall building. The edges of the building swayed as she walked up the steps— no doubt an illusion and the result of a sleepless night. She paused to gaze at the gently swaying shrubbery. Or was it another minor California earthquake? Not severe enough to break things, just enough to remind Northern California residents that Mother Nature was still in charge. After a few moments, the swaying ceased and her balance steadied. Agnes straightened her dress, squared her shoulders, and opened the heavy glass front door. Her heart pounded as she reached into her purse and was comforted by the cold steel against her fingertips.

Once inside the lobby, she shivered. Perhaps they'd turned on that new-fangled machine the city purchased last month—the one that produced cool air, like at the diner out on Hwy 1. How ridiculous that some folks thought that one day something like that would become a household necessity. It was clearly an advertising gimmick to attract tourists into diners along the highway. Agnes tightened her sweater around her neck, tucked her purse higher up her shoulder, and strode down the hall. As she neared the elevator, her heart picked up a pace, likely a case of last-minute nerves. *Steady old girl. It has to be done.*

"Mornin' Miz Odboddy." Jackson Jackson stepped from the elevator. His welcoming grin was a comfort, and Agnes's pattering heart stilled. She resisted any second thoughts about her plan to reduce the number of city council members, in hope of a more reasonable outcome. Specifically, without Mr. Horatio Pustlebuster.

For a moment, she wondered whether he had any redeeming qualities she should consider before sending him to meet his Maker. She thought over the latest city council's decisions, recently posted in the *Newbury Gazette*. There was the daycare lady who babysat with the factory workers' kids. Mr. Pustlebuster stated it was illegal to run a business from her home inside the city limits, and forced her to close her daycare. Without child care, several women were forced to give up working at the munitions plant, resulting in a loss of production for the war effort. That certainly was not in the best interest of the country.

And, hadn't Mr. Pustlebuster's city council forced the closure of the Railroad Diner after the owner was sent *up the river* on assault and battery charges? Mr. Pustlebuster claimed the owner's wife couldn't keep the diner open because the business license was in her husband's name. And, they wouldn't reinstate the license in her name because…her husband was going to jail. The diner was forced to file bankruptcy, several waitresses lost their jobs, and a woman was left without a means of support. No. Even at Heaven's Judgment Throne, Pustlebuster would have no redeeming qualities in his favor. He pushed the city council into making too many improper decisions, making life miserable for too many Newbury citizens. It was a wonder someone hadn't done him in already.

"Morning, Jackson. Beautiful day, isn't it?" Agnes greeted her friend, as she stepped into the elevator. She glanced at the poster on the wall announcing Edward Reep's art show coming soon to Newbury. She regretted not being involved at that event, after all. With no other options to save the tiger, as her last desperate act, she was determined to put an end to Mr. Pustlebuster. Once the deed was done, perhaps she'd be able to talk to a *Newbury Gazette* reporter and explain her reason for committing murder. Perhaps such a touching newspaper account would attract national attention, and someone would step forward with a solution for Shere Khan. Wasn't it at least worth a try?

"You goin' to see Chief Waddlemuker, ma'am?" The elevator doors closed. Jackson's face blurred and he appeared to sway from side to side. Agnes blinked to clear her vision. She put her hand to her forehead, moist with perspiration. Another headache pounded across the top of her head. She took a deep breath. "Not today. Take me to the second floor. It's time to fix a problem that has plagued the city for some time." She would not let physical frailty deter her mission. She would finish it with her last breath.

"You gonna protest about that poor ol' tiger, ma'am?" Jackson said. "Shore wish there was sumpin' I could do. Lots of folks come through here every day. I could ask them to sign a petition, if that would help." Jackson pushed his cap back and scratched his head. Then, he leaned forward and peered into Agnes's face. "You looks mighty poorly. I hates ta see you discomfited like this, ma'am. Does you want me to call Miss Katherine?"

"That's very thoughtful, Jackson, but I'm fine. I'm afraid that tomorrow is the city council's deadline for Shere Khan, and it's too late for a petition. No. I have a more permanent solution in mind." A wave of dizziness struck. Her heart pounded. She leaned against the wall. She couldn't think about her ailments now. The deed would soon be done.

"If you're sure, ma'am." Jackson pushed the button, and the elevator began to rise.

Agnes closed her eyes and pushed thoughts of Katherine and Maddie from her mind. There would be a trial. Public humiliation. Jail. Sniggers from certain townsfolk who 'knew all the time, she was crazy.' Godfrey would be mortified to call her his girlfriend.

Would anyone understand her intention to bring national attention to Shere Khan's plight? Or would Chief Waddlemucker spirit her away without a news conference, throw her in jail this afternoon, and comply with the city council's extermination decree tomorrow without a word to the press? What if it was all for naught?

She shook her head. Where did these doubts come from? She was so sure she was doing the right thing when she left home and even when she stepped into the elevator. Why second thought now? If there was even a small chance that Pustlebuster's murder would get picked up by national newspaper coverage… She could almost see the headlines now. *Will Murder Save the Tiger? In a heroic last ditch effort to save Shere Khan from an unrighteous death, elderly, home town patriot and revered almost regular church-goer, Agnes Agatha Odboddy, tossed life and limb to the wind and bravely murdered the conniving, unscrupulous city council president, Horatio Pustlebuster, who called for the scurrilous destruction of the innocent tiger. Odboddy's brave effort, though charged as first-degree murder, made headlines across*

America and has resulted in seventeen zoos offering the unfortunate tiger a lifetime refuge. Though headed for the gas chamber, our heroine, Mrs. Odboddy will long live in our memories as the single ...

"We here, Miz Odboddy. Second floor." The elevator door clunked open.

Agnes opened her eyes and shook her head. "Thanks, Jackson. You've been a good friend." She squeezed his arm, and stepped into the hall. "Thanks for all your help over the years." She paused.

Off to the right was Chief Waddlemucker's office. Off to the left and down the hall was the Newbury City Council office.

Another pain shot through her head. Her knees weakened. She had to hurry and finish this, before she fainted dead away and lost the opportunity. She turned left. When she reached the city council office, she peeked through the window in the door. There stood Mr. Pustlebuster, a cigar in his mouth, his fat stomach pressed against the counter. Of course, he was yelling at the poor receptionist, who looked ready to burst into tears.

Perspiration rings formed under Agnes's arms and around her dress collar. Chest pressure made it difficult to breathe. Wasn't it just her luck that she might die of a heart attack before she could commit murder? Would that be some sort of poetic justice? She swallowed a lump in her throat. Enough procrastination! There was no other way. Destiny must be fulfilled.

Her gaze moved toward laughter down the hall near the chief's office. She considered heading there. Was it possible he found a way to save the tiger at the eleventh hour? Not likely.

She turned back toward the city council office. Counting on the results of her actions was a gamble, but it was a risk she must take. Agnes opened her purse and pulled out her pistol. She whispered, "Just do it and get it over with, Agnes!" *Agnes ... Agnes ... Agnes ...* Her name echoed in her head. If only she didn't feel so weak and sick to her stomach. Her head pounded like the woodcutter's hammer on a cuckoo clock. Within minutes it would be over and she could rest.

Likely behind bars, nevertheless, there would be a cot where she could lie down and close her eyes. Perhaps a bologna sandwich for dinner…

The walls began to weave. A hanging light swayed overhead. A picture of President Roosevelt tumbled from the wall and crashed to the floor. She closed her eyes against a blinding light smashing through her head. She forced open her eyes again. "What's happened?" Agnes gazed around the hallway and then down at her hand. She was standing outside the city council office, but… what was she doing with her WWI service pistol? The floor swayed. She put out her hands to steady her balance as her knees buckled and the pistol flew from her hand and clattered to the floor.

"Mrs. Odboddy!"

Agnes turned toward the voice. *Jackson?* He ran toward her, lurching left to right as the building shook and the walls pitched backwards and forwards.

Agnes fell to her knees and spread her hands to break her fall. Cracked mortar tumbled from the ceiling and chunks of sawdust and plaster sprayed onto her head. Jackson pulled her into his arms and knelt over her to protect her from falling debris. "I's gotcha'. Don't worry." Bits of plaster dotted the floor around them.

Shrieks and cries came from the nearby offices. Doors flung open, staff workers stumbled into the corridor and fell against the walls as the building continued to sway. Dr. Schatzsman lurched from the city council office, tripped and tumbled to the floor next to Agnes and Jackson.

Officers and staff rushed from Chief Waddlemucker's office. Some headed for the stairs. Others knelt along the hallway and held their arms over their heads in the manner that school children were instructed to shelter beneath their desks in case of an air raid.

Pustlebuster staggered into the hall. He stooped beside Agnes and Jackson. Within a minute, Mother Nature ceased her tantrum and the rumbling stopped. Jackson straightened up and brushed dust from his head. "You okay, ma'am? Is you hurt?"

Already woozy and disoriented even before the earthquake, Agnes stammered, "I…I'm fine. Just shook up, I think." She wiped debris from her face. "Oh!" Cold fingers tickled her cheeks. Like a floodlight over a football field, the intended purpose for being in the building flashed into her mind. Rational sense prevailed. *Why would I even… Why… What made me think it would save Shere Khan if I killed the councilman?* Goosebumps prickled her chest and arms. If it hadn't been for the earthquake… Was the earthquake a *God-thing* to bring her to her senses and stop her from committing murder? It was as clear as if the words were scrawled across a star-studded sky. Killing the councilman to save the tiger? How could that possibly change the inevitable? What an absurd idea. The doctor was right with his warning. The concussion must have caused a brain bleed, and now she was truly losing her mind.

Chapter Thirteen

Agnes gazed wide-eyed around the hallway. Dust and chunks of plaster were strewn about. A chair lay on its side and broken glass from dislodged pictures lay in heaps along the edge of the walls. People began to rise from the floor and mill about. Some were in tears. Others comforted and tended those with minor injuries.

The pistol! Where was it? She brushed debris off her shoulders and sat up, near panic rising in her chest as she felt the floor beneath her skirt. How could she explain the blasted thing to Officer Dimwiddie when it was found lying at her feet? *Where's the blasted pistol?* She turned and swept her hand through chunks of ceiling plaster, jerked to her feet and kicked at some of the larger chunks. Her gaze swept the corridor, moved past the men and women stumbling around, and came to rest on Pustlebuster, leaning over a woman near the wall. Too bad the ceiling hadn't collapsed on that particular part of the hallway.

Her thoughts leapt back to her service pistol. She searched left and right. What would she say if someone else found it? *Oh, never mind about this here little bitty pistol, ya'all. I was on my way to murder Mr. Pustlebuster, but thanks to the intervention of the good Lord and an earthquake, now I've seen the light!*

"It's okay, Miz Odboddy. Here's your purse, over here." Jackson blew off the sawdust and handed it to her.

Her fingers shook as she grasped it. Her purse was the last thing on her mind. "Thank you." Agnes's head throbbed. Her gaze darted around the debris littering the floor again. The pistol must be somewhere, perhaps buried under the rubble, but soon enough, it would be discovered. It couldn't have disappeared into thin air. Perhaps it bounced across the hall and someone else picked it up?

She had to comply when Officer Dimwiddie took her arm and led her into the police department. "I don't think you should drive home, Mrs. Odboddy. Let's call your granddaughter to come and fetch you. You don't look well at all."

Wasn't that the understatement of the year! *Looking unwell* didn't begin to describe the turmoil that surged through her mind as she sat in the lobby waiting for Katherine.

While Agnes waited, she dwelt on what she had almost done. She always considered herself to be a reasonably level-headed woman. Why had she even contemplated such a plan? Perhaps she *was* losing her mind. Godfrey hinted as much. The concussion she experienced, falling from the apple tree, must have been more severe than she imagined. Maybe she *was* hallucinating when she saw Dr. Schatzsman remove paintings from the house on Cherry Blossom Way.

Though she clearly remembered every detail of her actions this morning, it was hard to understand what made her walk into city hall with a loaded pistol, intending to kill a prominent citizen. No matter how much she hated his political decisions, and no matter how much she grieved the decision to destroy Shere Khan, it was totally out of her character to resort to violence. When in her seventy-something years had she ever considered solving her problems that way?

She shook her head and rubbed the chill bumps up and down her arms. If not for the earthquake, would she have gone through with it? She wanted to believe that she would have come to her senses on her own, but recalling her determination, she didn't think so.

She felt the need to talk to someone, but whom? Katherine would be out of her mind with worry if she knew how close her grandmother came to killing the councilman. Katherine would never leave her alone again. Would Godfrey understand? What about Mildred? Agnes was sure of her loyalty and friendship, but it was doubtful Mildred would be sympathetic once she learned what happened.

Over the next few minutes, she considered and discarded the idea of discussing the situation with Chief Waddlemucker, Pastor Lickleiter or any of the ladies at The First Church of the Evening Star and Everlasting Light. None of them would have an explanation for her bizarre behavior or any idea how to prevent a recurrence.

No. It was best to keep her actions locked in her heart, but what a terrible secret to bear alone. In the future, she vowed to keep her emotions in check and never again allow anything to become an obsession. Perhaps the best thing to do was take a couple more of Dr. Schatzsman's pills. That should ward off any further bleeding in her brain or a recurrence of her ridiculous notions.

She brushed specks of sawdust off her skirt. The earthquake stopped her from committing murder, but she had accomplished nothing to help Shere Khan. His situation was worrisome, but at the moment, the more pressing concern—where the blazes had the pistol disappeared, and would they know it was her pistol when it was found?

Katherine and her friend Myrtle burst into the office. Katherine threw her arms around Agnes. "Office Dimwiddie called the shop and told me what happened. Are you sure you're all right, Grandma?"

"I'm fine, dear, just a little shaken. Was there much damage to the beauty shop?"

"A few bottles of shampoo knocked off the wall, but nothing like this. We felt the aftershocks, but I don't think it hit the shop as hard as the city hall building." Once assured that Agnes suffered no permanent injury from the earthquake, they guided her through the rubble, down the stairs, and into Katherine's Buick. Myrtle followed behind, driving Agnes's car home.

As they drove across town, they noticed a few businesses with broken windows. Agnes closed her eyes as they passed the house on Cherry Blossom Way where she saw Dr. Schatzsman carry out the paintings. In light of her recent episode at city hall, she couldn't bear to look at the house. Was it real memory, or *was* it a hallucination?

Chapter Fourteen

"Grandma will save the tiger." Maddie

S aturday came—the dreaded day. Her best efforts to save Shere Khan had come to naught. Agnes rose with the sun, dressed as quietly as possible, grabbed an apple, and left the house. Careful not to awaken Katherine, she released the brakes on Ol' Betsy, and let the car roll down the driveway. When it reached the street, she started the car and pulled away from the house.

What did she hope to prove by going out to the Higgenbottom farm? Must she bear witness to the travesty of justice about to take place? She'd appealed to the council, appealed to the chief, and done everything in her power to locate a permanent home in a zoo. Having exhausted nearly all her resources and every possible avenue of relocation, she had run out of ideas how to prevent Chief Waddlemucker from carrying out the city council's decree. It would have been easier to ignore the inevitable and hide her head under a pillow. The thought made her stomach churn. As dreadful as witnessing the event would be, she had to be there to make a last appeal.

She stopped at a stop sign, looked left and right, and then moved through the intersection. Maddie's sweet face came into her thoughts. What could they tell the child? Like it or not, they would have to lie. It was in Maddie's best interest to hear they found a zoo and Shere Khan left on the morning train, long before she awoke, and therefore there was no chance to say good-bye. Agnes's eyes stung as she imagined how Maddie would react to such a story. There would be tears and tantrums, and likely nightmares for nights to come. Would she believe them? If she guessed the truth, it could do irreparable damage to her trust in Agnes and Katherine. Hadn't Maddie evoked Agnes's promise and believed? 'Grandma will save Shere Khan.' *Haven't I done everything humanly possible to make it happen?* How could she make the child understand that sometimes things are impossible, even for grandmas.

Agnes grappled in her handbag, pulled out a hankie and dabbed her eyes. It wasn't a good idea to drive with tears streaming down and blurring one's vision. She blew her nose and tucked the hankie back in her purse. *Don't think about it. Think of something else.*

Maybe she should concentrate on the art show coming to town. Once this tiger thing was behind her, she'd have time to devote to the artist's show. She even thought it might be a good opportunity to...

Her car passed the white picket fences surrounding the Higgenbottom farm. A small herd of black and white Holsteins clustered along the fence. Up ahead, the silo connected to Mr. Higgenbottom's barn came into view. She turned into the long driveway. Dust kicked up around Ol' Betsy's tires as she bumped along the dirt drive. She pulled up alongside the chief's black and white patrol car. Several reporters and their cameramen milled around near vehicles belonging to the *Boyles Springs Citizen*, and *Newbury Gazette*. A reporter and his cameraman from the *Gazette* must have recognized Agnes's car and rushed toward her.

Agnes's hands trembled on the steering wheel. *Bloodthirsty paparazzi!* Was she too late? Had the chief already completed his dreaded assignment, and Agnes wasn't even there to lend her moral support to the poor tiger? Maybe it was for the best that she didn't have to witness the terrible deed.

Agnes pulled her car to a stop. The reporter tapped on her car window. "Mrs. Odboddy," he shouted through the glass. "I'm from the *Newbury Gazette*. How do you feel about what happened here this morning?" A flashbulb exploded in Agnes's face. Apparently, Chief Waddlemucker arrived earlier than she expected. Shere Khan was already dead!

Agnes stepped out and put up her hand to shade her eyes. "I'm appalled at the decision and such shocking behavior!" She slammed the car door and started toward the barn.

The reporter hurried alongside, his pencil poised over a tablet. "So, you don't support the outcome? Do you have a quote for the newspaper?"

Agnes stopped and glared at him. "If you mean was I hoping to get here before the chief complied with the demands of an egomaniac like Horatio Pustlebuster, the man with a God-complex who controls the city council? Then yes, I guess you can quote me as saying I'm appalled."

The reporter lifted his eyebrows, pushed back his hat and scratched his head. "I don't think I follow, Miz Odboddy. Are you saying that Councilman Pustlebuster is responsible for—?"

"Of course he's responsible. If it weren't for him, this would never have happened. I did everything I could to change things, but you can't fight city hall." She spotted Chief Waddlemucker standing with Sergeant Dimwiddie and hurried over, leaving the reporter writing frantically on his tablet. Her nails bit into her palms as she clenched her fists. "We've had our ups and downs in the past, Chief, but this time, you've gone too far. So help me, if I live to be a hundred, I'll never trust you again. We're through!" Agnes spun on her heel. Uncontrolled tears flowed down her cheeks as she dashed back toward her car. Hampered by blurry vision, she grappled at the door handle.

"Agnes! Wait." The chief followed. Reaching her car, he grabbed her arm, spun her around, and put his hands on her shoulders. "I don't understand. Why are you angry with me?" She twisted to free herself. The chief gestured across the barnyard. "Do you know anything about what's happened here?"

Her hand swept across her damp cheeks. "You tell me. You're the one who just killed an innocent animal that never harmed a flea on his back."

"I killed... What—?"

"You must be proud. It must have been like shooting fish in a barrel. The poor tiger, trapped behind bars. He didn't stand a chance. I suppose you'll mount his head on your wall, or are you going to make a rug from his skin?" Agnes grabbed the door handle, yanked open the door, and dropped into the seat, sobbing into her handkerchief.

"Wait. We need to—"

She dabbed her cheeks with one hand and fumbled with the key in the ignition with the other. "I need to go home before I say something you'll regret," she said, pressing the starter. Ol' Betsy's engine roared to life.

Chief Waddlemucker reached through the car window and grabbed the keys. "Now, you hold on a gol-darned minute. You're talking like you think I've shot that tiger of yours."

Agnes mopped the tears off her face. "Well, haven't you? That's what you all came for. Every reporter in the county came to take pictures of a dead tiger to post on the front page of their newspaper. The ghouls!" She shuddered and dabbed her eyes again. Sorely tempted to draw back her fist and punch him in the nose, she resisted the tempta… What was the chief smirking about? The reporter stood nearby, his pencil poised, apparently waiting for more breaking news.

The chief chuckled. "Now, I understand what's got you so riled up."

The nerve! Was he actually laughing at her distress? Heck with resisting temptation. She knotted and drew back her fist.

"I didn't shoot your tiger, Agnes. When we got here this morning, Charles, the tiger, and his caravan were gone. Mr. Higgenbottom says Vincent came before dawn, hitched the caravan to his truck and drove away. I don't know where they went, but he's gone, thank goodness, so my job is done. I was about to tell everyone to clear out when you showed up."

The reporter scratched on his notebook, flipped it shut and stalked away.

Agnes's mouth dropped open. "Vincent took the tiger?" She ran her hand over the tingles crawling across her cheeks. "He said he was working on a plan, but wouldn't tell us what it was," she mumbled. "He must have found a way. Oh, my goodness. Oh, thank you, Lord!"

Where ever Vincent took him, at least for the moment, Shere Khan was safe from Horatio Pustlebuster. Agnes hoped she wouldn't find the tiger's caravan parked in her driveway when she got home.

Chapter Fifteen

"I'd have thought you'd be there for moral support." Katherine

gnes sang at the top of her lungs as she drove Ol' Betsy home from the Higgenbottom farm. Plans for celebrating the tiger's unexpected rescue with Katherine and Maddie raced through her thoughts. She'd call Godfrey and have him come over for breakfast. She'd make waffles. Maddie loved waffles. Vincent must have taken Shere Khan somewhere out of the county, but where? The rascal! Sneaking into the Higgenbottom farm before dawn and not telling anyone. Why hadn't he shared his plans? He knew how worried they all were. Maybe he thought if word got out, someone would try to stop him.

Agnes cranked down her car window and breathed in the cool crisp air. The flowering cherry trees along the highway near town were already in bloom. She glanced at her watch. Only quarter to seven. She might even get home before Maddie was awake. Likely, Katherine was up and wringing her hands, knowing Agnes had gone to the farm, since today was the date of the city council's edict.

She probably should have wakened Katherine before she left the house, but since she and Maddie shared a bedroom, there was the risk of also waking Maddie. She left without even a cup of coffee.

As Agnes passed a grove of birch trees, a flock of Swifts, rose up and blackened the sky, as though driven by a single mind, darting hither and yon, making undulating patterns in the sky. Unlike Shere Khan, they were free to fly and raise their young wherever they chose. Living in a cage and performing like a trick pony wasn't the best life for Shere Khan, but likely he knew no other, and as long as he was well-cared for and fed, wasn't that enough? Agnes shook her head. No. It shouldn't be enough. Returning to the jungle where he belonged was not possible, but where could he be free to be a tiger? It wasn't right to be forced to perform tricks, an object stared at, no matter how much he enjoyed the attention.

Was she approaching this from the wrong angle? Vincent spirited Shere Khan away before dawn, but to what end? Suppose she found a zoo willing to take him. He'd still be on display for adults and children to jeer at, point at, throw peanuts at. No peace and quiet. No hills to roam. Fed at the end of a stick, confined to a small, barred cage.

Tears stung her eyes. Why had she gotten involved in a situation where there was no good solution? Would it be better to turn her eyes from injustice, prejudice or discrimination, knowing that getting involved would change nothing? Should she have looked the other way when she learned of Shere Khan's plight?

Her head continued to spin with more questions. Would their energies be better spent trying to prevent traveling carnivals, circuses and zoos from displaying wild animals?

Carnivals and zoos gave the public a chance to see animals they would never see otherwise, but what about the animal? Taken from their natural environment, often mistreated or with questionable care, put on display like a performing monkey… Would there ever be a day when society actually abolished circuses and traveling carnivals and provided more natural habitats for the wild animals? That was likely years away, or more likely, never.

Agnes shook her head. It was all upside down, and too confusing to sort out. Too many 'what ifs.' For today, she would consider it enough to have saved one animal. Sadly, Shere Khan's best option lay in the chance to live in a zoo, as unsatisfactory and problematic as that might be.

Hopefully, Vincent had a longer range plan in mind. Otherwise, it was prolonging the inevitable.

She dismissed all the depressing thoughts. She was supposed to be in a celebratory mood. Vincent saved the tiger from certain death, but, in her heart she knew, as satisfying as today's success, it was not nearly enough.

Katherine walked over to Agnes's car window when she pulled into the driveway. "I was on my way to the farm." She placed a trembling hand on her grandmother's window sill and lowered her head. "Is it over?"

Agnes stepped out of her car. "You didn't hear from Vincent? That rascal got there before dawn. He and Charles took the tiger away before anyone arrived." She grinned. "Crisis averted."

Katherine put her hand to her heart. "Thank God. Vincent hasn't called. Where do you suppose they went?"

Agnes leaned back into the front seat to retrieve her pocketbook. "I'm so glad the chief didn't have to ... well, you know. Now, come on in the house. Do we have enough eggs to make waffles?"

"I think so." Katherine followed her up the steps, unlocked the door and went inside.

"Where's Maddie?"

"I sent her over to play with Mavis's puppy. I couldn't take her with me to the farm. I'll call and have her come home."

"Let her stay for a while." Agnes nodded toward the wall phone. "Let's invite Godfrey to breakfast. I have a hunch he may know more about Vincent's plan." She opened the icebox and removed the milk jug and a carton of eggs.

Katherine called Godfrey while Agnes mixed the waffle batter. "He'll be right over. He says he can catch a ride with his neighbor."

"Good." Agnes pulled the waffle iron from a lower cupboard, and plugged it into the wall socket. "There. As soon as he gets here, we'll eat." She opened the icebox and brought out the Oleomargarine and the homemade strawberry jam, and then, the honey jar from the cupboard.

"Grandmother," Katherine said. "Before Godfrey gets here, can we talk? I have some concerns." She stared at the table and slid the salt and pepper shakers back and forth.

"What concerns would that be, dear?" Agnes measured coffee into the pot. She lit a wooden match, touched it to the burner as she turned the stove knob, igniting the gas beneath the burners. A blue flame danced around the prongs. Adjusting the knob lowered the flames under the pot. "That's about right." She turned and crossed her arms. "You have my full attention. Are you worried about marrying Vincent?"

"It has nothing to do with—"

"I know things have been difficult since Dr. Dew-Wright left town." Agnes pulled out a chair and sat, remembering Katherine's previous fiancé who left her to become the head surgeon at a prominent Sacramento hospital. "I thought things were going well with you and Vincent. Is there a problem?"

"I said, it's not about—"

"Then, it must be Maddie. In my opinion, she couldn't have a better role model. Don't give it a second thought. You're doing a great job with her."

Katherine shook her head. "It's got nothing to do with—"

"Coffee should be ready any minute now." Agnes glanced at the chicken clock on the wall over the stove. She jumped up. "I'll pour. Get the milk from the icebox, would you, dear?"

Katherine sighed, and picked up the milk jug from the counter. "It's already sitting right here. Now, Grandma, stop changing the subject. You know I'm not talking about Dr. Don or Vincent or Maddie! I'm talking about your continued headaches and fainting spells since your fall."

Agnes pulled her mouth into a scowl. "What did Godfrey tell you?"

"Don't get mad at Godfrey. He told me what happened in Chief

Waddlemucker's office the other day. He's worried about you, too. We both think you should go back to Dr. Schatzsman."

"When H-E-double-hockey sticks freeze over! I told you I'd take his flaming pills, but I won't see that fraud again. Next time I need a doctor, I'll see Dr. Thigpen in Boyles Springs."

"Then, maybe you should call and make an appointment. Even after a concussion, it isn't normal to continue having problems for so long." Katherine's cheeks turned pink. "There could be something else going on in your thick head."

Agnes set Katherine's coffee mug on the table. "My dear, I had no idea you were so concerned. You mustn't worry. I'm perfectly all right, I assure you. I'm taking Dr. Schatzsman's pills, just like he said." She patted Katherine's hand. "In fact, I even take an extra pill from time to time, for good measure."

"An extra one? Is that a good idea? Maybe you shouldn't—"

Agnes's neck and cheeks flushed. "Confound it, Katherine. Make up your mind." Her eyebrows squinched together. "First, I'm not doing enough to take care of myself, and now I'm doing too much?" She turned on her heel. "If Godfrey gets here before I'm back, tell him I've gone for a walk." She stomped into the living room and out the front door, slamming it behind her.

Katherine opened her mouth and clamped it shut again. One minute Grandma was fine and the next she was snapping and snarling like a cornered badger.

Ling-Ling wandered into the kitchen, stopped in the doorway and sat on her haunches. Her crossed blue eyes stared in Katherine's general direction.

"What just happened?" Katherine said.

Ling-Ling's head turned in the direction her mistress had gone. Her expression seemed to say, *'Beats the heck out of me. She's your grandmother.'*

Living with Grandma's willfulness and eccentricities was always a challenge, but usually their personal relationship was good. Quarrels were few and short-lived. Get mad—get over it, was the philosophy they chose to live by. It wasn't possible for two strong women to live in the same house and not have occasional tiffs. The addition of a child to the household created additional stress and with the advent of Shere Khan's situation—even more.

Since Grandma's fall, she was more cantankerous and challenging than usual, notably her irrational mood swings and her unreasonable behavior toward Councilman Pustlebuster and Dr. Schatzsman. It was hard to guess whether these changes were due to her fall or dementia, but it put Katherine in a delicate position. Put up with Grandma's nonsense, or consider a separate living arrangement. How could she afford a place for her and Maddie on her income from the beauty shop and the occasional money she received for doing the hair and makeup for the dearly departed at Whistlemeyer's Funeral Home? It appeared Grandma needed someone around to help her, now, more than ever.

Bing Bong

"It must be Godfrey." Katherine dabbed her eyes, blew her nose, and hurried to open the door. "Well, I see you've graduated to a cane. Bet you're glad to be rid of those crutches. Come on in. There's fresh coffee in the kitchen."

"Morning, Katherine." Godfrey stepped into the living room and paused just inside the door. "You okay? You look like you've been crying." He glanced around the room. "What's wrong?" The muscles around his mouth tightened.

Katherine gave a dismissive wave of her hand. "Oh, there's nothing to worry about. Grandma and I had a little spat. It wasn't important. She's taking a walk to cool off."

They both knew that dealing with Agnes was often like riding a run-away train, barreling down the track toward a washed-out bridge.

Godfrey nodded. "I'll have that cup of coffee and we'll chat for a while." He followed Katherine into the kitchen and pulled a chair from under the table.

Katherine poured a cup of coffee and set it in front of Godfrey. "I'm surprised you didn't go to the farm with Grandma this morning. I thought you'd want to provide moral support."

"As it happens, it wasn't necessary. Besides, Agnes didn't call me before she left. There wasn't much we could have done to stop the chief. He had orders from the city council. Thankfully—"

The front door squeaked open. *"Yoo-Hoo!* I'm home." Agnes bounced into the kitchen, all smiles, rubbing her bare arms. "It's a bit chilly out, to be sure. I should have taken a sweater." She leaned down to kiss Godfrey's cheek. "Where are your crutches? Did Katherine tell you we have waffle batter all ready? Now, let's see if we can feed this hungry man." She poured herself a cup of coffee. "Katherine! Godfrey likes a dollop of milk in his coffee."

"Well, I—"

"Never mind. I'll get it. So, tell me, Godfrey. Have you talked to Vincent? The most amazing thing happened. When I got to the farm this morning, the tiger was gone. So were Vincent and Charles. Of course, I was relieved, since the chief didn't have to do the unthinkable, but it would've been nice if Vincent told us what he was up to. I could hardly sleep last night for worry. Katherine sent Maddie over to play with Mavis's puppy, but she'll be home soon. I'm sure you're anxious to see her. She's one of your girls too, you know, as much as Katherine."

Katherine took her grandmother's arm and gently eased her into a kitchen chair. "Sit, Grandma and calm down. You sound like Flash Gordon's rocket ship, about to blast off to Mars. The waffle iron is ready. I'll have a waffle ready in a jiffy."

Katherine ladled batter into the hot iron. Something was definitely wrong with Grandma. First, flying off the handle over the smallest thing, and now sounding like she was plugged into an electric light socket. Katherine exchanged glances with Godfrey and nodded toward Agnes.

"Vincent called before he headed for the farm this morning," he said. "He filled me in on his plan. I thought he called you."

"Well, I should think. It would have been nice to know what he had in mind instead of leaving us in the dark and worried half the night."

"I think he only got the final approval from Colonel Farthingworth at the Boyles Springs Military Base around midnight," Godfrey said. "He didn't want us to get our hopes up if it didn't work. As soon as he heard from the colonel, he drove to the farm and spirited Shere Khan away."

"If Vincent had come an hour later, the tiger would have been a goner. Chief Waddlemucker was at the farm before six o'clock this morning. So, what's the long-range plan?"

Katherine plopped a waffle onto a plate and handed it to Godfrey.

"Apparently, the tiger's caravan can stay at the military base. Vincent and the colonel have worked it all out with Washington."

Katherine refilled Godfrey's coffee cup. "So who's going to take care of Shere Khan? He needs someone who understands his needs. What's Charles going to do?"

"That's the best part of the colonel's plan. They're hiring Charles to take care of Shere Khan. They've offered him a stipend and housing in exchange for staying on. It's temporary, but at least it buys us some time. That's what took so long. Working out Charles's arrangements."

"That was kind of the colonel. *Huh!*" Grandmother stared out the kitchen window, as though lost in thought.

"The plan," Godfrey said, "is that Shere Khan will be part of a morale boosting program. The colonel convinced Washington it would increase war bond sales. They'll take the tiger to various fairs, or conferences, and local events and let him perform. Just like at the carnival, they expect the tiger to draw in the crowds. Then hopefully, they'll be more inclined to buy war bonds." Godfrey spread jam on the waffle on his plate. "Thanks. This looks great."

Grandmother leaned across the table and patted Godfrey's hand. She turned and beamed at Katherine. "It's wonderful news. Good old Colonel Farthingworth! I thought of taking the tiger to the military base, myself. I was getting ready to suggest such a plan to the colonel, but it looks like Victor beat me to it."

"Really, Grandma?" Katherine set a waffle in front of Agnes. "Here's your breakfast."

Chapter Sixteen

"Must you demean me so early in the morning?" Agnes

T he clock over the mantle struck eleven o'clock. Katherine and Maddie had gone to bed and Agnes stood in front of the bathroom mirror, tying her hair in little rags, in hopes of having a bit of wave in the morning. She peered at her reflection, bared her teeth in a grimace and then rubbed cold cream into the winkles beside her mouth. Not that the cold cream had any effect on alleviating wrinkles, but after seventy-plus years, it gave one a measure of hope, no matter how futile.

She turned from side to side, pulled her nightgown against her breasts to evaluate her figure and sighed. The girls were heading south, no doubt about it, but she'd seen worse on women of a certain age, and she still considered herself a fine figure of a woman. There was no point bemoaning the hand Mother Nature dealt. The ringing of the kitchen phone pulled her away from her lament. "Who could that be at this hour?"

"Hello? Odboddy residence. Whatever you're selling, I already have one."

"Agnes? It's Chief Waddlemucker. Sorry to call so late, but it's important—thought you'd want to know."

"Whatever it is, there's not much I can do about it at this hour."

"Guess not, since you put it that way. Well, then, sorry to bother you. I'll call Mildred Higgenbottom, being as she's the vice president of the Ladies Society down at The First Church of the Sunset and Never-ending Light and—"

"That would be The First Church of the Evening Star and Everlasting Light, and you'd know that if you ever brought your heathen-self to church on Sunday. I'm the president of the Ladies Society. Now, what's this all about?"

"First Church of the... What You Said. Thought you ought to know there's been a burglary at the church. A neighbor heard glass breaking and called it in. When we got there, we found the window busted. The thief emptied the Ladies Society Missionary moneybox in the front of the church and—"

"Oh, horse feathers! That was for the Puerto Rican missionaries. Is that all they took?"

"'Fraid not. They also took a painting from behind the choir loft."

"Not our Bernhard Plockhorst painting of the Good Shepherd!" A physical pain shot through Agnes's chest, remembering the hours spent at church rummage sales and bake sales earning the money to purchase the painting. When she first saw it offered for sale in a San Francisco newspaper, she convinced the Ladies Society to make it their 1937 Ladies Society annual project. At a cost of over $200, even an early framed lithograph of the beautiful painting was sure to gain value over time.

"Were you personally attached to that one?" Chief Waddlemucker said.

"Sorry to say, yes. I've always loved that picture of Jesus, holding a shepherd's staff in one hand and a lamb in the other." Agnes's eyes pricked with tears. "It's the most iconic rendition of Christ recognized by most Christians, even to the point of accepting his face as that of the true Christ. The painter has quite a history."

"I'm not familiar with it."

"Bernhard Plockhorst was from Germany, famous during the latter part of the 1800s, and copies of his paintings are practically a US household item."

"Now that I think of it, my mother had a Good Shepherd picture in her living room when I was a child."

"I'll bet you didn't know that he also painted the Guardian Angel watching over two children as they traversed a dangerous cliff."

"Don't know what to say, Agnes. So you're not so worried about the missing money? How much was in the missionary box?"

"I don't know. Maybe thirty dollars. We can always bake more cakes and replace the money. How can we replace our Good Shepherd? It was priceless. Well, maybe not priceless, but expensive, and it was ours! Who would do...?" Agnes's hand flew to her forehead. Dr. Schatzsman! Of course! The thief who never saw a good painting he didn't try to steal. He probably had connections to an underground network to sell his ill-gotten items.

Why, just last Sunday, he'd came to church for the first time in a month of Sundays, sat right up close to the pulpit, and ogled the painting during the whole service. When Agnes noticed him gawking toward the front of the church, she'd assumed he was eyeballing young, pretty Alice Magrooter, sitting in the front row of the choir, wearing a dress with a much-too-revealing neckline for Sunday morning service. In hindsight, the doctor was likely scrutinizing The Good Shepherd painting and thinking how he might sneak back some dark night and purloin the prodigious Plockhorst painting. The scumbag! She almost felt an ownership to it, since she'd been instrumental in its purchase.

Now, the question was, did she dare share her suspicions with the chief? Was he likely to agree with Godfrey and Katherine's opinion that seeing Dr. Schatzsman burgling the house not so long ago in the dark of night was a result of hallucinations brought on by her fall? Or would he believe she was an eye-witness to a burglary? "Chief, I can tell you who had the audacity to break into the church and swipe our Good Shepherd painting, but I'm too tired to go into it right now. I'd rather—"

"You know who the thief is?"

Agnes sighed and glanced up at the clock on the wall. "It's late. Suppose I come down to your office first thing in the morning and we can discuss it in detail."

"But, Agnes. If you have information we could use to catch the thief, I need to know now. We can't have thieves running amuck through Newbury. What do you know?"

"Good night, Chief. I'll see you first thing in the morning." Agnes hung up the phone. It wasn't nice to hang up on him, but an explanation would take too long. On the other hand, hopefully it wouldn't keep her tossing and turning all night, going over how she witnessed Dr. Schatzsman carry the painting from the blue house with the white shutters. Or was it the white house with the blue shutters? *Oh, bother.*

Agnes stood on the front porch as the paperboy cycled down the street, tossing early morning newspapers to each house. She retrieved her paper and rolled the rubber band off the cylinder as she carried it into the kitchen. She opened the newspaper and scanned the headlines. "Not a word about the burglary. No surprise."

Katherine scurried around, chopping celery and carrots and making a peanut butter and jelly sandwich for Maddie's lunch. "What are you growling about, Grandma? You sound like a bear with his paw stuck in the honey pot." Katherine ladled Cream of Wheat into a bowl. "Maddie! Come right now. Your breakfast is ready."

"There's nothing in the paper about the church break-in and our Good Shepherd painting being stolen."

"What about it. What happened?" Katherine slid into a chair. She poured milk over her cereal and sprinkled brown sugar on top.

"Chief Waddlemucker called late last night. Someone broke into the church and took the painting and emptied out the missionary box."

"That's terrible. What is the world coming to these days?"

Maddie hurried into the kitchen and sat. "Morning, Grandma." She tossed a ribboned braid over her shoulder.

"Good morning, sweetheart. You look nice today." Agnes took

a sip of coffee and set her cup on the table. "I'm going down to the police station this morning to talk to the chief. I expect we'll join forces to bring the thief to justice." She smiled at Maddie and jiggled her eyebrows.

Katherine coughed as she sipped her coffee. "Really? Since when did the chief ask you to assist him in their open criminal investigations? I suppose you think this is related to the burglary you thought you saw the other night."

Warmth tinged Agnes's cheeks. She set her coffee cup on the table. "Well, if you'll recall, my intuition and resourcefulness has played a major role in solving a number of cases. Maybe it would be better to call them situations rather than actual police cases."

"Actually, I recall that it was more like sticking your nose where it didn't belong and having the good fortune to come back alive," Katherine snapped, "rather than playing an active role in assisting the police, wouldn't you say?"

"Katherine, that's a mean thing to say. Especially, in front of the child. Must you demean me so early in the morning? After all we've just been through?" She pushed back her chair, leaving her cereal half-eaten, and then flounced down the hall and into her bedroom.

"Wait! I didn't mean... I'm sorry," Katherine called.

"*Humph!*" Agnes slammed her bedroom door. Maybe Katherine was right, describing her previous crime-solving activities as more inadvertent, than purposefully planned. More often, she'd stumbled into criminal activity, and when all was said and done and the results were favorable, she'd claimed the outcome was her plan all along. Surely, her efforts played *some* part in bringing various criminals to justice. Great Caesar's ghost! Couldn't Katherine give a little credit where credit was due? Katherine tapped on Agnes's bedroom door. "We're leaving. I'll drop Maddie at school. Can we talk later, Grandma?"

Still miffed at Katherine's reprimand, Agnes mumbled, "Good bye."

"Okay. Have it your way," Katherine called. The front door

slammed shut.

So she'd apologized, but was it necessary for Katherine to make such a claim in the first place? Oh, get mad! Get over it. She'd bake some brown sugar cookies this afternoon, and by nightfall, there'd be no need to revisit the situation. All would be forgiven.

Her gaze roamed around the bedroom and paused at the yellowed newspaper clipping pinned to the side of her dressing table mirror. It pictured Mrs. Wilkey's son, a local boy who gave his life for his country. Poor Mrs. Wilkey. She pulled down the yellowed clipping, wadded it up and tossed it in the wastebasket.

The clipping reminded her of the article she'd read on the front page of the *Newbury Gazette* this morning, another account of the military artist she'd read about in Mrs. Wilkey's grocery store. She returned to the kitchen and found the article. "Yes, here it is. Multiple award-winning United States Army combat painter and photographer, Edward Reep, is coming to Newbury next Saturday and will be displaying his artwork in the Crest Theater lobby. Mr. Reep's art is considered one of 1943's most promising investments. His most notable creation is an eight foot by twenty-four foot mural at the Soldier's Club in Monterey, California."

Agnes snapped the paper, folded it in half and snorted. "With this kind of advertising, he'll sell plenty. That is, unless good doctor Schatzsman breaks into the theater and empties out all his precious paintings." Agnes tossed the paper onto the table. "Hey, wait a minute." A sly smile creased her lips. "If I can convince Chief Waddlemucker… With the help of his detectives, we can bring down this scoundrel."

The sun glinting through the kitchen window struck the cut glass vase in the middle of the table, casting a glaring beam into her eyes. She jerked her head away, and put her hand over her eyes as a blinding pain shot through her head. She stood and strode down the hall toward the bathroom. Perhaps she should take a headache powder before she left for the chief's office. And she mustn't forget to take her morning dose of Dr. Schatzsman's cursed pills.

Chapter Seventeen

"Hang on, Agnes, don't go arse over teakettle now." Agnes

That's about it, Chief. I saw Dr. Schatzsman carry a painting from the house on Cherry Blossom Way. I read all about the burglary in the newspaper the next morning." Agnes folded her arms across her bosom and frowned. "It was him, as sure as the devil. What's the odds that he didn't steal our Good Shepherd painting, too?"

Chief Waddlemucker laced his fingers behind his head and leaned back in his chair. "So, why am I only hearing about it now, for goodness sake? Knowing you, I should think you'd have been pounding on my door with this information the next morning before daybreak."

Agnes lowered her gaze. "Well, it was the morning after I fell out of the tree, as you'll recall, and I was feeling poorly. Katherine and Godfrey said I was hallucinating for a while during the night. They had me half-convinced that I didn't see what I saw, so I was hesitant to bring it to your attention... *um*... but then I read about the house getting burglarized, and I knew I'd seen what I thought I'd saw... seen."

"But, Agnes, you and Godfrey came down here a day or so later. If you were so convinced by then, why didn't you mention it that day? Now you come in at this late date... why should I believe your story now?" He lowered his chair back to the floor, picked up a pencil and tapped it on the desk. His bushy eyebrows furrowed and the lines in his forehead resembled horizontal craters on the moon.

Agnes's hand fluttered. "I felt faint the day I came to your office. Godfrey said I was having a flashback to a nightmare, and I couldn't go into it then. I didn't think you'd believe me. But, I'm better now..."

Agnes blinked several times to bring the chief's face into focus. Truth was, he looked a little blurry, and she wasn't feeling better at all. The effort of getting dressed, driving across town and the anxiety of wondering how the chief would receive her story was taking more of a toll than she cared to admit. "I swear it's the truth. I'm telling you that the doctor is running a burglary ring. I suspect he's the one who stole the painting from the church last night, too. He's probably fencing his high-end merchandise in San Francisco. Maybe he thinks his reputation protects him from suspicion, but I saw him on Cherry Blossom Way with my own eyes." She clenched her hands to stop their shaking. *Hang on, Agnes, don't go arse over teakettle now.* She could feel the tell-tale signs, but she had to keep from fainting dead away if she was to convince the chief or there was no hope of him helping her bring the scalawag to justice.

The chief ran his fingers through his thinning grey hair and folded his hands on the desk. "Now, Agnes, you've been under a lot of stress recently, what with your fall and then all this clap-trap over the tiger. That kind of stress can play tricks on your mind, but I can assure you, Dr. Schatzsman is innocent. He's highly respected. Why, he's a pillar of the community and serves on the city council. I can't act on your accusation, seeing as how it all happened during a time you were suffering from a concussion.

"Now, here's what I'm going to do." He leaned solicitously toward her. "Suppose you run along home and I'll have a little talk with the doctor. I'll see if I can't get to the bottom of things in a way that satisfies your concern. Now, how does that sound?"

Agnes's neck warmed as she grabbed her purse and rose from her chair. "Sounds like a trailer-load of donkey doodle to me. I should know better than to bring my concerns to you." She strode to the door, turned and blustered. "Apparently, if that scoundrel is ever brought to justice, I'll have to do it myself." She opened the door into the outer office and was assailed by the sound of murmuring voices and the click of typewriters.

"Now Agnes, don't go off half-cocked and do something stupid. The doctor has rights. If you harass him, it'll go bad for you."

"Are you going to arrest me? I'm not the one who burgled a house on Cherry Blossom Way and more recently stole a picture of our Lord Jesus Christ from The First Church of the Evening Star and Everlasting Light. I'm the one who's trying to tell you about a…a viper in our midst. Good day, sir!"

Agnes tromped out of the chief's office and slammed the door. She dropped onto a bench in the hallway. Now, wasn't this a fine kettle of fish? She hadn't convinced the chief about Dr. Schatzsman's shenanigans and would get no help from the police department in bringing him to justice. Worse yet, the chief was going to 'speak to the doctor,' alerting him to her suspicions. That would make it even harder to expose his crimes and bring him to justice.

She wiped beads of perspiration from her forehead and tucked the handkerchief back into the neck of her dress. Though she had a vague idea that Edward Reep's show might tempt the doctor into a compromising situation, she would need help if there was any hope of her plan succeeding. Godfrey and Katherine already voiced their disbelief about witnessing the burglary. How could she convince them to help her expose the doctor?

Agnes rose from the bench and walked down the stairs to the first floor. Though she enjoyed the company of the elevator attendant, Jackson Jackson, at the moment, she had no desire to engage in small talk.

Satisfied that Shere Khan was out of imminent danger and in good hands at the Boyles Springs military base with Charles, Agnes spent the remainder of the week volunteering with Edward Reep's staff, shuffling papers and making phone calls to promote the art show that weekend.

On Sunday morning, before the theater opened to the public, the volunteers set up the art work. Mr. Reep would arrive later that evening to attend an 'invitation only' champagne soiree for Newbury's most prominent citizens, most likely to purchase paintings and photographs. Those invited included the mayor, the city council members, Dr. Schatzsman, and the CEO of Newbury Hospital. Mr. Bernard Whistlemeyer, owner of the local mortuary where Katherine provided hair styling and makeup would be there along with Chief Waddlemucker, Officer Dimwiddie, and their wives.

The theater was to open at 2:00 P.M. Sunday afternoon for Alfred Hitchcock's Shadow of a Doubt, starring Joseph Cotton, and Teresa Wright, two of Agnes's favorite movie stars. The public could view the artwork in the lobby on their way into the feature.

Officer Dimwiddie would guard the lobby throughout late Sunday afternoon, until the champagne party at 7:00 P.M. Having learned the hard way that his artwork attracted opportunistic scalawags, Mr. Reep hired an additional security man during the champagne social, who would remain stationed outside the theater throughout the night.

Agnes gazed around the lobby. With all the artwork placed on their respective easels, the carpets shampooed, every surface dusted and polished, the champagne glasses stacked in a pyramid on a table near the door, everything was as neat as a pin, waiting for the moviegoers to arrive.

The following morning, the volunteers would pack up the artwork and load it into a moving van headed for the next venue.

With his penchant for valuable artwork, how could Schatzsman resist such an attractive target as the famous Reep lithograph? Surely, he would attempt to pinch the prized painting for his own inappropriate purposes...so to speak. With the artwork in the theater for such a brief time, the devious doctor most likely would make his move tonight after the last champagne glass was drained and the last guest was gone!

Since Chief Waddlemucker gave no credence to her warning about the doctor's true calling, it was incumbent upon her to capture the rogue herself. Agnes planned to keep watch throughout the night, catch the thief in the act, turn him over to the authorities and be vindicated with regards to her accusations. What a shame she lost her service pistol during the earthquake. Perhaps Godfrey would loan her his pistol.

Agnes gave no thought to exactly how she planned to go about capturing the doctor. With Godfrey's help, it would all work out.

Agnes ran her hand over the frame of an eighteen by twenty-four inch lithograph, a likeness of Reep's famous painted mural at the Monterey Soldier's Club, the most publicized item in the show, and probably the most valuable. It was likely to be Schatzsman's prime target. Agnes set the easel strategically close to the back hallway where she could keep an eye on it while she lay in wait for the thief.

Now, all she had to do was convince Godfrey to keep watch with her!

Agnes knotted her fists on her hips and stamped her foot. "But, Godfrey. You're not listening. I've explained a dozen times. You need to help me catch the doctor in the act. You know he'll try to steal the Reep lithograph tonight."

"Honey-biscuit, *you* don't understand. I've told *you* a dozen times. You're wrong about the doctor. You just think you saw him stealing paintings. You were probably having a nightmare. You can't go around accusing folks of crimes without proof. Come on, plum-bunny, be reasonable." Godfrey wobbled across his apartment on his cane. Agnes, arms crossed, leaning against his Youngstown metal kitchen cabinets.

"Don't honey-biscuit-plum-bunny me, Godfrey Baumgarten…" Her voice took on a tone that usually preceded her throwing a fit.

Godfrey took a step backward. His cheeks paled. Agnes knew he was all too familiar with the warning signs, having been on the receiving end of her temper-tantrums. He put up his hands. "Okay!

Okay! Do whatever you want, but, you're on your own. I'm not getting involved. What do you plan to do, anyway? Tie him up and beat a confession out of him? You know this is all nonsense."

"Really, Godfrey. I can't believe you'd think that of me. What I have in mind is much less violent. The doctor won't be able to pass up the famous Reep lithograph. It's too valuable. With it right under his nose, he's sure to take the bait. I plan to catch him in the act." Agnes lowered her head and picked at her fingernail. "If you won't help me..." She lifted her head. "I really don't want to set up a sting operation by myself." Having recently read another Ellery Queen novel, the concept and terminology came easily to her lips. "Can I borrow your pistol?"

Godfrey's mouth turned down. Was he frustrated or fearful for her safety? A defeated sigh escaped his lips. "No, you cannot. What's wrong with your pistol, as though you'd need one in the first place?"

"It's... *um*... I'm not sure where I've put it." Her cheeks burned.

"If you insist on going through with this, at least get someone else to go with you. Have you talked to Vincent?"

Agnes lifted her eyebrows. "I hadn't thought of asking him. I was so sure you'd... but I see that dog won't hunt." She turned on her heel, stalked out the door and down the theater stairs, to where her Model A was parked.

Godfrey leaned over the railing. "Agnes, wait! Honey-bun. Can't we talk about this?"

Agnes yanked open her car door and yelled, "All talked out!" She slid into the seat and jammed the key into the ignition. Ol' Betsy rumbled and shook. Agnes shoved the floor gearshift into reverse, looked over her shoulder to check for traffic and backed into the street. "I don't know when I've ever been so disappointed in a man," she mumbled. "Oh, wait. What am I saying? It's Godfrey. One way or another, about all he's ever done is disappoint me."

She drove across town, lost in thought. She hadn't a clue how to convince Vincent to get on board with her scheme.

Chapter Eighteen

*A*gnes squirmed on the packing crate, trying to restore circulation to her bum. She leaned the fireplace poker she brought from home against her crate, reached for her thermos bottle, poured the lid half full of coffee and took a sip. *Yuck!* Lukewarm already! She twisted her wrist until a stream of light from the front window fell across her wristwatch. 2:45 A.M. Oh-dark-hundred! She'd only been there since eleven-thirty when the last visitor left the cocktail party in the theater lobby. Already bored, stiff from sitting on a packing crate for three hours, and still there was no sign of the expected thief.

She glanced around the silent, shadowy hallway and into the theater lobby, dimly lit by the light inside the popcorn machine. Where was the blasted doctor? The biggest scoundrel in Newbury was sure to be tempted by such a delicious prize. She'd wait. He'd come sooner or later, without a doubt. She was never wrong…well, mostly, never wrong.

She stood, flexed her knees, and gazed into the quiet lobby. Only several hours before, the room hummed with chatter, bursts of laughter, and the clink of glasses, as the local high school performed a medley of show tunes for the local mucky-mucks. Agnes sat back on the crate, remembering the *oohs and ahhs* over the numerous chilling photographs and watercolors Mr. Reep produced, depicting the human misery, battle scenes, and exhausted men at rest or in prayer. The horrors of war were at the center of many chilling conversations as older Newbury citizens recounted their own WWI experiences. Agnes had mingled with the guests and engaged in murmured conversations, referencing complaints about meat shortages and gas rations. With much soul-searching, the guests compared their current grievances against the suffering of the men depicted in Mr. Reep's art work.

She leaned her head against the wall. What was Godfrey doing tonight? Why did he refuse to help her? If Godfrey was so sure she was wrong about Dr. Schatzsman, he might have at least agreed to keep her company tonight. She hefted the fireplace poker and spun it between her hands. She should have borrowed Godfrey's pistol, but, that prompted his question, 'where is your pistol?' That was a question she was unwilling and unable to answer at present. She wondered what the janitor thought when he swept up the debris and found her pistol among the rubble at city hall. It was odd there hadn't been a whisper of gossip about it.

What about Vincent? Her efforts to convince him to join her tonight had fallen on deaf ears. Even with his background as an FBI agent, it didn't take a rocket scientist to see through his feeble excuses—a meeting with his FBI counterparts in Cloverdale... Yeah, right!

And, Katherine? She'd outright refused, 'If you want to sit down there in the cold all night and make a fool of yourself, go right ahead. I won't be a party to it.' Ungrateful girl! After all they'd been through together, too. And this was the thanks she got?

Rather than involve either of her two elderly lady-friends, Mavis or Mildred, Agnes opted to come alone.

Agnes heard a skittering sound near the back door. She jumped to her feet and grabbed the fireplace poker. *It must be the doctor.* Up until now, she'd neglected to consider how she was to apprehend the doctor. Now that the game was a-foot, doubts assailed her mind. Would he surrender just because she verbally confronted him? Not likely. Could she get close enough to whack him over the head with the fireplace poker before he noticed her in the shadows? Less likely. Would the night watchman circling around the building hear her if she yelled for help? What if the doctor was armed? The thought made her light-headed. *Oh, Agnes, you idiot!* Godfrey and Katherine were right. She'd been foolish and headstrong. Why did enlightenment always come when it was too late?

Thoughts of her comfortable easy chair by the fireplace, with Ling-Ling on her lap, and a cup of cocoa loomed. She'd exchanged such a pleasant evening for a hard crate in the dark, and confronting a hardened thief. Why had she ignored her loved ones' warnings? She flattened her back against the wall, the blood throbbing through her head, and peered through the darkness toward the back door.

Several minutes passed. When nothing amiss occurred, Agnes's heartbeat slowed. She realized she'd been holding her breath and gradually blew it out, set the poker back on the floor, and sat back on the crate. False alarm. It was probably a rat in the alley. Maybe Godfrey needed to call an exterminator. Better yet, he could use the services of a good cat to patrol the theater at night. She determined to call Mr. Higgenbottom at the farm first thing in the morning and see if there was a barn cat he could donate for a good cause.

With pleasant thoughts of the numerous black and white kittens at the farm, Agnes's heart rate slowed and she dismissed the disturbing concerns of five minutes before. When the doctor came, she would stop him, single-handed...somehow. To make sure she would have no further anxiety attacks or lightheadedness, she opened her purse, retrieved one of the doctor's pills, and popped it in her mouth. Another sip of lukewarm coffee and down it went. There! That should assure she'd have no ill effects from the stress of this night's efforts, no matter how excited she got.

Tomorrow, she expected to read the details of her heroism on the front page of the *Newbury Gazette*. She could almost see the headlines now. *DOCTOR BROUGHT DOWN BY PATIENT CITIZEN* ...a little play on words there... The story would go something like... *Agnes Agatha Odboddy, self-appointed pursuer of justice and local revered citizen, has once again captured a criminal caught in the act of skullduggery, attempting to steal a painting by the famous American painter, Edward Reep. Following the champagne soiree celebrating the renowned artist, and defying risk to her person, and having declined any help whatsoever from her relatives and friends, despite multiple offers to assist, Mrs. Odboddy, single-handedly, without assistance, staked out the Crest Theater and apprehended the no-longer highly respected local Dr. Schatzsman, as he attempted to steal the famous lithograph based on the twenty-foot Reep mural.* Maybe they'd add a few paragraphs about her previous successful efforts exposing black-market conspiracies and Nazi foes.

Agnes glanced into the lobby again. A shadow passed the front door. Then a flash of light lit up the lobby and moved on. Over the past several hours, the night watchman circled the building every eleven minutes. Occasionally, he'd stop at the front entrance, rattle the doorknob, checking that it was locked. She assumed that with each circle of the building, he checked windows, doors, and flashed his light around the alley before moving on.

Agnes counted the guard passing the front window twice more. Her head nodded and her eyes drooped as the day's activities and lack of sleep caught up with her. Her eyes snapped open at a ruckus at the back door. Instantly awake, adrenaline surged through her limbs. She jumped off the crate and grabbed the poker. The back door rattled. It wasn't a rat this time. Something was going on in the alley behind the theater. Was that the sound of a tool picking the lock?

Agnes held the fireplace poker over her head and backed into a deeper shadow. The doctor was coming! Why hadn't the watchman stopped him or scared him away? Had the scoundrel overpowered the guard? Should she try to reach a phone before he broke in, or remain in her current hiding place? There was a telephone in Godfrey's office, but to reach it, she'd have to pass by the back door where the thief would likely enter any second. Her breathing quickened. She could feel a flush rushing up her arms, into her neck and face. The poker trembled in her hand.

The lock gave way and the back door slowly squeaked open. A man stepped through the door and crept down the hall toward the lobby, coming directly toward her. Too dark to actually see…but it looked like… It must be Dr. Schatzsman.

She blinked rapidly to clear her blurry vision. Her head throbbed as blood rushed into her temples. She couldn't hold the heavy poker over her head much longer.

The shape of the thief drifted from side to side as he crept closer. What was happening? It was exactly as if… A pain shot past her eyebrow, moving upward. Was she going to…to… *Not now, Agnes!* She couldn't faint now. *Don't…*

The dark hall spun as if she was in the center of a whooshing vortex. Unable to hold her weight, her knees buckled. She heard a muffled clunk as the poker hit the rug, and then blackness surrounded her. She tumbled down, down, and then there was nothing.

Chapter Nineteen

"That looks like…my missing pistol!" Agnes

gnes opened her eyes. Was it moments, or hours later? The coarse threads of the rug pressed against her cheek. She noted the silence…the darkness, as if nothing had happened. As though she hadn't tumbled down in a dead faint when the doctor forced the door and entered the hallway. She ran her hand down her arm and legs. Nothing felt amiss. Apparently, the doctor had done her no harm.

The Reep lithograph! She sat up and blinked, clearing the dizziness from her vision. The fireplace poker lay on the rug by her side. From her vantage point, she could see into the dimly lit lobby, but nothing appeared disturbed. She leaned on the nearby crate and struggled to her knees, and then to her feet. Using the poker like a cane, she wobbled into the lobby, although she knew what she would find. Or rather, what she would not find.

A shaft of moonlight fell across the empty easel where, only minutes—or was it hours before—the Reep lithograph was displayed. It came as no surprise that Schatzsman had made off with it, after all.

Agnes staggered down the hall to the back door, now slightly ajar. "Hello? Hello?" Where was the night watchman? She peered into the dark alley, stepped outside, and walked to the corner of the building. Why hadn't she brought her late husband's flashlight? Deep shadows touched the exterior of the building where the wall was lined with wood pallets and boxes stacked at precarious angles. She hurried on. "Hello? Sir? Where are you?" A sense of dread jiggled through her chest. Something was terribly wrong. Rounding the second corner of the building, she nearly stumbled over the guard, crumpled next to the wall, his flashlight lying beyond his out-stretched arm. "Oh, my stars!" Agnes knelt and touched the blood on the back of his head. She felt for a pulse. "Still breathing. Thank God."

Her head whipped around at the sound of a siren. Help was on its way! Within seconds, a police car squealed around the corner. As it barreled down the alley, its headlights illuminated Agnes and the man on the ground. She stood and waved. The car screeched to a halt and two officers bounded from the car. "Don't move, lady. Keep your hands where I can see them," the officer bellowed, his hand on his holster, ready to draw his weapon at the first sign of resistance.

Agnes took a step back. She glanced down at the blood on her hand. "Wait. You don't think… I just found him a minute ago. I didn't have anything to do…"

The officer in charge nodded toward the injured man. "Simmons. Check him out." He turned back to Agnes and glanced at his wristwatch. "If you're so innocent, what are you doing here at this hour? Headquarters received an anonymous call about a break-in at the theater and… here you are."

"I didn't call. I was inside and…" Realizing the futility of explaining her suspicions about the doctor, the missing lithograph, or why she was found next to the injured guard in the middle of the night, she shrugged. She lifted her chin. "Call Chief Waddlemucker. He'll vouch for me. Tell him it's Mrs. Odboddy." It was no surprise the officers thought she attacked the night watchman, finding her leaning over the injured man. She wiped her hand on her leg, leaving a red streak on her skirt.

Officer Simmons examined the guard. "He's alive." He stood. "We need an ambulance. I'll call it in."

Agnes pointed toward the back door. "There's a phone in the office right inside the door."

"Don't need it. I can call an ambulance from the car. He hurried back to his vehicle.

The remaining officer removed a flashlight from his belt, flicked it on and gestured toward his car. "Get in the car, lady. I'm taking you back to headquarters. We'll listen to your story there." He cast his flashlight up and down the alley, and then into the shadows near the boxes, where the beam glinted off something metal. "Hello? What have we here?" He leaned down, pulled his handkerchief from his pocket, picked up a .32 caliber Colt revolver, and held it at arm's length. "The guard isn't wearing a holster, so this can't be his. It must be the weapon that clunked him on the head. Got anything to say about this?" The officer held up the gun.

Agnes gasped. It looked like... her missing pistol. But, how could it get here? The last time she'd seen it was during the earthquake at city hall. She swallowed the bile gathered in the back of her throat. *Don't get ahead of your skis, old girl.* All pistols look pretty much alike, especially in the dark, especially when your heart is in your throat, and even more especially when you're found leaning over an injured man with blood on your hand.

Agnes stared at the large mirror on the opposite wall of the interrogation room. She squirmed in a hard metal chair and clasped her hands around the paper cup on the scarred table. She studied the grey walls and the tiled floor discolored with indistinguishable stains. She could already imagine what Katherine would say when she arrived. 'Didn't I tell you it was a fool's errand to go to the theater tonight? Now look at the mess you're in.'

Agnes contemplated her situation. She was in trouble. She could be charged with breaking and entering, and perhaps even for attempted murder of the security guard—worse yet, if he should die. Perspiration darkened the armpits of her dress. Perhaps she ought to make contact with the Almighty before—

The door opened and Chief Waddlemucker entered the dismal room. Agnes glanced at her watch. "Well, it's about time, Chief. I've been sitting here for over two hours." She stood, stretched and swept her arm toward the table. "Your people have been very considerate, but this swill you call coffee leaves much to be desired, and, if you have no objection, I'm desperate to use the ladies' room."

Chief Waddlemucker's cheeks flushed. "Sorry to keep you waiting, Mrs. Odboddy. I just got here. I'll have someone escort you to the *joh…uh…*washroom. We don't exactly have a ladies' room." He opened the door and gestured to an officer down the hall. "Show Mrs. Odboddy the facilities, and then bring her back here. We're dying to hear her reason for being behind the theater next to an almost dead night watchman at 3:30 A.M."

Minutes later, Agnes peered at her reflection in the soap-spattered mirror in the tiny restroom. She shook the water from her hands and pulled on the wrinkled blue towel looped beneath the metal box on the wall. The used section of towel wound under and back up into the box. She dried her hands on the clean section of towel and gave it another pull. A clunk, and the portion of towel she used looped under, leaving a smooth, blue section. At least the next person to visit the facilities would have a cleaner option when they washed their hands. *Guess that's my good deed for the day.* She needed every point she could score with the Big Guy considering recent events.

Clearly, being found leaning over the night watchman's body made her appear responsible. Once they discovered the Reep lithograph missing, they would blame her for that, as well. She shuddered to think the pistol found in the alley might be the one she lost during the earthquake. It was all so annoying, considering her fainting spell and her inability to catch the doctor in the act. Now that Chief Waddlemucker had arrived, perhaps the matter would be cleared up and she could go home. Her stomach growled and her head ached from lack of sleep.

The officer brought Agnes back to the interrogation room and plunked her into a chair across from the chief. He had replaced her cold coffee with a fresh, hot cup. She wrapped her hands around the warm cup. "Chief? I suppose you want an explanation for how I happened to come across the night watchman?"

"Good start. But, I can't say I'm surprised. Whenever I'm called out to a crisis, day or night, it's a safe bet you're right squack in the middle of it. Pray tell, enlighten me. What were you doing in the alley at three-thirty in the morning?" The chief took a sip of coffee, grimaced, and set the cup on the table. He leaned back in his chair, hands clasped behind his head. His expression was one of expectation, as though looking forward to yet another convoluted and not quite believable explanation.

"Well, Chief, it's really quite simple. I was on a stake-out inside the theater, waiting for Dr. Schatzsman to break in and steal the Reep lithograph." A faint smile twitched the corner of her lips. So far, the chief appeared receptive. This wasn't so bad, after all.

The chief tilted his chair back to the floor. "You were... Wasn't that the night watchman's job? To make sure nobody broke in? And, now he's lying in the hospital, half-dead from being attacked in the alley. What do you know about that?"

Agnes drew back. "Nothing. I assure you. I'm so sorry he was hurt."

"Yes, well. Tell me again, with more detail this time, exactly why you were there?"

"As it happens, you know I was volunteering with the art show staff. I stayed behind after everyone left the soiree. If you'll recall, I warned you that Dr. Schatzsman would try to steal the Reep lithograph. And, I was right. Sure enough, he broke in the back door. Unfortunately, when I saw him coming down the hall, I got so nervous, I fainted." She lowered her head and put her hand to her forehead. "I've been doing that a lot lately."

The chief nodded. "Go on."

"When I came to, the lithograph was gone. I rushed outside to alert the night watchman, and found him in the alley. That's when your officers arrived. Unfortunately, I got caught in the crosshairs."

"The lithograph is, indeed, missing. You say you were inside when the thief broke in. So, you saw Dr. Schatzsman in the theater, right?"

"Well, I… It was dark, but I'm sure…" Agnes glanced at her watch. Her cheeks warmed. She couldn't lie. In reality, she hadn't seen the thief's face. Her stomach churned. She glanced at the clock on the wall. "Saints preserve us," she said. "Look at the time. So, if you don't mind, I'll be running along now. I'm tired and hungry and I really don't feel very well." She stood and reached for her purse. "Katherine will be having a cat fit wondering where… I am." A wave of dizziness sloshed through her head. She dropped back into the chair. "Oh, dear. I… I feel a little lightheaded. In fact, I…" Not again. Why was this happening?

Beyond her best efforts to remain coherent and in control of the situation, the posters on the walls rippled and swayed. The chief's face faded into darkness. She crumpled forward, and her head smacked onto the table. She felt Chief Waddlemucker grab her before she could slip from the chair, onto the floor.

Chapter Twenty

gnes opened her eyes and stared into Dr. Schatzsman's face. "…coming around now. She's going to be all right. Fetch me some water, will you, Chief?"

Panic gripped Agnes's chest. "What? Why?" She jerked her head. *Help me!* The chief's face moved into Agnes's line of sight. "What happened?"

"Right-oh. Water, coming up." Chief Waddlemucker stood and hurried across the room. Agnes forced herself into a sitting position and glanced around. She was in a different room. Grey walls, a small table and three chairs in the center, and a single sofa bed she was lying on. A wall poster overhead stated *Loose Lips Sink Ships.* Another by the door declared, *We've Just Begun to Fight!* The chief leaned over a water cooler nearby.

This must be the staff lounge. But, why was Dr. Schatzsman there? She ran her hand over her face. The chief's voice broke into her thoughts. "…then you fainted, and we carried you in here. Lucky for you, the doctor lives nearby and Officer Dimwiddie asked him to check you over." He handed Agnes a paper cup. "Drink this. You'll feel better. Doc says you'll be fine."

Agnes's gaze locked on the doctor's face as she drank the water. No doubt the chief told the doctor all about finding her at the theater. But, he already knew that, since he must have stepped over her lying on the floor on his way to steal the painting. This was most unsettling.

Didn't he appear as calm and cool as a spring breeze? She would match his performance, as if there was no history between them, save doctor and patient. "So, Doctor," she said with a chuckle. "Am I going to live? Can I go home now?" Agnes's mouth twitched in a half-hearted smile, pleased by her confident performance.

The doctor frowned. He leaned toward her. His eyes narrowed. "Whether you live or die depends on you, my dear. If you continue on your current path, your future health is somewhat doubtful, if you get my drift. I strongly recommend a radical change in your conduct. Let's say, a complete end to such provocative behavior."

Yikes! A shiver touched the back of Agnes's neck. To Chief Waddlemucker's ears, the doctor's words sounded like solicitous and heart-felt advice to take better care of her health. But, knowing what he really meant frightened her to her core. He intended it as a threat. Shocked into silence, Agnes opened her mouth to respond and clamped it shut again. She lay back on the sofa and closed her eyes. The doctor's words buzzed in her head. '*radical change—provocative behavior—health somewhat doubtful.*' "Will you please call my granddaughter to come and drive me home, Chief?"

The chief hopped out of his chair. "No need, Agnes. I've already notified Katherine. She's on her way. There are a few matters we still need to clear up. I'm not entirely satisfied with your previous explanations."

Agnes shook her head. "I've already told you all I know. I have nothing more to add." She glared at Dr. Schatzsman.

"Well, be that as it may," the chief said, his cheeks flushing again. "Under the circumstances, I'll let it go for now. Katherine can take you home, but we're not finished. We'll need to discuss this more fully in the near future." He and the doctor left the room and pulled the door shut behind them.

Agnes lay on the sofa. Without the support of Godfrey or Katherine, the chief's complete disregard of her story, and Dr. Schatzsman's veiled threat, maybe it was time to give up. How did the old saying go? *You can't fight City Hall?* An image of the church's beloved painting of The Good Shepherd entered her mind. Her heart wrenched when she remembered how hard the ladies worked to earn the money to buy it. No. She wouldn't let the doctor get away with his shenanigans. Another old saying popped into her head. Her mouth curved into a grin. *Retreat and Live to Fight Another Day.* She liked that old saying better. She would appear cowed by the doctor's threat and go home, docile and repentant. But, if that's what he believed, he didn't know Agnes Agatha Odboddy.

Katherine gripped the steering wheel and peered through the windshield, her chin jutted forward, as she drove across town toward home. The sun was peeking over the horizon, promising a glowing dawn and the coming day. "All right, Grandma. What have you got to say for yourself this time?"

As much as Katherine loved her grandmother, she was getting exasperated by her eccentric behavior. Once again, Grandma was up to her neck in some hair-brained scheme that went awry, leaving others to pick up the pieces. *What about my reputation? Will I be considered guilty by association?* Maybe it was time for her and Maddie to find their own apartment, far enough that only occasional letters and cards would find their way to her doorstep—preferably about 180 miles from Newbury. Katherine scowled and glanced at Agnes, picking at her fingernail. "Well? I'm waiting. I asked what you had to say for yourself."

"Well, I—"

"How many times must I come and collect you from some obscure place you had no business to be in the first place?"

"Now, Katherine, you knew I intended to—"

"This nonsense has got to stop. I won't stand for any more of this behavior. What do I have to do to make you understand how inappropriate and dangerous your actions are?"

"I know you mean well, but—"

"The chief said you passed out in his office… again. How many times does this make? Four? Five? Can't you see that you're not well, and this behavior is…is…" Katherine swiped her hand across her cheek. She pulled the car to the side of the street, pulled on the brake, and switched off the motor.

"Katherine, I'm sorry." Agnes lowered her head.

"Sorry isn't going to pay the bulldog, Grandma. You know I love you and I'm worried about you. What am I supposed to think? Are you getting senile? Losing your senses?"

"Katherine! What a terrible thing to say!" Agnes lifted her chin and crossed her arms across her chest.

"I mean it, Grandma. You're not acting like a rational person. All this nonsense about Doctor Schatzsman is embarrassing. I won't even mention every other irrational thing you've done over the past couple years. I suspect I don't even know about all the monkey-shines you've been up to."

Agnes's face flushed.

"You're acting like a foolish old woman without the ability to…"

Agnes turned her face to the window, then gripped the door latch and opened the car door. Katherine reached over and grasped the edge of her sleeve. "Now, where do you think you're going? Do you plan to walk home?"

"I don't intend to sit here and listen to another word. Don't you think I don't know I've made a mess of things? Nothing worked out the way I thought it would. If you or Godfrey had come with me last night, as I pleaded with you to do, you would know I was right. You could have helped me catch the *good* doctor in the act. Instead, he attacked the night watchman, broke into the theater and stole the Reep lithograph right under my nose, and left me to take the blame. So you see, my notion wasn't so hair-brained after all."

"You saw Dr. Schatzsman there in the theater? What happened to the night watchman?"

"You didn't bother to ask, 'what happened, Grandma? Or, 'are you all right, Grandma?' You started right in, scolding me for being a foolish old lady. Well, you're right. I am a foolish old lady for trying to do something alone. I shouldn't have tried without back-up. Now, the Reep lithograph, The Good Shepherd, and items from Cherry Blossom Way are all gone and apparently, there's nothing I can do about it."

Katherine drew in a breath. "We really should discuss—"

"I've said my piece and I don't intend to discuss it any more. If you can't drive me home without another cross word, I'll get out and walk." Agnes stared at her with an intensity she'd never seen before. Was she wrong? Hadn't Grandmother's behavior been inappropriate and foolish? *Don't I have the right to call out her impetuous behavior?* Just like so many times before, somehow, Grandma managed to turn the situation on its head, making Katherine feel guilty, as if she should apologize. Warmth rose in her face. She shook her head, released the brake, started the car and pulled back onto the street.

They drove home in silence. At the house, Agnes got out of the car, and stomped up the sidewalk past Ling-Ling, sleeping on the porch swing. She opened the door and slammed it behind her, leaving Katherine standing on the porch steps.

It appeared that World War II now extended from the battleships in the Pacific to a tree-lined street in the sleepy little town of Newbury, California.

Chapter Twenty-One

B ing ... Bong ...

"Maddie?" Katherine called over her shoulder, her hands wrist deep in a pan of dish water. "Would you answer the door? I'm finishing the dishes."

The volume on the radio of another thrilling episode of The Lone Ranger dimmed. "Oh! Hi, Officer Dimwiddie. Katherine's in the kitchen. Come on in."

Overhearing Maddie's conversation, Katherine came into the living room, wiping her hands on a dish towel. "Officer Dimwiddie. What brings you here this afternoon?"

The officer pulled off his cap and wiped his feet on the porch mat. "Good afternoon, Miss Katherine. May I have a word with Mrs. Odboddy?"

"What's wrong? Didn't they get everything straightened out down at the station this morning?" Katherine gestured toward the sofa. "Have a seat."

"No, thank you, ma'am. This is official. I need to speak to Mrs. Odboddy."

Continuing her day-long sulk, Grandmother had appeared in the kitchen only long enough to fix a sandwich at noon and return to her room. Apparently, her current snit was going to take a while longer than her usual commitment to 'get mad—get over it'.

"She's in her room," Katherine said. "She's not feeling very well today. I'll get her."

Katherine's hand trembled as she knocked on Grandmother's door. "Officer Dimwiddie is here. He's asking for you."

"Tell him I don't feel like seeing anyone. Just leave me alone." Agnes's voice quavered.

Katherine knocked again. "I don't think he's going away, Grandma. He said it was something official. You'd better come out and talk to him." She turned back toward the living room.

After several minutes, Grandma entered the living room, arms crossed. "What's so all-fired important that you have to wake me? I was up all night as you'll recall. I'm not feeling well, and I'm under doctor's orders. You were standing right there when he told me to get more rest." This, with a defiant glare directed toward Katherine.

Officer Dimwiddie's cheeks flushed above his short, red beard. "I'm sorry to bother you, Mrs. Odboddy, but Chief Waddlemucker sent me." His boots shuffled on the carpet as he twisted his cap. "He sent you home to rest for a while because you fainted, but, now he wants you to come back to the station and finish your interview."

"He has more questions? We already discussed everything this morning. What does he want now?"

Officer Dimwiddie shrugged. "All I know is, he sent me to fetch you and said 'don't come back without her.' Will you come peacefully?"

Agnes tossed her head. "What other way is there? In handcuffs?"

The officer lowered his gaze. "If needs be, ma'am. Chief Waddlemucker's orders. I don't want to restrain you, but I will if I have to. Please, don't make this any more difficult for either of us." He twisted his hat in his hands.

Agnes turned to Katherine. Visibly shaken, her face paled.

"It's okay, Grandma. You should go with the officer." Why should Grandmother be so nervous about talking to the chief? All she'd done was sit up all night in the theater on a wild goose chase. She'd mentioned something about Mr. Reep's lithograph going missing, but, with the few words they exchanged in the car or since they came home, there must be some vital details the chief still needed to clarify.

Katherine patted Grandmother's arm. "Call me when you're through, and I'll come and fetch you."

Agnes pulled a sweater off the coat rack. "Never let it be said I was anything but cooperative in aiding the police with an ongoing investigation." She retrieved her handbag from her room. "If the chief needs my input to solve this matter, I'm more than willing to help."

Officer Dimwiddie's eyes cut toward Katherine as he opened the door. "This way, ma'am."

Wasn't that just like Grandma? Pretending she was needed to solve a crime when in fact, she was being hauled from her house against her will, and taken to police headquarters for questioning.

"Thanks for coming back, Agnes." Chief Waddlemucker pulled up a chair and sat across the table from her. "Did you get some sleep?" He slid a glass of water across the table toward her.

"*Humph!* Your officer gave me little choice. He threatened me with handcuffs if I didn't come peacefully." Agnes picked up the glass and sipped. "What's this all about? Am I under arrest for sitting up all night in the theater?" She set the glass on the table, folded her hands, and attempted a sarcastic smile. It came across more like a tremble of her lips, matching the jitters in her stomach.

"Well, that's to be determined." The chief wiped his hand across his chin and mouth. "I'm afraid something has come up. I'm sure we'll be able to clear things up in a snap, if you'll answer a few more questions."

"Always willing to give the police a helping hand." This time her smile was more successful. She leaned back in her chair and folded her arms across her ample bosom.

"Good. Maybe we can talk a bit more about the missing Reep lithograph. Now, Agnes, before you get your bloomers in a bunch, I haven't forgotten your accusations against Dr. Schatzsman. But, you admitted you were the only one in the theater when the lithograph disappeared. And, you admitted that you really couldn't identify the doctor as the person you claim came through the back door. You can see why I have to ask."

Agnes shoved back her chair and stood. "Let me get this straight. Are you insinuating I wasn't truthful about seeing someone in the theater, and that I had something to do with the painting going missing? I told you Dr. Schatzsman broke into the back door and—"

"As a matter of fact, you never told me a great deal, because you fainted before we could get to the bottom of things. I sent you home to get some rest, and now I need you to give me some more answers. So, are you telling me now, that it *was* Dr. Schatzsman in the theater?"

"Well, I… I…didn't exactly see him, it was too dark. I saw someone come in the back door…" She lowered her gaze, "… before I fainted. I seem to be having a problem with that since my fall, especially when I'm stressed. When I came to my senses, the painting was gone. It had to be Dr. Schatzsman." Her face brightened. "Didn't you find the lock picked on the back door? I heard him picking the lock. That should convince you I'm telling the truth."

The chief checked his notes. "We saw scratches on the lock, but anyone could have done that any time. There's no proof it happened last night."

Agnes drew in a sharp breath. "What about the night watchman? Maybe he heard someone picking the lock before he was attacked."

The chief shook his head. "We haven't been able to question him. He's still unconscious. Now, Agnes, I know this is going to be upsetting, but there's something else I need to ask." He glanced at Agnes and then quickly looked away. "We found a pistol in the alley with blood on the handle. Apparently, it was the weapon used against the night watchman."

Agnes's hand went to her mouth. Blood pulsed through her temples. *Please don't say it was my…*

The chief opened a box on the table and pulled out a pistol. "This is a .32 caliber revolver like the ones used during WWI. We've heard gossip around town that you were some sort of secret agent during that time, and that it was the weapon of choice by such persons. We could check the serial number on the pistol, but that's going to take a while. I have to wonder if this is your service revolver."

He drew a deep breath, turned the pistol over and laid it back in the box. "I'm sorry, Mrs. Odboddy, but we think you picked the lock on the back door to cover the theft, and spirited away the Reep lithograph. Perhaps the night watchman discovered your attempt to get away, so you attacked him with your service pistol. When you heard the police car coming, you tossed the gun away. You were found leaning over his body. You've admitted being in the theater. Now, you're making wild claims, blaming the doctor for everything. There is more than circumstantial evidence that you are responsible for the crime. Unless you can convince me otherwise, I'll have no choice but to charge you with assault and battery. We could even charge attempted murder." Chief Waddlemucker lowered his gaze.

Agnes sucked in her breath, her greatest fear now a reality.

Almost under his breath, the chief added, "These charges could put you away for a very long time." His lip trembled with remorse. Over the years, the two of them had been at odds on multiple occasions and particularly over the displaced tiger, Shere Khan. But, there was always mutual respect, if not downright affection, between them. His drawn lips and pale cheeks suggested the situation caused him a great deal of pain. If Agnes was guilty, she'd betrayed his trust. If she was innocent, he was causing her a lot of grief.

Agnes glanced between the chief and the door. *Lord, I need Your help now more than ever. Please give me wisdom to know what to say in this moment of trial.* "First of all..." Agnes swallowed what felt like a golf ball-sized lump in her throat. "If you'll recall, I told you that I suspected Dr. Schatzsman was responsible for the burglaries around town. I thought the Reep lithograph was too much of a temptation for him to pass up, so I planned a sting operation. I figured a friend and I could wait in the theater and catch him in the act, but I couldn't get anyone to join me. Go ahead and ask Katherine and Godfrey and Vincent. They'll tell you I asked, or maybe you think they're thieves, too?

"I expect that my thermos bottle and our fireplace poker are still at the theater where I sat. If I planned to break in and steal the painting, why would I have brought them to the theater? Why would I purposely leave evidence of picking the lock? And, if I stole the Reep lithograph, where did I hide it before the police found me in the alley? Also, if I attached the night watchman, why would I stay with him when I heard the sirens? If you think about it, you'll have to agree that if I did all these things I've mentioned, I must be the stupidest crook you've ever met. How could you possibly think I'm responsible for all this?"

During her explanation, the chief made notes on a tablet. Now, he tapped his pen on the table. Had her explanations made any points? Did he believe her?

The charges of breaking and entering were one thing. Finding her pistol in the alleyway with the watchman's blood on it was a horse of a different color. How could she confess to losing her pistol at city hall during the earthquake? Delusions, a mental breakdown, and plotting a murder were different than explaining away the events surrounding her behavior at the theater.

The chief raised his eyebrows. "I can almost believe your explanation, Agnes, except for the pistol. If it's yours, how do you explain it being in the weapon used against the night watchman? Is it yours or not?"

Indeed, the pistol. She couldn't explain it. She thought back to the day she lost the pistol during the earthquake. Dr. Schatzsman must have found it in the hallway rubble. After he stole the lithograph and attacked the night watchman, he'd left the pistol in the alley. Perhaps he left it to incriminate Agnes, thus preventing her from giving him any further trouble with her accusations? She was caught like a bug on a roll of flypaper. She could deny it was her pistol, but, eventually the serial number would prove the truth. Did she dare gamble that after twenty years, the government wouldn't be able to locate the information identifying her as the owner? How could she lie and claim it was stolen when she just asked God for divine intervention on her behalf? To confess losing her pistol at city hall, and admitting her delusional plan to murder Councilman Pustlebuster to save the tiger was sure to put the last screw in the jailhouse door.

Before she could open her mouth to speak, the door crashed open and Officer Dimwiddie burst into the interview room, his eyes wild, and his arms flailing. "We got a call from Boyles Springs Military Base! A Japanese submarine attacked a lumber freighter, the Samoa, on its way down the coast! They sent an SOS, and then the transmission went dead."

Chief Waddlemucker jumped up, knocking his chair backwards. His face paled. Perspiration popped out on his forehead. "Lord, help us!" He headed for the door. "Have an officer drive Mrs. Odboddy home. Initiate Operation Home Front. Assemble the militia at the vet's hall, but, don't tell them why. We don't want hotheads running amuck before they're organized and properly informed. "

Officer Dimwiddie nodded, his hand still on the doorknob. "Yes, sir."

Agnes leaned forward. "How can I help, Chief?"

The chief turned at the door. "Could the church ladies make coffee and sandwiches for the men down at the vet's hall? We'll likely be there all night."

"Yes. I'll get right on it." *A Japanese submarine attack.* Was war coming to their shores after all? It was on everyone's mind since the Pearl Harbor attack. If there ever was such an invasion of the homeland, the California or Oregon coastline was the most likely location. Memories of serving as an undercover agent in Europe during WWI flooded her mind. She was no stranger to danger, and now, even as a senior citizen, she saw herself as a home front warrior.

"Thanks, Agnes," the chief said. "That would be helpful, but I don't want this gossiped around town. We don't want folks to panic before we know all the details. We'll assemble at the vet's hall and wait for more information from the Boyles Springs Military Base." He rushed from the room.

"Come with me, Mrs. Odboddy. I'll take you home." Detective Dimwiddie offered his hand.

Agnes rubbed the prickles on her arm, picked up her purse, and followed him into the outer corridor. The sound of their footsteps echoed on the linoleum as they trod down the hall, past faded propaganda posters and wanted posters with curled edges. Several individuals on the posters sported penciled-in mustaches and beards, likely added over time by bored detectives.

Doesn't God move in mysterious ways? What an extraordinary turn of events. A Japanese submarine attack on a lumber freighter! Hadn't she prayed for deliverance, having to explain the presence of her pistol at the scene of a crime? Not that she approved of a Japanese submarine attack as His means for her rescue, but it did delay any further questions about her pistol. Perhaps, given a bit of time to cogitate, she could come up with a plausible and semi-truthful excuse for why her revolver was used to attack the night watchman.

As she climbed into Officer Dimwiddie's 1939 Dodge police car, she considered the current state of affairs. Too bad her pistol was now in an evidence locker. She would need it over the next few days if the Japanese invaded. Would Chief Waddlemucker let the church ladies join the militia? She saw herself at the head of a group of women warriors, armed to the teeth, hiding behind a makeshift barrier, facing an enemy platoon. There is nothing more formidable than a woman protecting her family. She touched Officer Dimwiddie's sleeve. "Instead of driving me home, I'd appreciate it if you'd drive me back to the theater where I left my car. I'll need it later tonight if I'm to bring refreshments to the vet's hall."

"I can do that. Say, you make the best apple pie, Mrs. Odboddy.

Suppose you could bring a couple pies along with those sandwiches?" Desire for the requested pie shining in his eyes, Office Dimwiddie glanced sideways at Agnes.

"Pie? You want pie? *Humph!*" How frustrating. The only way Dimwiddie could imagine a woman helping overcome a Japanese invasion was to organize the church ladies to make sandwiches and bake an apple pie.

Chapter Twenty-Two

atherine paced the living room, wringing her hands, glancing repeatedly at the clock on the mantle. *I should have gone with her. Why haven't they called?* Wasn't Grandma about the most frustrating person she ever met? And, didn't she love her almost more than any other person in her life?

From what she learned earlier that morning from Grandmother's limited information, she was found in the theater alley when the police responded to a call regarding a break-in. *I should have gone with her to the theater last night.* Katherine figured when no one showed up to steal the art work, Grandma would quickly realize her accusations against Dr. Schatzsman were ridiculous. She should have insisted that Officer Dimwiddie explain why he was taking Grandma back to the station this afternoon. Katherine made another loop around the living room.

Ring ... Ring ...

Finally! Katherine raced to the phone. "Hello? Grandmother?"

"It's me, Vincent. You were expecting Agnes?"

"Haven't you heard? She's at the police station—"

"Listen. I just have a minute. I wanted to make sure you were okay. Something's happened. I wasn't supposed to tell anyone, but a Japanese submarine attacked a freighter off the coast. Gossip is running high. Folks are afraid of a possible invasion."

"A what?" Katherine's stomach did a somersault. Her gaze moved down the hall toward the bedroom where Maddie was playing with Ling-Ling. *What's keeping Grandma?*

"Chief Waddlemucker has called up the militia. I'm headed down to the vet's hall now to see what I can find out. Everyone's going crazy. Where's your grandma, anyway?"

"You won't believe it. You remember, she sat up at the theater all last night expecting to stop a burglar. Apparently, someone broke in and stole a painting. They're questioning her about it now. It sounds like they think she's responsible. What should I do?" Katherine leaned through the kitchen door into the living room. "Wait a minute. I hear a car out front now. Maybe that's someone bringing her home. Hold on." She dropped the receiver. It swung back and forth at the end of the phone cord.

She threw open the front door. Grandma rushed into her arms, squeezed her tight and with a little hiccup, said. "My dear, you're safe. Close the door. Where's Maddie?"

"She's in her room. Hold on! I'm on the phone with Vincent." Katherine hurried away. Grandmother followed her into the kitchen "Hello? Grandma just came in. I have to go. Will you call me later when you hear anything more about…the…thing?"

"I will," Vincent said. "Stay inside and lock your doors. You're safe enough now. I suspect the military will let us know pretty soon if there's any real danger. Now, remember. No gossip. Keep it to yourself about the freighter, okay? Good bye, dear."

"Good bye." Tears stung Katherine's eyes as she hung up the phone. "Stay safe," she whispered. She turned to Grandmother. "Vincent said… *um*… Oh, I'm sure it's okay if I tell *you*. Vincent said a submarine attacked a freighter." Chill bumps careened across her chest at the thought of what a Japanese invasion could mean to a small town less than ten miles from the ocean.

"I heard," Grandmother paced from the kitchen stove to the back door. "Someone called the police station. That's why they sent me home. Dimwiddie drove me back to the theater to my car. Does Vincent have any more information?" Agnes flipped on the burner under the teakettle. "I'm dying for a decent cup of tea."

"Do you think the Japanese are likely to invade? Oh, Grandmother! What should we do? Pack up and move inland?" Katherine's gaze swept the kitchen as if the answer would be found somewhere within the comforting sight of the icebox, the stove, or the table with its red-checkered tablecloth.

"I don't think we should rush to such a conclusion. We don't even know for sure it's true. Maybe it's just a rumor. We should stay calm and wait for the military to give us instructions." Grandmother flipped on the kitchen radio and dialed it to a local news station. She filled a tea ball with loose tea and poured boiling water into a mug. "Do you want a cup?"

"Yes, please. First, I'll run and check on Maddie."

"I doubt she's disappeared from her room in the last ten minutes," Grandmother said with a smirk. She moved the tea ball into another mug for Katherine. After setting the kettle back on the stove, she sat at the kitchen table and wrapped her hands around the warm cup. Katherine joined her at the table. "I've got to start a phone chain. The chief wants us to bring sandwiches to the vet's hall. He's gathering the militia there to plan their next step."

"A phone chain? Vincent said we're not to say anything about the … you know…"

"How am I supposed to ask the women to prepare food for the militia if they don't know why?"

Katherine shrugged. "You'll figure it out."

Grandmother dialed her friend, Mildred, and after explaining the situation, said, "So that's all I know, Mildred, but don't tell a soul what I said. That's just between you and me, okay? The chief said he doesn't want folks to know about the attack before he has a chance to announce a plan to the militia. He's waiting for orders from Boyles Springs."

"Don't lecture me, Agnes. I guess I know how to keep a secret as well as you."

"Just call the ladies on your phone chain and have them bring sandwiches to the vet's hall. I'll call Mavis and Mrs. Lickleiter. We should each make up a half-dozen sandwiches and meet there at 6:00 P.M. We'll know more then, okay? I'll see you later, Mildred." She hung up the phone.

Katherine removed a knife from the block, pulled bread from the bread box and sliced it. "What kind of sandwiches shall we make?"

Grandmother peered into the icebox. "What do we have to work with? There's a bit of liverwurst left. And, strawberry jam. How about a couple liverwurst and the rest, peanut butter and jam?"

"We could boil some eggs and make a couple deviled egg sandwiches. They're always well-received."

Agnes nodded agreement and chose four eggs. "Officer Dimwiddie asked me to bring an apple pie. Can you imagine? I should bake an apple pie after the night and day I've just had? He'll be lucky to get some day-old cookies."

With her picnic basket loaded with sandwiches and cookies, and the sandwiches Mavis contributed when they dropped Maddie at her house, Katherine drove toward the vet's hall. Agnes yawned as she balanced the picnic basket on her lap, deep in thought about the recent events. With no sleep the previous night, and only a brief nap earlier today, her eyes felt gritty. Sooner or later, Chief Waddlemucker would have her back in the hot seat with questions about her pistol. It was time she put some thought as to how—

"You never explained what happened at the police station this morning." Katherine kept her eyes on the road, not meeting Agnes's.

"That's a conversation that will take a lot longer than we have right now, so let's discuss it later. Right now, we have other fish to fry." They drove in silence for a few blocks until they reached the corner of

Main Street and Blue Willow Way. "What on earth is going on over there? Do you suppose those men heard about the submarine attack?"

A cluster of men were gathered under a light pole on the corner. Each carried a rifle and from the looks of the rowdy bunch, they were ginned up to a mob mentality. Several men whooped and hollered, shoving and slapping each other on the back. One of the men lifted a brown paper bag to his lips. Apparently, the bottle inside was providing the liquid courage he needed to face a potential enemy.

Katherine slowed the car as she approached the intersection. "Isn't that, Horace Faggenbacher, the guy who owns the Flying Red Horse gas station at the edge of town?"

"Why, he's as drunk as a skunk! They all are. Maybe you shouldn't stop."

"It's okay. I know Horace." Katherine's confident smile did little to calm Agnes's concern.

Horace passed the brown bag to his friend, and with his rifle balanced over his shoulder, staggered toward Katherine's car. She rolled down the window. "What's going on, Horace? What's the meaning of this? You all look like you've had a few too many."

Horace leaned on the car window sill and wiped perspiration from his brow. "You little ladies better run on home now. Got no business on the streets tonight. Iz man's work." He hiccupped. Katherine jerked her head back. Horace turned, pointed his rifle toward the top of the light pole and pulled the trigger. The men jumped back, laughing uproariously, as shards of glass rained down on their heads and plummeted to the sidewalk.

Katherine gunned the engine and her car roared away from the corner. She turned to glare at Agnes "I have a feeling that the word is out. How do you suppose that happened? I thought the chief told you to keep quiet. What have you done?"

"Me? I'm not the only one who knew. I know how to keep a secret. I told Mildred, but I told her not to say anything." Agnes crossed her arms and stared out the window. "I'm sure it didn't come from me…"

"*Uh-huh*! And when Mildred called the ladies about the sandwiches, I suppose she told them not to say anything, too. Of course they told their husbands, and now the cat's out of the bag. Those idiots are armed and drunk, thinking they can stave off a Japanese invasion. Who knows what they're apt to do tonight in their state?" She hunched over the steering wheel, sped around a corner, and pulled up in front of the vet's hall. A group of men with rifles, and a few women were gathered around the chief's police car parked at the curb. Vincent came through the front door and motioned for everyone to come inside. He hurried over to Katherine's car.

Agnes stepped out of the car with the picnic basket in hand and followed Vincent into the building. "Anything more you can tell us, Vincent?"

He shrugged and took Katherine's hand. "The chief will bring us all up to date. So far, so good." He pulled Katherine into the hallway beside the door and gave her cheek a quick peck.

Agnes glanced around the vet's hall. Off to the right, Mildred and Mrs. Lickleiter were filling the coffeepot and laying out the makings for tea, sandwiches, and desserts on a table near the kitchen. Agnes handed her basket to Mildred. "I brought more sandwiches. Do you need any help?"

Mildred shook her head. "We have it handled. Go and sit down. Godfrey's over there."

Godfrey and several others had pulled chairs from a stack at the back of the room and set them in rows. Some of the men and women were already seated near the front.

"Quickly, now." Chief Waddlemucker stepped onto the stage. "Everyone, let's all sit down so we can get started."

Before long, everyone found a seat, their rifles at their sides, twisting and fidgeting in their chairs. Godfrey limped across the room and sat beside Agnes. He took her hand and squeezed it. A man in the second row stood, "What's going on? Why did you bring us in?" Apparently, he was not one of the husbands from Agnes's phone chain.

Several snickers from the more knowledgeable and slightly inebriated husbands followed. A general rumble of muttering ensued, prompting Chief Waddlemucker to clap for attention. "Gentlemen. Gentlemen. Don't get your bloomers in a bunch. I'll tell you why you've been called in tonight. Some of you already know a Japanese submarine attacked a freighter a bit up the coast." A few gasps and exclamations were heard from the less informed.

The chief continued. "Our information is still sketchy, because we lost contact with the freighter directly after the SOS was received. Colonel Farthingworth, from Boyles Springs Military Base, asked me to assemble the militia and be on alert tonight, just in case…"

Mumbles and exclamations erupted again until the chief waved them into silence. "Many of you have volunteered at the coast watchtowers for several years, and you know we've always been mindful of a potential Japanese attack. The Japs have attacked harbors along the East Coast since the beginning of the war. With this strike on the Samoa, they've brought some of their tricks to our part of the country. The Colonel has already dispatched several teams along the coastline. As a measure of further caution, he felt it prudent for our militia to be on stand-by tonight. I'll take questions, but remember, I have no more information about the freighter than already mentioned."

"Was the freighter sunk?" A voice from the rear.

Chief Waddlemucker huffed. "What part of, 'I don't have any more information' don't you understand?"

Agnes put her hand over her mouth as snickers and mumbles came from various parts of the room. The man next to Agnes raised his hand. "How long will we be here? I have cattle to feed in the morning."

The chief moved from behind the podium. "We'll be here until the military tells us to stand down. We plan to be prepared, but that doesn't mean we should imagine the worst and panic. If we're still here in the morning, those who have livestock can take turns returning home."

Barnaby Merryweather, owner of the shoe repair shop, raised his hand. For a brief moment, Agnes was reminded of the moment she opened her eyes after falling from the tree and peered into Barnaby's concerned face. It also reminded her of the shoes in her closet that needed the heel replaced. "If there is a Japanese invasion," Barnaby said, "what could the few of us possibly do to stop them?"

The chief coughed. "I never suggested an invasion, though, of course, it's possible."

A shiver raced up Agnes's neck. Barnaby was right. Thirty men and six women couldn't stop a Japanese invasion if they came ashore on a local beach. Hopefully, Colonel Farthingworth's troops at the ocean would be the first to encounter such an attempt and call for reinforcements.

"It's true. We couldn't do much," the chief said, "but we'd be able to notify Washington, and we could slow them down enough for others to be warned…if we had to."

Barnaby's face turned as pale as buttermilk. The chief stepped off the stage and onto the floor. "Now, Barnaby, let's think about this. What would be the point of a Japanese invasion at a rural site like Boyles Springs or Newbury? By the time their army advanced to any potential target area, say, San Francisco, the whole country would be up in arms. An air assault on San Francisco, or the ships and submarines at Mare Island in Vallejo makes more sense—or even the naval base near Astoria, Oregon, essentially the same latitude from Japan as we are. Actually, no land invasion on American soil makes much sense, considering its size. The Japanese are strategic, sneaky, and wise. Look at Pearl Harbor. They caused the most damage in the shortest amount of time on a small but tactical target. Officer Dimwiddie is standing by the telephone. He'll let us know as soon as we hear anything from Boyles Springs Military Base with more information."

Barnaby settled back into his seat and turned to smile at his son, Benjamin, both apparently relieved they weren't expected to fight off the entire Japanese army.

The chief continued. "So, let's relax and enjoy some of the food our ladies have prepared. It will be a long night, but I think we can pass the time pleasantly. Let's break out a few checkers and chess boards. There's a stack of records over by the record player."

The men stood and either headed for the food table, or paused to jaw with friends. At the moment, few seemed interested in the other entertainment. Perhaps as the night wore on there would be more interest in a rousing game of checkers.

Agnes and Godfrey approached Chief Waddlemucker. "Chief," Agnes said. "We've prepared tea and sandwiches on the back table. Unless you need me, I'll head for home. I'm exhausted from being awake all last night. And, I might add, all alone." She turned and frowned at Godfrey, as if to say, *No thanks to you since you wouldn't come and sit with me!*

"No doubt," the chief raised an eyebrow. "As soon as this situation is over, we must continue our conversation that was unfortunately interrupted."

Agnes lifted her nose. "You know where I live. Give me a call." She turned on her heel. "Katherine? Are you coming?"

A hand on Agnes's arm made her turn and face Carolyn Biddle, the night watchman's wife. "You have some nerve showing your face here, Mrs. Odboddy, while my poor husband lies unconscious in the hospital. I heard all about how you attacked poor Daniel. You should be in jail."

Agnes's chest seized. Carolyn had every right to be upset. Circumstantial evidence suggested her guilt. How could she convince Carolyn of her innocence? "I know it might look like I was responsible for Daniel's attack, but believe me, Carolyn, I'm being framed. I was inside the theater, but I wasn't anywhere near Daniel when he was hurt. You've got to believe me."

Carolyn's eyes squinched and her nostrils flared. She clenched her fists. "I don't have to believe anything you say. Everyone knows what kind of person you are. You've managed to get away with it so far, but your luck won't hold forever. One of these days—"

"Here, here, now! What's going on? No need to carry on like that,

Carolyn." Officer Dimwiddie pulled Carolyn a few steps away from Agnes. Carolyn buried her face in his shoulder and burst into tears. He peered over her shoulder and smiled at Agnes. He mouthed the words, "I'm sorry," as he walked Carolyn toward the rest rooms.

Agnes nodded and smiled. "Well, I guess on that note I'll take my leave. Vincent can drive Katherine home later." Agnes turned to Godfrey. "How about you? Do you want to come with me? I can give you a ride home."

"I'm not ready to leave yet. I may not be much help taking on a Japanese platoon, but it's my duty to stay. At least I can keep the fellows company. Here, let me walk you to your car." Godfrey hobbled beside Agnes out the door and through the darkened parking lot to Katherine's car. He opened the car door and gave her cheek a peck. "Good night, dear. Now, be careful and go straight home. Don't give another thought to Carolyn."

"Don't worry about me. I can take care of myself. Even with your sprained ankle, I'm not surprised that you're staying. Besides, I can't blame you for not wanting to be seen with an accused attempted murderer." She slammed the door in Godfrey's face.

Chapter Twenty-Three

"Better to wear stockings with patriotic holes than go without." Agnes

*A*gnes awoke before dawn the next morning. Although certain she wouldn't sleep a wink due to the threat of Japanese invasion, she had fallen asleep almost as soon as her head hit the pillow. She vaguely remembered hearing Katherine bring Maddie home from Mavis's house and put her to bed.

She chided herself for sleeping so soundly all night while others remained vigilant down at the vet's hall, guarding the town's safety. She lay in her bed and listened. Silence. No pistol shots. No cannons. No sirens. No aircraft overhead. Apparently, fears of an enemy invasion were exaggerated and the attack on the freighter a rogue strike by a lone Japanese submarine, as Chief Waddlemucker suggested the night before.

She threw back the covers. Would Godfrey be home yet? She put on a bathrobe and tiptoed past the girls' bedroom to the kitchen. After dialing Godfrey's number, she pulled the telephone cord to its full length through the kitchen doorway into the living room, lest she awake the girls. Godfrey's phone rang several times without response.

Agnes gazed at the clock on the mantle. 6:10 A.M. Perhaps Godfrey was still at the vet's hall. She hung up the receiver, filled the coffee pot, measured in three scoops of coffee, placed it on the stove, and lit the stove burner.

She stepped out onto the back porch. The sky off to the west glowed red. *Red in the morn, sailors warn.* It looked like they might be in for a bit of rain. Off to the right, stood the empty chicken coop where Mrs. Whistlemeyer, Chicken Mildred and the other chickens had lived until their move to the Higgenbottom farm. Thinking about her chickens brought a smile to her lips. Thoughts of the farm reminded her of Shere Khan, his caravan now parked at the Boyles Springs Military Base. It was odd that she hadn't heard from Charles since he moved the tiger to the temporary location at the base. Hopefully, he was satisfied with the housing and the stipend offered by Colonel Farthingworth. Considering Charles's wandering lifestyle up until now, she worried a bit that he might get the wanderlust again and abandon the tiger. Her brow deepened.

As long as Shere Khan continued to draw a crowd to a war bond booth and sales were brisk, the military would welcome his promotional role. If the cost of his upkeep and Charles's salary exceeded the war bond sales, who knows what Colonel Farthingworth would decide regarding the tiger's future? It was imperative Shere Khan find a permanent home, not contingent on his ability to generate income.

President Roosevelt kept up the country's morale on his nightly radio broadcasts, touting military successes in various theaters of war. He encouraged the public to look to the day when the war would end and the country could begin to tend to the needs at home. As wonderful as that day would be, it could mean that Shere Khan's usefulness to the military would eventually cease. What might happen to him then?

Bing bong...

Shortly after the girls left for work and school, Agnes opened the front door and was surprised to find Chief Waddlemucker. "Well, I'll be. What brings you here so early in the morning? Come on in and have a seat. I thought you were dealing with a Japanese invasion."

"Seems there was nothing to get all riled up about. The Japanese submarine is probably half-way to Japan by now, so Colonel Farthingworth told us to stand down. Since you and I had some unfinished business, I came by to finish our talk." He covered his mouth and yawned as he sat on the sofa.

The blood in Agnes's temple began to throb. *So soon?* With all the excitement of the freighter being attacked, she'd no time to concoct a plausible story explaining why her pistol was found next to the injured night watchman. *Delay! Delay! Think.* "I have coffee. Could you use a cup? I can warm it up in a jiffy."

"That would be great. Might keep me awake long enough to put this business to bed…which is where I'd like to be."

Agnes returned in a few minutes with his coffee. He sat, straddle-legged, holding the cup between his hands. Still in her bathrobe, Agnes fidgeted on the sofa chair beside the fireplace. "You've caught me unawares, Chief. I'm not even dressed yet. Katherine and Maddie just left." She glanced at the clock on the mantle. 7:15 A.M.

"I apologize for the early hour. I should have called first. I thought you'd be more comfortable here at the house instead of down at the station." He opened a notebook and pulled a pencil from his inside pocket. "You'll recall, before we were interrupted by the news of the submarine attack, you were about to tell me how your pistol came to be behind the theater."

Cold chills slithered up the back of Agnes's neck. Her cheeks flushed and she gulped down a lump in her throat. It was time. She had no choice. She would have to confess everything to Chief Waddlemucker. Perhaps their past good relationship would work in her favor, no matter how fantastic her story sounded. It had to be the truth or he would never understand why she'd carried the pistol to city hall and lost it during the earthquake. "It's a long story, Chief, but here goes…"

The chief sat red-faced as he listened, scribbling notes in his notebook. From time to time, he shook his head, as though having a hard time believing her incredible tale. He stared, wide-eyed, when she described her delusion that killing the councilman might gain national attention that would in turn, save Shere Khan.

"Are you serious? You actually planned to commit murder?" His mouth dropped open when she asserted that Dr. Schatzsman must have found her pistol in the rubble and used it to attack the night watchman. Chief Waddlemucker's hand trembled more and more as he made notes. "Never in my life would I have believed you could do something like that."

Agnes wiped away tears when she reached the completion of her tale. "So, that's the whole story, Chief. The only way my pistol got behind the theater was because Dr. Schatzsman attacked the night watchman and left it there to incriminate me. He knows that I've been saying he's the art thief. It was retaliation because I denounced him, pure and simple."

Ling-Ling sauntered into the living room, her tail as straight as a flagpole. She jumped onto the sofa and brushed her head against the chief's sleeve.

"*Ah..ah..choo!*" The chief wiped his eyes and blew his nose. "Cats! Love 'um but I sneeze every time they come near." He laid his notebook on the coffee table, leaned his head back against the sofa, and closed his eyes.

Agnes shooed Ling-Ling off the sofa. "Scat! Run on and play." Ling-Ling dashed back into the kitchen.

The chief sat up straight and tucked his handkerchief back into his back pocket. "I've known you for a long time, Agnes. I never thought for a minute that you attacked the night watchman. But, you see how it looks. I have to follow the evidence. This morning, I heard that Daniel has regained consciousness and should make a full recovery, thank goodness. Unfortunately, either he never saw the attacker or he can't remember anything about what happened."

"I'm glad he's going to be okay. He's been in our prayers."

With a nod, the chief gathered his paperwork and struggled to his feet. "I'll write up your statement and pass it along to the district attorney. I have no idea how he'll proceed. You'll have to admit, it sounds pretty fantastic, but I promise, we'll take a closer look at the doctor. Maybe we'll find something to substantiate your claims. In the meantime, don't plan any overseas vacations." Almost a grin cracked his jaw.

"I wasn't planning to visit Italy any time soon."

The chief took his hat from the coat rack and reached for the doorknob. "Will you be okay here by yourself? You're not worried about the invasion scare, are you?"

"I'll be fine. I expect Godfrey will stop by later. I suppose there is nothing to stop our routine activities?"

"None that I can think of. I'll let you know if the district attorney decides to file any charges, but we'll have to wait and see." The chief waved and stepped onto the porch.

"Thanks for stopping by." Agnes closed the door and turned. Ling-Ling sat in the kitchen doorway. "*Meow.*" Chief Waddlemucker's unexpected visit delayed her breakfast and she let Agnes know such delays were completely unacceptable.

"*Phew!* Thank goodness that's over. It went better than I thought." Agnes hurried into the kitchen to feed the demanding cat. She looked up from Ling-Ling's bowl at the sound of the front door opening.

"Hello! Your knight in shining armor has arrived, sans trusty steed." Godfrey stepped into the kitchen as Agnes returned the milk jug to the icebox. "All's well that ends well. The Japanese scare is over…or at least put on hold until next time. My neighbor dropped me off on his way home. How are you this morning?"

"I'm okay. I have a little headache from lack of sleep. Coffee?" She reached for the coffeepot and gave it a shake. "There's a little left. I made extra this morning since I thought you'd come by. Chief Waddlemucker stopped on his way home. He wanted to bring me up to speed from last night's scare." She grinned, and neglected to mention the remainder of the chief's reason for visiting. "You look tired. You're not going home to sleep?"

Godfrey grabbed the coffee pot and shook his head. "I'm used to all-nighters. I'll nap later. You sit down. I'll get the coffee. Do you want more?" He pulled a mug from the cupboard and poured a cup, then opened the icebox for the milk and added a dollop to his cup.

"No thanks. I've had enough." She headed for the hall. "Excuse me. All this company this morning and I'm not even dressed. Be right back." She gave his cheek a peck and hurried into her bedroom. Fortunately, it seemed she'd dodged a bullet with Chief Waddlemucker. It remained to be seen how the district attorney would view her story.

Agnes pulled off her robe and gown and chose clean lingerie. An oversized brassiere, a corset with ribbons and laces in front to pull in her unruly waist and control her recalcitrant stomach and hips. Next she dropped a pink, slightly frayed, silk slip over her head, Mildred's Christmas present several years ago, before all the silk was sent to the war effort to make parachutes and other items. The women of America would rejoice when the war was over, the boys came home, and for the return of silk lingerie.

She sat on the edge of the bed and pulled on her worn nylon stockings, one with a hole in the heel and the other with a hole above the knee. Better to wear stockings with *patriotic holes* than to go without. Donning a pink flowered dress with buttons up the front and matching belt of the same material completed her ensemble.

Fully dressed, she stepped into the bathroom, ran a comb through her hair, wound it into a bun and tucked the two steel chopsticks through the back. Quickly washing her face and brushing her teeth, she glanced into the mirrored medicine cabinet over the sink and applied a touch of lip rouge. Satisfied that she had done all humanly possible considering what she had to work with, she gave her hair a final pat and returned to the kitchen. Godfrey sat reading the newspaper and sipping his coffee. He looked up. "You look lovely, dear."

She pulled out a kitchen chair and sat. "Thank you. So, what do you want to do today?"

"It depends, dear heart. Do you feel like going out? Perhaps you'd rather stay home and put together a puzzle. Or take a nap? We could probably both use a nap." He ran his hand over his thinning hair. "I need to get a haircut, such as it is, but not necessarily today."

Agnes shook her head. "Here's an idea. Why don't we make sandwiches and picnic in the park. We can stop at the barber on the way home."

"Sounds like a plan." Godfrey stood, drained the last sip of coffee from his mug, and set it in the sink. "You sit and relax and tell me what kind of sandwiches you'd like. It there's one thing I'm really good at, it's making sandwiches and opening a can of soup."

Chapter Twenty-Four

"Isn't it just a God thing?" Agnes

Following a picnic in the park, Agnes drove Godfrey to the barber shop. "Afternoon, Chester," Agnes said, opening the front door. She glanced up at the bell over the front door and gazed around the shop. "I see you've spruced up the place since I was here last." Godfrey took a seat under the window. The barber's client and Godfrey's faces were reflected in the large mirror that ran along one wall in front of the barber chair.

Chester reached for one of the horsehair brushes that lay on the counter beside a tall container of clear liquid holding combs and razors. "Morning Agnes, Godfrey," Chester dusted the hair from his client's neck. "What are you two up to today?"

"We've just come from the park. We took a picnic and fed the squirrels," Agnes said.

Chester whipped off his customer's cape and helped the elderly man step down from the barber chair. He straightened up and removed a fifty cent piece from his pocket, then added another dime and smiled. "Here's for the haircut and extra for the conversation. Good day." He took his hat from the rack and left the shop.

Chester turned to Godfrey. "Are we here for the works? I can give you a shave for an extra twenty cents." He gestured to his chair. "Have a seat."

Agnes took Godfrey's cane as he limped over to the chair and climbed in. He lifted his feet onto the footrest and leaned his head back. "Thanks, just a haircut today." Agnes sat on the smooth wooden bench in front of the window and picked up an *Esquire* magazine.

"So, how's the theater business?" Chester wrapped the cape around Godfrey's neck and laid a clean white towel across his chest. "Any good movies coming up? Wife and I take in a movie a couple times a month." *Snip... Snip... Snip.* Chester's scissors moved across Godfrey's neckline as snippets of hair tumbled onto the cape and then to the floor. "I love that John Wayne war movie. Helps me think we're winning the war."

Agnes thumbed through the magazine and tuned out the conversation. Advertisements... war stories... government propaganda encouraging the purchase of war bonds. She smiled. They should run a story about Shere Khan, helping to sell war bonds. She turned the page. Her attention was drawn to an article written by journalist Hugh Hefner, currently working for a military newspaper. Her breath caught as she gazed at a picture of a sophisticated man peering into a lion's cage. The caption read *Oregon Philanthropist Zeigerman Provides Home for Displaced Big Zoo Cats.*

So excited by the words that her vision momentarily glazed over, Agnes gasped, and pulled her reading glasses from her purse. Godfrey lifted his head. "You okay, babe? Something wrong?"

Agnes shook her head without looking up. "I'm fine. Just reading." She didn't want to miss even one word of the article. Almost unable to believe her eyes, she read the caption twice. Blood pounded behind her eyes. Was this the answer to her prayers? She quickly scanned the article.

Multi-millionaire philanthropist, Myron Zeigerman, an esteemed Oregon businessman, amassed a fortune in the hotels and restaurant industry. Anxious to share his good fortune, he finances various philanthropic projects overlooked by other investors.

When he learned wartime rationing affected multiple zoos, forced to euthanize many of the nation's big cats, Mr. Zeigerman opened his popular hunting lodge to provide sanctuary for a number of endangered animals. Multiple lions, panthers, ocelots, jaguars and various other big cats temporarily reside at the Zeigerman Hunting Preserve. 'They are an American treasure and must be saved. They will be returned to their home zoos when the war is over. How could I turn my back on these beautiful creatures when I have the means to save them?' (Myron Zeigerman)

On his nature preserve of 60,000 acres, licensed hunters hunt wild pigs, bear, elk, deer, cougars, and other species in season. Providing an environment similar to pre-war African big-game safaris, Mr. Zeigerman's preserve accepts discriminating hunters with appropriate Oregon licenses. Strict guidelines govern hunting practices under government conservation requirements, assuring the continued viability of each species. Excess unwanted meat partially provides food for the residing animals.

Zeigerman's unique program includes a modern bunkhouse, all meals, and experienced guides to a select number of participants. Contact The Zeigerman Hunting Preserve at 3479 Zeigerman Road, Shaniko, Oregon for availability, cost and specific—

"Agnes? Did you hear me? How you are feeling? Godfrey says you took a bad fall."

"What?" Agnes laid the magazine on her lap. "Oh. I'm fine, Chester. Thanks for asking. Are you about finished, Godfrey? Something important has come up. I've got to get home right away and make some calls."

"Right now? I thought we were stopping at the grocery store."

"No time." She held up the magazine. I may have found a place for Shere Khan." She stood and paced the small barber shop. "Lord willing, all our problems are solved." *Maybe I can get a phone number from information and call Zeigerman.* "Godfrey! Let's go."

Chester brushed the hair off Godfrey's neck and pulled off the cape. "You better get moving, ol' man. I've known Agnes for twenty years, and once she sets her sights on something, she means business."

"Coming, little moon-flower." Godfrey stood, tossed a fifty-cent piece at Chester and grabbed his cane.

Agnes was already half-way out the door. "Can I take this magazine?"

"Sure." Chester waved it away. "Take it. Thanks, Godfrey."

She held the door for Godfrey. "There's no time to stop at the grocery store. I need to get home. Maybe Katherine will take you when she drives you home, okay?"

"What's up, babe?" Godfrey limped to the car and slid into the passenger seat. He picked up the magazine and thumbed through it. "What did you find that's got you so jazzed up? A zoo?"

Agnes turned left onto Cherry Blossom Way. She nodded toward the magazine. "Look at the story about the Oregon Hunting Preserve that houses big cats. Maybe he'll take Shere Khan." She beamed at Godfrey. "Isn't it just a God-thing? I would never have seen that Esquire magazine if we hadn't stopped at the barber shop."

Godfrey flipped to the story and scanned the page. "Yeah... It may be a God-thing, but I have to wonder... What's in it for him? Nobody's that generous. Why didn't any of the zoos you wrote to tell you about this place? And, since Shere Khan's perfectly situated at the military base, I don't think we should mess with things now."

"Our letters to the zoos described Shere Khan as a carnival tiger. Maybe they thought he wouldn't qualify for this program. Besides, when the war ends, what will happen to him? We could be right back where we started." She pulled into her driveway, turned off the motor, and opened the door. "Can you manage, or do you need help?"

"If I can get up the stairs to my apartment, I can manage two steps onto your porch."

"Of course you can. That's why you tripped on the porch step last week and sprained your ankle in the first place, right?" Agnes took his arm and walked him up the sidewalk, but her thoughts were on the Zeigerman Preserve. She tried to push away consideration of Shere Khan's current satisfactory housing situation and Godfrey's disturbing questions, but she couldn't help wonder... What *was* in it for Zeigerman? Pure altruism? Or something else?

Chapter Twenty-Five

W hile Godfrey put the kettle to boil, Agnes dialed the long distance operator. As the phone rang, she sat and stretched the telephone cord until it reached the table. Her heart raced with anticipation. Was finding the article about the animal preserve really a God-thing? And would Zeigerman agree to take Shere Khan?

"Long distance. Number, please."

Agnes's voice shook. "I don't have a number. It's the Zeigerman Hunting Preserve in Shaniko, Oregon. Can you help me?"

"Thank you, ma'am. I'll check our local listings." Agnes heard voices in the background—other operators, she presumed—and a series of clicks. The operator came back on the line. "I've located the number, but at the moment, there's no available line. I'll call you back when I'm able to connect your call."

"Oh? How long will that take?" Agnes mouthed a 'thank you' to Godfrey as he set a mug of tea in front of her and sat across the table.

"I can't say, ma'am," the operator said. "Usually within half an hour. Sometimes less. Will you be able to take that call?"

"I'll be right here. Thank you." Agnes hung up the phone and turned to Godfrey. "Now we wait." She leaned back and drummed her fingers on the red-checkered tablecloth.

Several minutes passed. Godfrey asked about her headaches, and Agnes questioned what movie was showing at the Crest Theater. Before long, they ran out of small talk, slid their cups around, and sat in silence for long minutes, listening to the ticking clock over the stove.

Agnes wondered if the Oregon preserve was really the answer to her prayers. Would Mr. Zeigerman reject Shere Khan because he didn't have room for another big cat? Would it be a good permanent home for him? Would Shere Khan miss the crowds and performing? He loved the children's attention when he performed. Would he miss Charles, his new caregiver? Charles already had a strong connection to the tiger and concern for his welfare. She shook her head. She couldn't worry about such details. Shouldn't it be enough that the tiger would be fed and cared for?

Agnes started when the phone jangled. Her heart thumped as she slid back her chair and grabbed the receiver. "Hello? Odboddy residence."

"This is the long distance operator. I have your party. Go ahead, please." The operator disconnected from the line.

"Hello? Zeigerman Preserve. Herman Stelling, manager speaking."

"Mr. Stelling? This is Agnes Odboddy, calling from Newbury, California. I read the article in the Esquire magazine about your animal preserve. As it happens, we are trying to find a home for a male Siberian tiger, displaced when a local carnival was shut down. He's very tame and performs tricks for children, and—"

"You want us to take the tiger?"

Agnes raised an eyebrow. "Well, yes. I've tried for several months to place him with a zoo, but you know how things are. None of the zoos are willing, what with the war and all." Pressure mounted in her chest as she verbalized all the difficulties she faced. Tears welled up and threatened to fall. She gulped them down, not wanting to sound as desperate as she felt. Would the Zeigerman preserve turn her down? "So, when I read about Mr. Zeigerman's efforts to save the displaced zoo cats, I wondered if he'd consider taking Shere Khan." Agnes held her breath.

"I think we can work something out. If you put him on a train to Salem, Oregon, we will send a truck to pick him up and transport him from there to the ranch."

Agnes turned to Godfrey with a grin and gave him a fist pump. "You will? Thank you. We'll look into that. I'll get back to you with the details."

Godfrey pulled on Agnes's sleeve. She tried to shake him off, but he persisted. "Just a minute, Mr. Stelling." She put her hand over the phone and whispered, "What is it, Godfrey?"

"He's willing to take the tiger, but you haven't asked anything about the facilities or what would happen to him after the war. Let me talk to him." He reached for the phone.

Agnes jerked it away. "I know what I'm doing." She turned her back to Godfrey. "*Uh,* Mr. Stelling. As a matter of curiosity, how many cats are on the ranch? What kind of accommodations do you have?"

Mr. Stelling coughed. "Oh, *um,* we do have a lot of big cats. I don't know exactly how many at the moment, but for sure, a couple lions, maybe two panthers, *uh*…several ocelots, I think. Yours would be the first tiger. That's why I'm so thrilled… I mean…rather…*um*… so far we haven't had a request from a zoo to take a tiger, so it would be good…you know, to save one. How soon can you get him here?"

Agnes raised her eyebrows. He hadn't addressed her concern about accommodations. For that matter, as the manager of the facility, he didn't seem to know much about the animals, not even how many they had. She ran her hand across her neck. "What kind of accommodations did you say you have for each animal?"

"Well, of course they're caged. Surely, you can understand, with so many, and under the circumstances, there's no way we could provide much more than a cage."

"Oh, I see. I was hoping…but I guess it makes sense. So, I suppose you have a vet on call, in case they get sick or something?"

"No vet. We try our best, but, *uh*…unfortunately, as can be expected, we have lost some. There's no guarantee, you know. But remember this. If we didn't take them, they'd likely all be euthanized at the zoo. So, their chances are better here, even if they aren't too comfortable. When the war is over, they can go back where they came from. That's good, right?"

Agnes glanced at Godfrey's frown. Why on earth wasn't he on board with the Zeigerman Preserve? Didn't he believe her when she declared finding the article was a *God-thing*? Hadn't they run out of long-term options for Shere Khan? He was safe enough for the time being at the military base, as long as the war lasted, but then, what?

She shrugged. Godfrey was just being contrary because he was always contrary when it wasn't his own idea. Anyway, Shere Khan was her responsibility and she would make the decision about his future, not Godfrey. "I read that you feed the unwanted meat from the animals the hunters kill. So, is that enough to feed the animals? Seems like it would take a lot more meat than what would come from the hunters. How can you buy more meat with the rationing situation affecting everyone else?"

"Oh, we have quite a few licensed hunters bringing in wild pigs, mountain sheep…sometimes a bear. We get by. Some days they don't get fed, of course, but it doesn't hurt them to go a few days without meat. You know, they often go a number of days without food in the wild."

So, some days, they go hungry. Don't go there, Agnes. Agnes chatted with Mr. Stelling until her concerns for how Shere Khan would be housed and cared for were somewhat alleviated. It wasn't the most ideal arrangement, but seemed like the best long-term solution she could hope for, under the circumstances. She didn't dare pass up the opportunity. There might not be another. "Thanks, Mr. Stelling. I won't take any more of your time. I'll look into travel arrangements and get back to you when I have a firm date."

"Sounds good. Looking forward to it. Thanks for calling." Mr. Stelling disconnected.

"So, did he answer all your questions?" Godfrey's forehead wrinkled. "I'm not sure about this. Maybe you should talk to someone in Oregon who's seen the place before you decide."

"That's not necessary. He said the animals were caged, but it was better than being euthanized. What did you expect him to say? Not likely they're living in the Ritz Hotel." She stood and paced the floor. She put her hand to her head. Another headache coming on... She turned and hurried to the bathroom. She couldn't remember if she took Dr. Schatzsman's pill this morning, or not. Oh well, if so, another one wouldn't hurt. She swallowed the pill and returned to the kitchen.

Godfrey stood when she came into the kitchen and pulled out a chair for her. "I'm not trying to rain on your parade, my dear. I want you to consider everything so you don't make a mistake. In my experience, when things sound too good to be true, they usually are." He looked down at his hands and picked at his cuticle. "I know how badly you want to help Shere Khan, but he is settled now, and at the present, there's no need—"

Agnes glared at Godfrey. "I don't have any delusions about this. I know what I'm doing. It's not ideal, but maybe it's the best thing in the long run." She reached for the phone book. "I'm going to call the Santa Rosa train station and make arrangements to send his caravan to Oregon. Maybe if we transport him in his caravan, they'd let him live in that, instead of a cage. He's used to it, and he'd be much more comfortable."

Godfrey frowned, stood, and went into the living room. "I'm going out on the porch for a breath of fresh air. I'll be back in a few minutes." The front door opened and closed. He was obviously opposed to the whole idea of moving the tiger and didn't wish to argue with her.

"Good," Agnes scowled. "Don't let the door hit you in the butt. And, don't come back until you get rid of that hang-dog face." *Now, why did I say that?* Godfrey was playing the devil's advocate. He had a right to raise concerns if that's how he felt, but he had to understand. It was her decision, not his. She dialed the operator, asked for the listing for the Santa Rosa railway station and was quickly connected. "Railway station? How much will it cost to ship a tiger to Oregon?" She chuckled under her breath, imagining the expression on the clerk's face.

Agnes ladled a splash of tomato sauce over a plate of spaghetti and handed it to Maddie. She served Godfrey's plate and then Katherine's. Lastly, she fixed her own plate and slid into her chair at the kitchen table. "Pass me the salt, please." Katherine handed her the salt and pepper shakers. Agnes turned to Maddie. "Did you have a good day at school today?"

"We're studying Columbia," Maddie said, winding her fork into her spaghetti. "That's where they grow coffee beans. Miss Hennasey says it's hard to ship coffee to the United States now because of the war." She took a bite and reached for a biscuit. "May I please have the strawberry jam?"

Agnes slid the jam jar in front of Maddie's plate. "She's right. That's why our coffee is rationed, because not many ships can get to America. Do you want a biscuit, Godfrey?" He took a biscuit from the basket. Agnes hesitated bringing up her conversation with Mr. Zeigerman's employee. She couldn't shield the plans for Shere Khan from Katherine and Maddie much longer, but she knew how the news would be received. It was now or never.

Her cheeks warmed as she lowered her head and stirred her spaghetti, avoiding Maddie's gaze. After talking with the railway employee, she had to scrap the idea of shipping Shere Khan in his caravan due to the cost. He'd have to go in his traveling cage, after all. The plan was to ship him at the end of the week. He'd live in another cage on the Zeigerman Preserve, like the other displaced cats. "I spoke to a man in Oregon on the phone today. He works at an animal preserve that takes care of some of the displaced big zoo cats."

Katherine laid her fork down and stared at her grandmother. "Oh! You can't mean for Shere Khan to go there now, do you? After Vincent went to such efforts to get him settled at the military base?"

Maddie's chin trembled. Her face clouded over. She stirred mounds in her spaghetti and then smashed peas into the mounds. A tear trickled down her cheek as she shoved her plate away.

Katherine stood and gathered the plates. "If you aren't going to eat, Maddie, please go to your room. Grandmother and I need to talk." Maddie stood, burst into sobs, and rushed out.

As Katherine tossed the dishes into the sink, the shattering of glass confirmed that one of the plates hadn't survived. "Now, see what you've done?" Agnes half rose from the table.

Katherine turned and glared at Agnes, "What *I've* done? Just leave it. I'll clean it up later." She hurried down the hall to Maddie's bedroom.

"Why are you mad at me? You're the one who scolded her for not eating," Agnes called after Katherine. She shrugged. "I guess she's upset about Shere Khan. Well, I'm sorry she's taking it this way, but she had to know. It's never easy telling kids things they don't want to hear."

Godfrey bit into his biscuit. "You can't blame her. I don't like it, either. I hope you know what you're doing. Have you talked to Colonel Farthingworth? He's not going to be very happy to let Shere Khan go. They went to a lot of effort to get permission and scheduled their whole war bond promotional program around the tiger. What about Charles? What's he going to do? Have you even considered these things?" He reached for the jam and spread a purple glob of grape jelly on his biscuit.

Agnes shook her head. "I'll have to drive over and see the colonel and Charles tomorrow morning. Charles might want to accompany the tiger to Oregon. With his experience, Zeigerman might keep Charles on the payroll. He must have employees taking care of all the big cats."

"That's an idea. At least Shere Khan would be with someone he knows. Charles could keep his eye on things." Godfrey popped the last bite of biscuit into his mouth. "These are delicious. Do you want that last biscuit?"

Leave it to Godfrey to be more concerned about his stomach

than about relocating a displaced tiger. At least he wasn't throwing a monkey wrench into her plans and making her question her decision any more than she was before. She shook her head to dispel the image of a terrified Shere Khan crouched in the corner of his small traveling cage, trembling in fear as the cries of unseen wild cats surrounded him. *I can't think of that now. I've made my decision.*

Chapter Twenty-Six

D espite his busy schedule, Colonel Farthingworth agreed to meet with Agnes for a few minutes before lunch the next day.

Grateful for all the errands Agnes had done while incapacitated, Godfrey agreed to accompany her to the Boyles Springs Military Base. "I want to be there to pick up the pieces," he said. "I expect plenty of fireworks when the colonel hears your plan for Shere Khan."

The beautiful drive along the coastline should have improved her spirits, but her eyes were gritty from lack of sleep, thanks to a headache and nightmares about Shere Khan starving in Oregon. She was unable to appreciate Godfrey's praise of the scenery or his delight in the seals on the rocks along the shoreline.

Godfrey pointed and chortled at the children frolicking in the waves and dancing back as the water splashed over their toes. Agnes hunched her shoulders, gripped the steering wheel in a death grip and avoided looking at Godfrey as he commented on the beauty of the pristine blue sky and colorful umbrellas on the beach.

She had awakened in the night and lain awake for an hour, unable to understand why she was so unsettled about the Oregon preserve. She'd prayed for guidance to find a permanent home for the tiger. She was so sure finding the article about the Zeigerman Preserve was God's way of answering her prayers. If that was the case, then why were Godfrey and Katherine so opposed? And, why did she have niggling doubts that she was doing the right thing? Her anxiety grew by the hour, once the train reservations were made.

Agnes glanced at her wristwatch as her car turned onto the military base. *11:20 A.M.* She signed in at the gate and headed toward the building where the guard indicated they would find Colonel Farthingworth. Agnes tapped at the door at exactly 11:30 A.M.

"Enter!"

Godfrey opened and held the door for Agnes as she stepped into the colonel's office. "Good morning, Colonel. Fine day, today. My, have you lost weight? I can't think when I've seen you looking so fit."

Colonel Farthingworth scowled. "*Humm.* Sounds like you're about to drop a load of donkey-doo on my desk. What's brought you here today? Something I won't like, no doubt." He gestured to a couple of chairs. "Have a seat."

Agnes's face warmed. The colonel could always spot balderdash a mile away. "Might as well get right to the point. It's about Shere Khan. It seems that—"

The colonel held up his hand. A big grin crossed his face. "No need to thank me for taking on the tiger and Charles. Best decision I made this year. He's a great guy."

"Yes. He is. But, something has come up, and—"

"That pair are a Godsend for the war bond effort, that's for sure. Can't tell you how glad I am that Vincent talked me into the idea." He glanced at his watch. "So, I'm very busy today. What's on your mind?"

"Well, actually, as grateful as I am that you took Shere Khan, I've felt it necessary to continue looking for a permanent home for him. No telling how soon we'll reach an armistice and then where will we be?"

"*Tut, tut,*" the colonel said, "No need to worry about that for a while. Not to say that the war effort isn't going well, but concerning your tiger, we're very happy doing our part for the foreseeable future. There's no reason to consider a change now." The colonel grinned and clasped his hands behind his head. He slid a spit-polished black boot onto the corner of his desk.

"Well, that's not quite true. You see, sir, it's like this," Agnes said. "There's an animal preserve in Oregon and I've made arrangements to send Shere Khan there, and—"

The colonel's foot slid off the desk and hit the floor with a clunk. "You've what? Send him away?" He leaned forward. "You want to take him away from us now? Just when it looks like I'll be able to make my war bond quota? You can't do that. Our first big event with the tiger showed sales increased by thirty percent. His antics put folks in such a jolly mood, they fell all over themselves buying bonds. Couldn't wait to reach for their wallets." The colonel's face paled. He stood and paced the room, his hands locked behind his back. He turned at the door. "What's brought this on? Has Charles complained about his housing or his salary? I'm sure we can pop that up a bit, if that's the problem."

"Oh, no. I haven't talked with Charles. It's all about the animal preserve I found. I haven't worried about Charles or the tiger since they've been here. Then, I saw this article about the preserve where they're housing displaced zoo cats, and it seemed as if God must have directed me to it, so that's why—"

"Well, Charles and Shere Khan are fine where they are. God can go and peddle his papers—"

"Colonel Farthingworth! For shame."

The colonel stopped pacing and put his hand over his mouth. His cheeks flushed. "Did I say that out loud? What I meant to say was ..." He paused, apparently gathering his thoughts. "There's no need to move the tiger. We're quite satisfied with the arrangements we've made, and I believe Charles is equally happy. So, if we're all happy and the tiger's happy, why would you consider making a change? Where is this place, anyway?"

Agnes gave him the name and address of the Oregon animal preserve. "I've already made the arrangements. He'll leave on the Santa Rosa train at the end of the week."

Colonel Farthingworth continued to pace the office. He turned.

"Why don't you hold off on your plan until I can make some calls and check out the preserve? You never know about such places."

Agnes's brow wrinkled. The colonel made sense. Why should she try to fix something that wasn't broken? But, the article! Didn't God put the magazine right under her nose? It was all so confusing. So far, everyone was against the plan. Maddie had cried herself to sleep last night, and Katherine hadn't spoken one word to her this morning before she left for work.

Agnes squared her shoulders and stood. *Sometimes you have to go against the wishes of others when you're sure you're doing God's will.*

"I'm sorry about your plans for the tiger promoting war bonds, Colonel Farthingworth, but my mind is made up. Vincent will come by early Friday morning and tow the caravan back to the Higgenbottom farm."

The colonel's mouth worked, but nothing came out. It was probably the first time he couldn't think of something eloquent to say to win his argument. Godfrey stood and opened the door. He glanced at the colonel and slowly shook his head. Agnes picked up her purse and followed him out the door.

"Are you sure you won't change your—"

Agnes couldn't hear the rest of the colonel's argument. She jerked open her car door and slid onto the mohair-covered seat. Godfrey entered the car and stared out the front window. "Didn't that go well? Now you have to talk to Charles." The tone of his voice chilled Agnes's heart.

When Charles heard Agnes's plan, it was all he could do to hold his temper. He railed against the idea. Having found suitable housing, a reasonable salary and a job where he felt important, not to mention his growing affection for the big cat, Charles was almost in tears to learn it was all going away practically before it started. Despite his arguments and downright pleading, Agnes stood firm in her decision.

Declaring a great affinity and familiarity with boxcars, Charles finally agreed to accompany the tiger to Oregon. He hoped to remain at the preserve, now that he had some experience in the care and feeding of Shere Khan. "I might as well give it a try," Charles said. "What other option do I have? If I stay here, I'm homeless and broke…again."

On the way back to Newbury, there was none of the usual camaraderie typical of the times Godfrey and Agnes spent together, since Godfrey seemed to have no argument to present that he hadn't already presented, and Agnes could think of no further excuses for her decision. Her heart ached, knowing one-hundred-percent of those closest to her disapproved of her decision. Godfrey was mad at her. Katherine wasn't speaking, except when spoken to. Maddie was despondent and frequently burst into tears. She found no support from her friend, Mildred, who had spent long hours writing letters to zoos. When Agnes shared the military's plans for Shere Khan, she was delighted. Now, with Agnes's new plan she felt all her efforts had been in vain.

Even Chief Waddlemucker questioned the wisdom of moving the tiger from the military station when he heard the news. 'He's happy as a woodpecker with a knot hole. Why move him now?'

She couldn't imagine Shere Khan living in a cage, because every time she did, she felt a pain in her chest. It was bitter hard doing what she perceived as the *Lord's will*.

"Agnes, dear heart, will you do a favor for me?" Godfrey touched her shoulder.

Agnes's head whipped around. "What?" The movement made her dizzy. She ran her hand over her brow and blinked. Godfrey's face blurred and then came back into clear focus.

"Will you talk to Pastor Lickleiter about believing the magazine was God directing you to do this? Everyone involved with the tiger since he first came into our care is opposed to the idea. Won't you please consider that you might be mistaken about God's will?"

What should she do? Bile gathered in the back of her throat. A wave of dizziness rushed through her head. *Could I have been wrong?* Agnes's gaze held steady on the road. Shere Khan's uncertain future loomed large in her mind. She remembered her uneasiness when she talked with Mr. Stelling at the Oregon animal preserve. Questions niggled as she recalled their conversation. Why was he so delighted at the prospect of getting a tiger? What an odd reaction. Agreeable, yes, but why such delight in one more mouth to feed? One more cage to scoop. One more displaced animal that needed care was an additional burden, not a circumstance to cause delight. And, why had he evaded her questions about the animals' facilities, health care and nutrition? His comment, 'better here than dead at a zoo,' wasn't exactly reassuring.

According to Mr. Stelling, the big cats would return to their former zoos at the end of the war, but where would Shere Khan go? He didn't have a zoo to return to. Would a zoo accept him in addition to their animals, or would he remain at the Oregon hunting compound? These concerns kept her awake long into the night and, once asleep, created images that turned into nightmares.

Perhaps she should speak to the pastor. Maybe he could help her understand whether the magazine was a God-thing or not. When we feel His divine direction to make a certain decision, are obstacles and a lack of validation from respected sources indication of the lack of *rightness*? When this happens, is it our own pigheadedness to continue in that direction, rather than heed the warnings? Or do we hold to the plan, rejecting the notion that we might have misread God's will?

Doubt filled her mind, but stubbornness filled her heart. How could she back down now without admitting failure, believing she was acting on God's will? After a few minutes of silence, Godfrey said, "I guess that's my answer. Why don't you drop me off at my apartment? I don't feel very well."

Chapter Twenty-Seven

"I've been irrational, quarrelsome, and I've been arrested." Agnes

The aroma of coffee wafted through the screen door, drawing Agnes back into the house. She poured a cup, dribbled in a dollop of milk, and carried her cup outside to the back porch. She sat on the top step to peruse her victory garden and try to put out of her mind the uncomfortable conversations with Godfrey, Colonel Farthingworth, and Charles during yesterday's outing.

She gazed at the pink and white blossoms covering the apple tree. It wouldn't be long until little red apples appeared. Raspberry bushes in full bloom clung to the back fence. Shoots of cabbage, zucchini and tomato plants pushed through the recently tilled soil. Twelve inches of green bean vines crawled up tripods of bamboo poles. Gazing at the fruits and vegetables in the garden calmed her restless spirit. Bless Jackson Jackson's heart! Again! Several weeks ago, he spaded the garden, determined to 'help one of Newbury's widda women.'

The yield from the garden would supplement their table throughout the summer. She would preserve any surplus to add to the jars of fruit and vegetables stored in the garage. Sadly, she couldn't make apple butter or raspberry jam this summer due to sugar rationing. So the extra apples and raspberries would be donated to others with less productive gardens.

Maddie and Katherine had planted the seeds and young vegetable plants, while she'd been in a dither over the tiger, gallivanting around town, causing trouble. Agnes's face flushed as Councilman

Pustlebuster's face came to mind. What could have possessed her to do such a thing? She shook her head to erase the memory of that awful day. Some days, it felt like she was losing her mind. "I must get those squash and pumpkin seeds planted. They're still on the back porch," she mused.

Ling-Ling dashed around the corner of the house; the crisp morning air putting her in a frisky mood. She swatted at a leaf, presumably chasing an imaginary beast, and then raced across the yard to leap three feet up the trunk of the apple tree. Agnes jumped up and snatched the cat off the tree. "Oh no you don't, young lady. You caused me enough trouble last time with this nonsense. We'll not have you doing that again. Oh, dear!"

Thinking of the day she fell from the apple tree reminded her that she hadn't taken one of Dr. Schatzsman's pills since yesterday, before leaving for the military base. Why was it so hard to keep to a regular schedule? She ought to go inside and take her medicine right away. With her coffee cup in one hand and the cat under her arm, she stepped onto the porch, dropped the cat, and reached for the screen door.

Humm! A thought niggled at her! Ever since she fell from the tree and started taking Dr. Schatzsman's pills, she'd been as irritable as a Billy Goat, endured almost continuous headaches, episodes of delusional thinking, and fainting spells, particularly whenever she was stressed. Now, she was at odds with Katherine and everyone she cared for about her decision to send Shere Khan to the Oregon animal preserve. Were Dr. Schatzsman's pills really doing her any good?

Wait another dad-gum minute! Dr. Schatzsman knew she had accused him of being the art thief and shared her suspicion with Chief Waddlemucker. Was it too much to question if the doctor would give her medicine that would do her any good? Or, was it more likely that... A shiver traveled from the back of her neck and into her arms.

"I need to get to the bottom of this." She glanced at the clock. 7:45 A.M.! Maybe Godfrey was awake. She went to the phone and dialed his number.

"Hello?" Godfrey's voice was wake-up scratchy.

"Godfrey? I need you to come with me. I'm going back to Boyles Springs. I'll pick you up in an hour."

"What? Agnes? What's so all-fired urgent in Boyles Springs? We were just there yesterday. You've already made the colonel and Charles furious. Who else is left to irritate?"

She could imagine his pouty face. She drummed her fingers on the countertop. "Go ahead. I'm waiting. You must have another snarky remark."

"*Um*... So, about Boyles Springs... What's the plan. Have you changed your mind about the tiger?" His voice lifted with a sudden hopeful ring.

"No. I'm going to see another doctor."

"I guess that makes sense. Why didn't you see him yesterday when we were there?"

"Oh, for Pete's sake! I decided I needed a second opinion about my concussion."

"Oh. Okay. I guess you want me to go with you? What time is your appointment?"

"*Uh*... I don't exactly have an appointment. I thought maybe if I dropped by, he'd see me. I suppose I should have called." She glanced at the clock. It was still too early to call a medical office. "Go back to sleep. I'll make an appointment for later today. Suppose we make a picnic lunch and we can stop somewhere along the coast. What do you say?"

Godfrey yawned. "Sounds peachy-keen. Call me later." He hung up the phone.

At 11:30 A.M., Agnes's car chugged along the narrow, winding road that hugged the ocean, headed back toward Boyles Springs. Eleven miles of beautiful ocean views, crashing surf, and the occasional sighting of seals resting on the rocks, and jagged cliffs kept Agnes's attention. Her mood was decidedly better than when they traversed the road the day before.

Despite the scenic drive, Godfrey's head nodded and jerked when the car hit a bump. His eyes flew open. "Sorry! I guess I dozed off. Can't seem to keep my eyes open."

"That'll happen when you stay up all night reading Sherlock Holmes novels," Agnes chided, but she smiled to suggest that she wasn't really angry. "You're missing a beautiful drive, but go ahead and take a nap. I'll wake you when we get there."

Godfrey responded with a sigh. "Don't mind if I do." He leaned his head back against the headrest and closed his eyes. "I'll look at the sights on the way home, okay, babe?"

Agnes pulled into town around noon and parked near Dr. Thigpen's office. She shook Godfrey's shoulder. "Wake up sleepy-head. We're here."

"I wasn't asleep. I was resting my eyes."

"Sure you were. You were snoring like a prize hog at the county fair." Agnes opened the car door and checked her wristwatch. "Let's go. My appointment is in ten minutes."

Agnes chuckled as she walked around the car and took Godfrey's arm. "Did you bring your cane?"

He shook his head. "I don't think I'll need it. I'm much better now. Just a little twinge when I'm on my feet too long." He stepped onto the sidewalk, pulled open the glass door on the front of the building. "After you, my sweet."

Dr. Thigpen's office was painted stark white. The waiting room held several Bombay style rattan chairs covered with brightly colored cushions displaying hibiscus flowers and palm leaves. Light colored wood frames held pictures of Polynesian birds and palm leaves. Copies of Life magazine lay on the coffee table. A Philodendron plant in the corner reached almost to the ceiling, its broad green leaves mimicking the palm leaves in the cushions and in the artwork framing the receptionist's window.

The glass slid open and a nurse leaned forward. "Good morning. Mrs. Odboddy. Have a seat. We'll be right with you." She slid a clipboard and paperwork through the window. "Would you fill out this form while you wait?"

Agnes sat down and glanced over the form. Name, address… That was easy. She filled in the requested information.

Next of kin… She tapped the pen on her lip and wrote down Katherine's name and phone number at the *Curls to Dye For Beauty Salon.*

Medical insurance… None. What a stupid concept! Other than the Veteran's Administration paying for military injuries and Worker's Compensation for people hurt on the job, folks should be responsible for their own health care. A ten-dollar office call wasn't going to break anybody's bank.

Medications… She left the question blank. It was none of the nurse's business.

Reason for visit… She left that blank too. She'd discuss her medical concern privately with Dr. Thigpen. Agnes signed the bottom of the form and handed it to the nurse through the window. "Here you go."

She returned to her seat, and ran her hand over the wide arm on the rattan chair. "Isn't this furniture pretty? Apparently, it's all the rage this year. Maybe I should redecorate my living room. What do you think, Godfrey?"

"I have no head for interior design," Godfrey said with a shrug. "Your furniture looks fine to me. As long as I can—"

"Mrs. Odboddy?" The nurse stood in the open doorway and smiled. "Doctor will see you now."

Agnes stood. "You wait here, Godfrey. This shouldn't take long."

She followed the nurse into the inner office where they met Dr. Thigpen in the hallway. He accompanied them into an exam room. The nurse left the room and closed the door behind her.

"Have a seat." The doctor motioned toward the exam table. "What can I do for you, Mrs. Odboddy?"

Agnes sat on the end of the exam table with her handbag in her lap. "Thanks for seeing me on such short notice." Her cheeks warmed. "I… I'm not sure where to begin." She crossed her arms over her purse. "I had a fall a while back and hit my head. Dr. Schatzsman in Newbury treated me. He prescribed some pills… said I was at risk of a brain bleed."

The doctor raised his eyebrows. "Well, let's take a look." The doctor picked up his ophthalmoscope, leaned toward her, and peered into one of her eyes and then the other. "Your eyes look okay. Were you unconscious after your fall?"

Agnes nodded. "I guess maybe for a couple minutes."

Dr. Thigpen's brow wrinkled. "So, what's the problem? Are you still having pain?" He took her wrist between his fingers and glanced at his wristwatch.

"I've had headaches, nightmares, irritability, insomnia, delusions…" She lowered her head. "I've been irrational, quarrelsome, and I've been arrested." She lifted her head. "This isn't who I am. Something is terribly wrong and I don't know what to do. I was hoping you could help me."

"Of course, I'll do my best. But, if Dr. Schatzsman is your doctor, why don't you discuss these concerns with him?" The doctor laid her hand back on her lap.

Agnes snapped open her purse and took out the pill bottle. "I don't want to work with him because… let's say I have my reasons which I'd rather not discuss. But, he gave me these pills. I wondered if I should continue taking them. They certainly aren't helping. I don't like to take medicine, particularly if it isn't doing me any good." She handed the bottle to the doctor.

He opened the bottle and poured four pills into his hand. "Why did he give you these?" He picked up one, held it to the light and peered at it. "What are they for?"

"Dr. Schatzsman said they were to prevent a brain bleed. Do you suppose that's what's happening? I'm down-right frightened by some of the crazy things I've said and done since my fall."

"I'm sure things aren't as bad as you think." The doctor patted her hand.

Agnes lowered her head and whispered, "I hate to say it out loud, and I hope you will keep this confidential, but I was even contemplating committing murder and almost carried it out…though it seemed like it was for a good reason at the time."

"No! What happened?" Dr. Thigpen's eyes opened wide.

"Fortunately, I came to my senses before I went through with it. You must understand. I'm not that kind of person. I abhor violence of any kind or anyone who breaks the law. Plotting murder is not in my nature. Is it possible I am having a brain bleed? Or am I going bonkers?" Agnes wrapped her hands around her elbows and rocked back and forth. "Do you think that's it?"

The doctor shook his head. "There, there. I don't think it's quite that serious. You wait here and let me check on something. I'll be right back."

"You're not going to report me to the authorities, are you?" Agnes clutched the neck of her sweater. Tear pricked her eyes. "I didn't go through with it. No one was hurt. Honest!"

"Of course you didn't. Never crossed my mind. I'll be right back." Dr. Thigpen left the exam room and closed the door behind him.

Agnes bit her lip. *Now, what have I done?* Maybe she shouldn't have confessed her murderous plans to the doctor. She wracked her brain. Weren't doctors supposed to keep confidences, like lawyers? Or was that something she'd read in a book or heard on the radio?

She stared around the small room at the posters on the wall. One depicted the skeletal arrangement of the human body. The other showed the detailed inner workings of the heart and lungs. Weren't our bodies impressively put together? Hard to believe it was all by chance, as some of the more modern opinions were touting, completely contrary to the common sense approach of creation as Pastor Lickleiter explained it. She was quite familiar with God's divine creation, the Garden of Eden, and Satan's persuasive appearance in the form of a serpent. With the state of the world at war, clearly, he was having a hey-day.

Agnes glanced at her wristwatch. What was keeping that doctor? Godfrey would be spinning out there in the waiting room. She drummed her fingers on the leather-covered exam table. Over the next few minutes, she thought back over her conversation with the doctor, wondering what she should have said and what she should have left out, and lamenting mentioning her erratic impulse to commit murder. That was liable to come back and bite her on the posterior.

Maybe it was time for more divine intervention. She bowed her head and began to pray. "Oh, dear Lord, it's Agnes Odboddy. I think I'm in terrible trouble...again... I know, I know. I don't say my prayers near often enough, except when I'm in trouble, but listen. It's not just about Chief Waddlemucker finding my pistol at the theater, and him thinking I might have attacked the night watchman. That's bad enough, Lord. Now I'm thinking that I might be losing my mind, considering all the stupid things I've done this week, not to mention telling this doctor all about my... *um*... lapse in judgment concerning the councilman.

"So, I guess I'm throwing myself on Your mercy again, and asking for Your help. Maybe it's not just Your mercy I need. Maybe I need a little healing too, considering the possibility that I'm probably having a brain bleed. Could it just be old age and senility setting in? Come to think of it, the prospect of that possibility is almost as bad as thinking I'm having a brain bleed. But, whatever it is, Lord, if You could help me, or cure me, or whatever You think best, I'd be eternally grateful. Well, that's about it this time. Thanks. Amen"

Chapter Twenty-Eight

"I guess I deserve whatever comes..." Agnes

Katherine put the last pin curl in Mrs. Plumbinder's grey hair and stretched a hair net over her head. "There we go. Now, let's put you under the hair dryer for a while, shall we, dear?" She directed the elderly woman to a nearby chair, pulled the large cone over her head and turned on the dryer. "Here's a magazine. I'll be back to check on you in a few minutes. Can I get you anything?"

"No, dear, I'll be fine. Thank you." Mrs. Plumbinder opened the magazine.

"Katherine?" Myrtle, the owner of the *Curls to Dye For Beauty Salon* leaned into the doorway. She beckoned from the back room, holding the wall phone. "You've got a phone call."

"I'll be right there." *Now what? Is Maddie locked out of the house again?* Katherine hurried through the curtained doorway to the phone. "Hello? Katherine Odboddy."

"Miss Odboddy? This is Dr. Thigpen, from Boyles Springs. Your grandmother is here in my office. She gave your name as her next of kin. If you have a few minutes, may I ask you a couple of questions about her health?"

"Dr. Thigpen? Oh! I'm a little surprised. I didn't know she was considering... Well, I knew she wasn't very happy with Dr. Schatzsman. How can I help you?" *What on earth?*

"Your grandmother mentioned a number of concerns, and I wonder if you can confirm some of her comments. It's not that I don't believe her, mind you, I'm just a bit concerned due to her age and the extent of... Well, let's deal with some health issues. First of all, she mentioned nightmares and dizziness, as well as fainting spells since her fall."

Katherine glanced around the salon. She raised her eyebrows, surprised by the nature of the doctor's questions and that Grandmother hadn't mentioned going to Boyles Springs. "*Um...*yes, she has complained of headaches and dizziness. She fainted several times after her fall. She told you about that?" She was acting a bit bizarre, but then again, with Grandmother, it was hard to know what was bizarre and what was just... Grandmother.

"Yes," the doctor said. "She also mentioned having uncontrolled delusions resulting in... shall we say... aberrant behavior that she claimed was not in her character. I can't go into further details, due to her confidentiality. Can you give me any insight into such a comment?"

"Well, yes. She has been more quarrelsome and irritable lately. I'm not sure that's aberrant to her personality, but it's certainly more pronounced since her fall. I'm not sure what... well, let me think. She has repeatedly made wild accusations about Dr. Schatzsman, but we didn't put much stock in them."

"I suspected as much," Dr. Thigpen said.

"Oh, wait. She was taken to the police station for questioning following an episode down at the theater. She refuses to discuss the details with me, so I'm not sure what that was all about. I understand a painting was stolen during the night, but..." Wheels began turning in Katherine's head. Surely, that wasn't why Grandmother was taken in for questioning. The chief couldn't possibly think she was responsible for the theft. He knew her better than that. "I'm afraid I haven't been much help. We are very concerned for her health. I think it's fair to say she hasn't been *herself* since the fall. Can I talk to her? Is she okay to drive?"

"I understand she came with a gentleman. I expect she can get home safely enough."

"Must be Godfrey, Grandmother's... friend. That's good." She sighed. With Godfrey there, Grandmother would get home in one piece. *I'm not so sure about her safety when she gets home.*

"Thank you, Miss Odboddy," said Dr. Thigpen. "You've been helpful. I'll speak further with your grandmother and decide how best to proceed." He hung up the phone.

Agnes started. Her mind had wandered and she hadn't heard the door open. The nurse beckoned. "What? Oh, right." She gathered her purse and followed the nurse down the hall to the doctor's office. *Here goes nothing.*

Likely, Dr. Thigpen called the police and there'd be a uniformed officer waiting to snap on the cuffs and arrest her for attempted murder. On the other hand, he would have had time to call the Boyles Springs Mental Hospital and there might be men in white coats waiting to haul her off to a rubber room. Either way, it could be a long month of Sunday's before she ever saw the light of day again. She hesitated outside the doctor's office. *I guess I deserve whatever comes.*

"Here we are, Mrs. Odboddy." The nurse opened the door to the doctor's office. "If you'll step inside?" Agnes took a deep breath, entered the office, and glanced around. No policemen and no men in white coats. *Huh!*

"Have a seat, Mrs. Odboddy." Dr. Thigpen sat with his hands folded neatly atop his desk. The nurse left the room and pulled the door shut. The wall clock ticked loudly as she and the doctor stared at each other for what felt like minutes, but most likely was only six or eight seconds before he spoke again. "I've been thinking about the things you've told me. Without an x-ray of your head, I can't guarantee you don't have a brain bleed. However, the symptoms you've mentioned aren't consistent with one, so I'm not too concerned at the moment. I am more concerned with this medication." He pointed to the bottle on his desk. "Without a label, I can't be sure what this is, but as a medical professional, what I can tell you is, there is no pill that would prevent a brain bleed."

Chills raced up Agnes's neck and bumps popped out on her arms. What exactly had Dr. Schatzsman given her, and why? Knowing of her accusations, could he have given her something that would mess with her mind, and create behavior that would discredit any accusation she made? Did the medication cause the delusions that led her to contemplate murder? She opened her mouth to question Dr. Thigpen's statement, but no words formed. She nodded. "Go on," she croaked.

"There are medicines that do a host of things such as lower your blood pressure or settle your upset stomach, but these…" He picked up the bottle and shook it. "I suggest you stop taking these immediately, at least until we can determine what they are. Perhaps I could speak to Dr. Schatzsman and—"

"No! I forbid it." Agnes jumped from the chair. Her hand shook. "I'll do as you say. Keep the bottle and figure out what it is, but don't talk to Dr. Schatzsman."

"My dear Mrs. Odboddy! Please sit down. I didn't mean to upset you. I won't call him if you object. I thought we might figure out what—"

"No! Please believe me, I have my reasons, but I beg you…don't call him." Agnes clutched her hands together in fear and concern. If Dr. Schatzsman knew she spoke to another doctor, what might he do? Bad enough he knew she shared her concerns with Chief Waddlemucker. She grabbed her purse. "I should go. I've taken up enough of your time." She stepped toward the door.

"Not at all, Mrs. Odboddy. I'm sorry I wasn't more help."

"Oh, but you were. You confirmed my suspicions about the pills. Since I won't take them anymore, my symptoms should improve in no time." She grasped the doorknob and smiled. "Thank you for respecting my wishes."

"I'll call you when I determine what they are." He shook the pill bottle. "Good-bye."

Agnes returned to the waiting room where Godfrey sat glancing through a magazine. She jerked her head toward the outer door. "Let's get going," she said, opening the front door.

Godfrey tossed the magazine on the table, followed her outside, and hurried to open her door and circled the car to his side. "Are you okay, my dear? You look a little pale. What did he say?" Agnes slid onto the mohair seat cushion and set her purse on the floorboard. She started the car, released the brake, and turned to check for traffic before pulling out of the parking space.

"Well? Is everything okay," Godfrey said? "What did he tell you, if you don't mind me asking?" His cheeks flushed.

"I don't mind you asking, as long as you don't mind if I don't answer." Agnes clutched the steering wheel and stared out the side window. "I'm not ready to discuss things yet."

How could she tell Godfrey that she thought Dr. Schatzsman gave her inappropriate medication? How could she tell him about her intentions to murder Councilman Pustlebuster, or about her gun being found at the theater and used to attack the night watchman? No. It was best to keep Dr. Thigpen's information a secret until she learned more about the pills.

"But, Agnes, my dear. You've suffered a concussion and that can have long-lasting effects. I'm worried about your continued headaches and dizziness. Thank goodness, Dr. Schatzsman gave you something to prevent a brain bleed. Did Dr. Thigpen concur with his diagnosis?" Godfrey's faced expressed concern.

Agnes's head jerked back to the road. "Oh, Godfrey. If you only knew. We'll talk soon about all this, but please, dear, not right now. Let's not spoil the day with unpleasant things. Let's stop at the beach on the way home and have our picnic." She grasped his arm and squeezed.

Godfrey raised his eyebrows. "As you wish. But, when you're ready to share, you can count on me. You know how much I care for you. I'll always be here for you." Godfrey blew a kiss to Agnes. She swiped her hand through the air, caught it and drew it to her lips.

Chapter Twenty-Nine

"Why would Dr. Schatzsman give me such pills?" Agnes

gnes no sooner arrived home from Boyles Spring and opened her front door, than the telephone began to ring. She tossed her purse on the couch and hurried into the kitchen. "Hello?" She stretched the telephone cord toward the table, pulled out a kitchen chair, and sat.

"Mrs. Odboddy? This is Dr. Thigpen. I'm glad I caught you. Do you have a minute to talk?"

"Oh, hello. I just got home. Did you figure out what the pills are already?"

"I did. I spoke with the pharmacist next door and he checked his drug books. We've identified the pills as an amphetamine—Benzedrine. That's not good. It's no wonder you've been having such adverse symptoms. It has nothing to do with treating a concussion. I can't imagine why Dr. Schatzsman prescribed those pills. They would have caused all sorts of side-effects."

"Oh my stars!" Beads of perspiration broke out on Agnes's chest. So, the pills were responsible for the headaches and nightmares and... Councilman Pustlebuster's face popped into her mind. *Oh no! What if I had gone through with...?* The doctor's voice broke into her thoughts.

"How long have you been taking these pills?"

"For over a week; twice a day since my fall from the apple tree. I only missed a couple of doses. Am I addicted? What's going to happen now that I've stopped taking them?"

The doctor sighed. "There are a number of factors to consider. Each individual might react differently. It all depends on how your body responds to stopping the medication. You might have some withdrawal symptoms. To be on the safe side, you should get plenty of rest and drink lots of water. That may flush the medicine out of your system sooner. Stay away from stimulants like coffee or alcohol. If possible, just use aspirin for any continued headaches. Let me know of any other physical symptoms you may have and we'll address them accordingly. It would be a good idea for someone to stay with you for the next several days, just in case… I'm so sorry this has happened. I can't imagine why Dr.… well, call me, day or night, if you need me."

"Thank you, Doctor Thigpen. I will." Agnes hung up the phone and slumped over the table. She stared at the icebox across the room. Amphetamines! It wasn't something decent people knew much about, except, maybe drug abusers. Dr. Schatzsman was trying to make her a drug addict!

Ling-Ling ambled into the kitchen toward her empty bowl. *Meow!* Agnes shook her head. *I need to feed the cat.* She stood, opened the icebox, took out the milk jug and poured a dollop into Ling-Ling's bowl. "There you go, sweetheart." She smiled, pleased with herself. If she had enough compassion to feed a hungry cat, she guessed she hadn't gone over the wall yet. She sat back down at the table, trying to think it through.

Why would Dr. Schatzsman give her pills that had nothing to do with her injury? Did he think they would make her act so crazy, no one would believe any accusations she made about him? That's it! Or worse yet, perhaps he thought she would do something life-threatening and he'd be rid of her for good. And hadn't he been right? The pills were responsible for making her think she should kill Mr. Pustlebuster when he opposed her plans to save the tiger. If she'd followed through on that delusion, she would have spent the rest of her life in jail… or worse and her accusations against the doctor would be totally ignored.

What would happen to her now? Dr. Thigpen hadn't exactly assured her that she wasn't already drug addicted. She would need Katherine and Godfrey's help over the next few days.

Her hand shook as she stood. She took the receiver off the phone and dialed Godfrey's number. "Hello? Godfrey? I'm sorry to bother you again so soon, but I desperately need you. I have something important I need to say. Can you come over right away?"

"My precious! You don't know how long I've waited to hear you say those words. I'll come as soon as I can."

Oh dear. What he must think. He'd jumped to the wrong conclusion again. "I'll call Katherine and ask her to leave work and come right home. She can pick you up on her way."

"But, love-bunny, what's wrong? You just dropped me off a few minutes ago. Can't you say what you need to tell me right now? I've waited so long—"

"I'd rather wait and tell you both together." Agnes hung up the phone and dialed the *Curls to Dye For Beauty Salon.* After Katherine heard her request, she agreed to pick up Godfrey and come straight home. Agnes moved into the living room and sat on the sofa, her head in her hands. How could she explain this to the two people whose respect she most desired?

Chapter Thirty

S o, that's the whole story. I'm sorry I didn't tell you before, and I'm not proud of what I've done, but it's not my fault." Agnes lowered her head and folded her hands on the kitchen table. "All my ghastly and bizarre behavior was caused by the amphetamines our good doctor Schatzsman gave me. It's a wonder I'm not dead!"

After describing all the nightmares, dizzy spells, fainting, panic attacks, delusions and acknowledging her irrational decision to stake out the Reep art show, Agnes finished her tale by confessing her attempted murder plot of the councilman. She sat back in her chair, her lip trembling and her heart doing the two-step as she glanced between Katherine and Godfrey. As the two most important people in her life, she couldn't help wonder what they would think, hearing such fantastic admissions. She hadn't mentioned quarreling with everyone regarding her decision to send Shere Khan to the Oregon animal preserve. Perhaps that was best left for another conversation.

Katherine sat in shocked amazement when Agnes relayed losing the pistol in the earthquake, Dr. Schatzsman's theft of the Reep lithograph, and how her pistol was used against the night watchman. Godfrey sat with his head bowed, staring at his hands in his lap the whole time, not saying a word. A quiver of anxiety rushed into her heart. *Why doesn't he say something? Just an hour ago, he promised he'd be there for me, no matter what.*

When, at last, Agnes concluded her shocking story, Katherine said, "This is incredible. I can't believe it. Why didn't you tell me what you were going through? It must have been terrible, keeping all this to yourself. You know we're both here for you." She glanced at Godfrey, seeking his agreement, but he had turned away.

"Really?" Agnes huffed. "How were you 'here for me'? As I recall, from the very first night when I saw the doctor stealing the Ledbetter's painting, neither of you believed me. You've dismissed anything I've said about him ever since. I begged you to go to the theater with me and you both refused. I believe 'foolish old lady' were the words you used. Why should I have troubled you with anything else?" She reached a trembling hand toward her cup of tea.

Katherine's face flushed. She laid her head on the table. "You're right. I didn't believe you. I thought your fall was causing hallucinations." She lifted her head, dabbed her eyes, and reached for her grandmother's hand. "I'm so sorry. How can I make it up to you? I have no excuse. It seemed so … so impossible." She glanced at Godfrey. "Neither of us thought…" Godfrey was gazing every direction around the kitchen, except at Agnes's face.

"Godfrey?" Katherine said. "Why don't you say something? You're as guilty as I am. You weren't much help either. You never spoke up for her." She pulled a hankie from her pocket and blew her nose.

The clock in the living room struck the hour. Godfrey pushed away from the table, and walked to the kitchen sink. He leaned against the counter, peering out the window into the garden. Agnes held her breath. Why wasn't he forthcoming with words of support? The pressure in her chest climbed into her throat.

At last, he spoke. "Looks like you'll have a bumper crop of apples this year. That tree is full of blossoms." He brushed his hair off his forehead.

Agnes gasped. Was that all he had to say? A bumper apple crop? No dismay over her being nearly poisoned by Dr. Schatzsman's pills? No sympathy for the emotional and physical suffering she had endured? No relief knowing it was only by the grace of God and an earthquake, she hadn't committed murder? Was it possible he didn't believe Dr. Thigpen's diagnosis and, thus, disbelieved that Dr. Schatzsman had given her amphetamines? Or, didn't he believe her symptoms and erratic behavior was caused by the drugs? He had declared his undying love a dozen times in a dozen different ways over the past few months, the most recent just this morning? There was only one reason for his silence. He didn't believe one word of her story!

"Well, I guess you've said it all without saying a word," Agnes said. "Katherine? Would you please drive Godfrey home? I don't think he plans to stay for dinner, after all. Obviously, he doesn't believe me, and has no concern for my needs." Her glare would have melted the ice cap in Alaska.

Godfrey whipped his head around, brow furrowed. His mouth trembled. "If that's what you really think, Agnes, so be it."

"It appears more the way you want it, Godfrey," Agnes called after him as Katherine rose and he followed her into the living room. Agnes held her breath, expecting, any moment, he would rush back to assure her that he had needed a few minutes to absorb all the disturbing information—to beg her forgiveness for doubting her word, and assure her of his complete support. The front door opened and closed.

She put her hands over her eyes and lowered her head. Of all the people in the world, weren't Katherine and Godfrey the dearest to her? To think that after all she had gone through this past week, he would withhold his trust and empathy. Why would she confess such horrible things if they weren't true? Her chest felt heavy with despair.

Agnes released her breath when Katherine's car doors slammed and the engine started. *He's not coming back.* This wasn't the first time he'd broken her heart, nor the second. How many times would she allow him to come into and out of her life? How many times…?

Over the next half-hour, Agnes paced the living room, going over and over her confession. Should she have been so frank? What details should she have left out? She had to tell about losing her pistol in the earthquake and explain how the doctor must have found it and left it at the theater to implicate her. She had to explain how the amphetamines were behind her bizarre behavior and her physical symptoms. What about her decision to send away Shere Khan? What was she going to do now that train reservations were already made for him to go to the animal preserve in a few days? It still seemed the best solution in the long run, or should she call and cancel...?

Why didn't Godfrey believe her? What should she have said differently to explain her actions? Maybe she shouldn't have confessed at all. She hadn't even asked for their help over the next few days before Godfrey got all weird on her. Why didn't he support her? That's what you do when you love someone. The only conclusion was that despite all his previous declarations of love, he didn't love her. Agnes threw herself on the sofa, pulled a pillow over her head and wept.

Katherine pulled away from the curb, her hands on the steering wheel, her gaze on the road. She stopped at the corner and turned to face Godfrey. "As I live and breathe, I have never in my life been so disappointed in someone. What on earth is wrong with you? I thought you cared for Grandmother." She rolled down the window, stuck her arm out, and signaled a left turn.

"You think I don't?"

"It sure didn't sound like it. She expected you to understand and comfort her and all you could say was something about apple blossoms? I nearly fell off my chair when you came up with that line." She crammed the gearshift into first, popped the clutch, and stomped on the gas. The tires squealed as she turned left through the intersection. Godfrey grabbed the armrest on the door to steady himself.

"You don't understand. It would have been worse if I'd said more," he said.

From the corner of her eye, Katherine caught a glimpse of his face as his hand moved to his eyes. He quickly turned his head toward the window. Was he tearing up? What was going on inside that wooly grey head? There was something more than what his words suggested. It was time to get to the bottom of this debacle.

"What's going on, Godfrey?" She pulled the car off to the curb, under the shade of a tree, shoved the gears into neutral, and shut off the motor. "Talk to me. Grandmother's feelings are desperately hurt. I could see that as plain as the nose on your face. There must be a reason you said what you did. Or, rather, didn't say what you didn't say."

Godfrey crossed his arms and jutted his jaw. "I thought you were taking me home."

"We aren't going to move from this spot until you come clean about what's bothering you. Don't you believe her? Do you think she made up Dr. Thigpen's diagnosis about Dr. Schatzsman's pills? You went to Boyles Springs with her. What did he say?"

"I don't know. She wouldn't let me go in with her. I asked what happened on the way home, but she wouldn't tell me anything. For all I know, he sent her back to Dr. Schatzsman."

"Grandmother says when he called a bit ago, he told her the pills were amphetamines. All those side-effects—the dizziness, headaches, fainting, and likely her bizarre behavior were likely caused by the drugs. It makes sense to me. I don't understand why you'd doubt her word."

Godfrey's cheeks reddened. "You don't understand. It made sense to me, too. It's not that I don't believe her. I know I should have explained…" He shrugged. "The fact of the matter is, I went over there thinking I would hear quite a different story. I guess I was mad when I didn't hear what I thought she'd called us home to hear. All that business about an attempted murder, and pistols, and amphetamines… It was enough to make your head spin."

"I'm not following you. I was as shocked as you were hearing her bizarre story, but what did you think you'd hear? She asked us to come home so she could tell us about her visit with Dr. Thigpen."

Godfrey didn't answer for a moment. "Godfrey? Talk to me."

"That's not what she said when she called *me*." He lowered his head.

Katherine leaned back and put her hands behind her head. "Oh, Lord! What are you talking about? What did she say? We're going to sit here until you tell me, Godfrey, so you might as well spill it. I have all day." She patted her mouth, as though yawning.

Godfrey sighed. He reached into his vest pocket and held up a small ring box. "I've been carrying this around for months, waiting for the right moment to ask Agnes to marry me."

Katherine's face warmed. "Oh my…"

"Every time I mentioned anything about the future, she'd put me off. Then all this business about the tiger and Dr. Schatzsman came up, and she seemed to pull even farther away. When she called a while ago and asked me to come back to the house, she said, 'Come quick. I desperately need you,' and I thought…finally! I thought since we'd been together all morning, maybe Dr. Thigpen's diagnosis made her come to her senses, and she was ready to…to…you know…let me into her heart. To take care of her. I was ready to propose."

"You thought she was finally ready to make a commitment? It must have been a shock to hear her story when you were expecting…" Katherine squeezed his arm. "I'm sorry. But, why didn't you say something? Why didn't you explain how you felt? She would have understood."

"Maybe I was disappointed, and a little mad, too. All those things happened to her, and never once did she confide in me or ask for my help. That's what people do when they love someone. I thought I meant more to her than that. I guess I was wrong." He lowered his gaze. "It all came to a head there in the kitchen and… I was overwhelmed and had no words to explain. I just…" He spread his hands and shrugged.

"I get it. But, I wasn't supportive of her either. We both turned her down when she asked for help. Now, you have to tell her how you feel.

She might not be willing to change her life and get married, but I know she loves you. I mean, she's probably thinking about me and Maddie as much as herself. Maybe she thinks if she marries you, it will disrupt our living arrangements." Katherine's heart quickened as she realized the extent of the situation. "If that happened... Oh my. She'd be right. Where would I go? I can't afford a place on my own. And now, there's Maddie to consider." She glanced at Godfrey and then looked quickly away.

"I never thought about it that way," he said. He lifted his head. "Maybe she thinks I wouldn't want you and Maddie to live with us." He reached for her arm. "She'd be wrong. I love both of you as if you were my own daughters. She should have explained if that's how she feels. Instead, she shut me down whenever I tried to get romantic."

Katherine turned back to face him. "Sounds like neither one of you are very good at telling how you feel. It reminds me of a Cary Grant movie I recently saw. The couple both misunderstood each other, so they quarreled and broke up. Of course, they got together in the end. Do you want to go back to the house? You really need to talk to her."

"I'm so embarrassed. I don't know what I'd say. What must she think...?" He shrugged.

"Just come back with me. I know Grandmother. She'll understand."

"Are you sure?"

"She's probably standing at the front window this very minute, waiting for us to come back." She turned the key and started the motor. "Ready?"

"Ready, willing, and able. Let's go!"

As soon as Katherine's car pulled into the driveway, she saw the living room curtain pulled back. Grandmother must have been watching through the window and heard them drive up. The front door opened and Grandmother flew out onto the porch.

Godfrey threw open the car door and the two met on the porch steps, both talking at once. Of course, Agnes would accept his apology. Of course, Godfrey loved her and poured out his heart to convey his sorrow and the reason for his poor reaction to her confession. Amidst hugs and kisses, they returned to the living room and sat holding hands on the sofa.

Katherine tip-toed away and hurried down the hall to her bedroom. She wasn't able to hear their entire conversation, but from a word here and there and then patches of complete silence, she determined they settled their differences and moved past their misunderstanding.

The biggest surprise of all came later that evening, when Agnes flashed an engagement ring and announced that she and Godfrey would be married later that summer.

Katherine forced a smile and congratulated the happy couple. Wasn't it the best news ever? Her smile wavered as she hurried from the room. *But, what about me and Maddie?* Godfrey said he loved them, but once he married Grandma, was it really practical that the four of them could live in this tiny house with only two bedrooms? Or would she be forced to leave the comfort she had grown to love and count on? Where would they go?

Chapter Thirty-One

"Why, Katherine. How you talk. You know I'm a gentleman." Godfrey

K atherine put the final pin curl in her regular Wednesday morning client's hair. She pulled a hairnet over Mrs. Whistlemeyer's grey curls and sat her in the chair under a hair dryer. "I'll set it to warm. If it's too hot, let me know. Can I get you a magazine and a cup of tea, Mrs. Whistlemeyer?"

The elderly lady nodded and smiled. "Thank you dear. That would be lovely."

Katherine brought the tea and handed her a Hollywood fashion magazine. She turned as the telephone rang in the back room. Her co-worker, Myrtle, answered the phone. "Hello? Just a minute," Myrtle handed the telephone through the curtained doorway. "It's for you, Katherine. It's that lovely young man you've been putting off marrying for entirely too long." She jiggled the receiver and grinned. "Why don't you marry him, already? A wedding would be a lovely way to brighten our spirits."

Katherine's cheeks tingled. What *was* holding her back? Vincent had proposed marriage enough times. Was it her two previous marriage proposals that both ended in disaster, one due to the misfortunes of war, and the other, basically being left at the altar? Unwilling to tempt fate a third time, she had put off Vincent's suggestions, at least until the war was over. With Grandma's recent engagement, perhaps it was time to give Vincent's proposal consideration.

Katherine took the phone from Mildred. "Hello? Vincent? Is

everything okay? You don't usually call the beauty shop." She stepped into the storeroom for more privacy.

"You're right," Vincent said. "I could have waited until tonight, but I was so excited, I had to call right away. It's about the Good Shepherd painting stolen from your church. I'm pretty sure I've located it."

"Really? What happened? How did you find it?"

"Well, that's where it gets interesting. You know how Agnes has railed against Dr. Schatzsman being behind the thefts here in town, including stealing the Reep lithograph, and the Good Shepherd painting?"

Katherine's cheeks warmed. "To be honest, for the longest time, we thought she was off her rocker. Now, I'm not so sure."

"Well, listen. I think she was right all along. I spotted an ad in the San Francisco Examiner. A guy calling himself Willard Shultz is offering the same size, same format painting of the Bernard Plockhorst Good Shepherd painting for sale. Suspicious, huh? Willard Shultz? Get it?"

"I'm not sure I understand what—"

"Since there are only a few Plockhorst paintings in that size and format, what are the odds this guy calling himself Willard Shultz is actually Dr. Willard Schatzsman? If I'm right, I'll owe your grandma an apology. I didn't believe her accusations against the doctor, either."

Katherine sucked in her breath. Another reason to believe Grandmother's story about the doctor and the pills being responsible for her recent behavior. "Well, what can we do about it? Did you notify the San Francisco police?"

"I suppose I could, but what good would that do? I can't claim that Willard Shultz and Willard Schatzsman is the same guy until we see him. Or, for that matter, how could we know that it's actually the same painting stolen from the church?"

"I can prove it. Grandmother has the receipt from when the church ladies bought the painting three years ago. It had the first owner's name written on the back in the lower right hand corner, and they recorded it on her sales receipt. If the name is on the back of the San Francisco painting, we could prove it's the church's painting. But, here's the problem. Once he sees me or Grandmother, he'd know it was a trap. He could refuse to let us in the door. He knows how Grandmother accused him to Chief Waddlemucker. Besides, Grandmother isn't able to go to San Francisco right now. She got a second opinion from Dr. Thigpen. Turns out, the pills Dr. Schatzsman gave her, supposedly to stop a brain bleed, are really amphetamines. That explains why she's been so nutsy the past few weeks. Of course, she stopped the pills immediately."

"Why, that dirty rat. Now, I'm more determined than ever to put him behind bars. Maybe we could send someone else to San Francisco to check out the painting."

"Grandmother will never stand for that. You know how she is. She'll want to be right in the middle of things. You can't blame her after what he's done. What should we do? We can't let him get away with it, and Grandma can't go to San Francisco to confront him."

"First of all, we keep our mouths shut. Not a word to Agnes. It's for her own good. We have to figure a way to check the painting without arousing his suspicion."

"Grandmother will be furious if she finds out we went behind her back."

"Once he's brought to justice, she'll get over it."

With a glance around the supply room containing hair products and, in particular, hair dye, Katherine said, "Wait. I have an idea how we can see the painting without him knowing it's us."

Vincent laughed. "You just said he'd recognize you. How could you check the back of the painting without him knowing it's you?"

Katherine lifted the bottle of hair dye. "You forget my expertise with make-up and hair. I'll make up my face to look like an old woman and dye my hair grey. I can fix it in finger waves like Mrs. Plumbinder, and wear one of Grandmother's dresses. I'll have to pad the front, of course. He'll never recognize me… Oh, Vincent, I can do this. He doesn't know you. You can pretend to be my son. You can make an appointment to see the painting. When he shows it to us and I see the name on the back, you can arrest him."

"I don't know if I have the authority. I suppose I could do a citizen's arrest and take him to the local police station." He paused. "Katherine, I'm not sure about this. It might be better to have one of my FBI friends approach him. It could be dangerous, once he knows he's caught."

"You'll be with me. What could possibly go wrong?" What, indeed. She'd lived with Grandmother long enough to know the results of some of her hair-brained schemes Was this plan any different? For a moment, she doubted their ability to pull it off. Maybe Vincent was right. Another agent could play the part of the buyer and… No! The idea of bringing the scum-bag to justice was empowering. She finally understood the motivation behind Grandmother's somewhat impetuous and usually disastrous, hair-brained, schemes.

"Agnes has asked me to pick up Shere Khan at the military base and drive him to the train on Friday," Vincent said. "But, I keep hoping before then, she'll change her mind about sending him to that animal preserve. What on earth is she thinking?"

"We're not exactly talking about Shere Khan these days. Even Colonel Farthingworth and Charles had a fit when they heard her plan, and they couldn't change her mind."

"How will we keep Agnes from discovering our plan to go to San Francisco?"

Katherine glanced at her wristwatch and peeked through the doorway curtain to check Mrs. Whistlemeyer. "She's so caught up in recovering from the amphetamines, and sending Shere Khan to Oregon, I don't think she'll even notice us. Besides, she's not supposed to leave the house for a few days, due to possible side-effects from stopping Schatzsman's pills. We can head on down to San Francisco after we drop off the tiger in Santa Rosa."

"So you're not going to do anything to stop her from going through with it?"

Katherine sighed. "What choice do I have? She's already talked to the colonel and made the reservation." Neither spoke for a bit.

Vincent cleared his throat. "I'll call Schatzsman and make an appointment to see the painting late Friday afternoon. We'll tell Agnes that after we drop the tiger at the train station, we're driving down to San Francisco for the weekend. I'll drop hints that we might be eloping. That way, she won't insist on coming with us. When we get to San Francisco, we can get a motel where you can change into your costume and make-up before we meet up with Schatzsman."

Katherine giggled and her cheeks warmed. "So that's all the motel room is for, right? Just a staging area?"

"Why, Katherine. How you talk. You know I'm a gentleman."

"We'll have to spend the night in San Francisco after we see Schatzsman. It will be too late to drive back home Friday night."

"We can get two rooms if you like. I wouldn't do anything you didn't agree to. Although, I'm sure we could find a Justice of the Peace somewhere in San Francisco, if you were so inclined."

"*Oops!* Gotta go." Katherine peeked through the curtain again. "Mrs. Whistlemeyer is waving at me. Call me later...or better yet, come by this evening and we'll spring our plans on Grandmother." She giggled. "She likes you. She'll be all for the idea of our eloping."

With the hints that they might be considering an elopement, it wasn't hard to convince Agnes to allow Vincent and Katherine to take Shere Khan to the train.

The night before Katherine and Vincent were to leave, Agnes tossed and turned all night, wondering if she should cancel the tiger's reservation to Oregon. Was it really the best long-term plan for Shere Khan, or had her decision been clouded by the effects of the amphetamines? Even as doubts about the wisdom of her plan circled in her brain for the past few days, her contrary nature prevented her from admitting she was wrong. Having dug in her heels against everyone's wishes, she couldn't back down now. It appeared poor Shere Khan would pay the price for her stubbornness and conceit.

By 6:00 A.M., in spite of her wakefulness, questions, and concerns, she was not convinced that she should change her mind. Vincent and Katherine would transport the tiger to Santa Rosa in his traveling cage, and then drive on to San Francisco. They said they were only going sight-seeing, but she knew better. They were eloping.

In the midst of the turmoil over Shere Khan, the one bright spot was that Vincent had finally broken Katherine's aversion to marriage and she would be safely married to a man committed to her and Maddie. Now, with her acceptance of Godfrey's proposal, wasn't it the best way to solve their living situation? She tried to push the image of Shere Khan's great golden eyes from her mind.

So, she pulled the pillow over her head and stayed in bed. She didn't have to be physically present when the tiger was sent to an uncertain future. It was hard enough to live with the pangs of guilt, without watching the train pull away from the station.

She thought about Charles's phone call the previous night. After first agreeing to accompany Shere Khan to Oregon, thinking he might stay on as Shere Khan's caregiver, he had changed his mind and decided to return to his hometown in Arkansas. Poor Shere Khan would be on his own in Oregon, with neither friend nor advocate to stem the tide of whatever fate awaited. Agnes closed her eyes against the image of him huddled in a small cage, hungry and frightened. It was hard to swallow the lump in her throat as her heart filled her with guilt and shame. *What is wrong with me? I hate myself for doing this.*

Chapter Thirty-Two

ust past dawn on Friday morning, Katherine and Vincent were on the ocean highway headed toward Boyles Springs Military Base. In a final attempt to get Grandmother to change her mind about sending Shere Khan away, Katherine had tapped on her door. She heard Grandmother inside, but she would not answer the door.

Fog rolled over the landscape, obscuring even the ocean waves against the rocks near shore, far below the cliff highway. It crept up and blanketed the road, limiting visibility to about twenty feet in front of Vincent's Model A pickup. Katherine gripped the armrest on the passenger door and prayed they wouldn't meet another vehicle heading around a curve. "I hate this road. Why doesn't the county at least put side rails along the edge of the cliff? No wonder they have so many accidents out here. This fog is murder."

Vincent didn't turn his head to answer, but kept his gaze locked on the few feet of white line he could see in the middle of the road. The pickup truck crept through the fog. Despite the chill in the truck, perspiration beaded his brow. "It will be better coming back with Shere Khan. The fog will burn off a little later. Don't worry. I've got this."

"You don't expect any trouble at the military base, do you? I mean, Colonel Farthingworth agreed to release the tiger, right?"

Vincent turned his head toward Katherine and then quickly back to the road. "I left a message with his aide yesterday, that we were coming this morning, but he didn't return my call. I guess he spoke to

Charles about having Shere Khan in his traveling cage."

"I wonder what Charles will do, now that he's out of a job... and a place to live." Katherine lowered her head. "I feel terrible about that, too. Actually, I feel bad about everything... The tiger going to Oregon. Deceiving Grandmother with our plans to confront Dr. Schatzsman about the painting. Quarreling with her this week over Shere Khan. Maddie's beside herself with grief. She's convinced Shere Khan will die in Oregon. Poor kid! I don't know what to say to her. I'm not so sure she isn't right. I'm worried about him, too." She ran her hand over her eyes. "I feel like crying every time I think about it." She turned her head away so Vincent couldn't see the tears puddled in her eyes.

"I know. I don't like it either. Look, the fog is lifting." He pressed the gas pedal harder and the pickup surged forward. "We'll be at the base in a few minutes." He sighed and glanced out to sea where the waves broke over the rocks near shore. A flock of seagulls rose above the cliffs and flew over the truck in groups of twos and threes.

Katherine pointed. "Look how they're flying. They almost look like Morse code dots and dashes for S.O.S. Three, three, three. Is it a sign?" A shiver crept up the back of her neck. "Vincent! Stop the truck at that pull-over spot. We need to talk before we go one foot farther."

Not wanting another last-minute argument over Shere Khan, Agnes had refused to speak to Katherine before she left the house. Exhausted from her sleepless night, Agnes arose, dressed and made a pan of oatmeal for breakfast. Maddie wandered into the kitchen, yawning.

Agnes glanced again and again at the clock as she hurried Maddie through breakfast. In her mind's eye, she could see Katherine and Vincent traversing the coast highway and nearing the military base where the tiger lay sleeping in his warm bed of straw, never suspecting his life was about to be turned upside down.

Agnes's brow wrinkled as pain pricked her forehead. She carried her coffee to the back porch and opened the door to breathe in the crisp morning air. She gazed out into the victory garden where the leafy shoots of radishes and cabbages peaked up through the dirt. A robin flitted in and out of the apple tree, picking bugs from the blossoms. As she gazed at the garden, her headache dissolved and her brow smoothed. In that moment, as if the floodgates of indecision and hardness in her heart opened and a surety of purpose emerged. She knew exactly what she must do. But, Katherine and Vincent were already on their way to Boyles Springs! Was it already too late?

"Maddie, honey, put your bowl in the sink. You can go in your room and color in your coloring book for a bit. Grandma needs to make an important phone call."

Her hand shook as she opened her address book and scanned the page until she found the number for Boyles Springs Military Base. She dialed the number and mumbled, "Hurry, hurry," as the phone rang. At last, a male voice said, "Boyles Springs Military Base. How can I direct your call?"

"Connect me with Colonel Farthingworth," Agnes almost shouted into the phone. "This is an emergency!"

"One moment please," the man answered, his voice relaying his boredom with her concern.

After several clicks, and what felt like an eternity, the phone in the colonel's office began to ring. On the fourth ring, a young soldier answered. "Colonel Farthingworth's office. May I help you?"

"I need to speak to Colonel Farthingworth, please. This is Mrs. Odboddy from Newbury. Please put me through immediately. This is a matter of life and death."

"I'm sorry. Colonel Farthingworth isn't in his office at the moment. May I take a message?

Agnes's hand holding the receiver shook with fury. "If he's not in his office, you'd dad-blamed better find him pronto, and get him here to talk to me or I'll have your hide for breakfast! Do you hear me?" The hollow in the pit of her stomach felt like the black hole of Calcutta.

Agnes's threats apparently struck home. "Yes ma'am. Right away, ma'am. I think he's in the mess hall. I'll run right over and fetch him." Agnes heard a *clunk* as the receiver hit the top of the desk. Next, a door squeaked open and slammed shut and then... silence.

Was it too late? Agnes raised her hand to her forehead. She could almost see Katherine's face as Charles and Vincent coached a sleepy Shere Khan into his traveling cage in the pickup truck. In a few minutes, they might be on their way toward Santa Rosa. Images of Shere Khan filled her mind. She could imagine him in the corner of the Oregon cage, alone, and missing Charles and his adoring fans. Why on God's green earth had she ever thought it would be in his best interest to take him from his familiar, happy life, and send him to a veritable death row prison in Oregon? Dr. Schatzsman amphetamines must have twisted her reason and made her do the most despicable things over the past few weeks. How she hated that man. Her system finally flushed of the pills, this morning she was clear-headed enough to see the error of her thinking. Not until she heard Vincent's truck pull away from the curb had all the consternation about Shere Khan clicked in her brain. Of course it made more sense to leave him in Boyles Springs. Now that she wanted to call a halt to the process, was it too late? Perhaps she could call the train station and cancel the reservation. Wouldn't that be interesting? Katherine and Vincent would have to take a tiger along with them on their honeymoon. She almost smiled at the thought as she paced the kitchen, stretching the length of the phone cord. Where in blue blazes was the colonel?

At last the sound of thumping boots, a door opening and closing, and the colonel's voice. "Hello? Mrs. Odboddy. I'm glad you called. I was going to call you this morning, myself."

"Colonel. Listen to me. Vincent and Katherine are on their way to—"

"Now, Mrs. Odboddy. I won't listen to another minute of your arguments. That tiger—"

"You don't understand. That's why I called. There's no time to—"

"No. *You* don't understand. I won't give up the animal. I'm claiming eminent domain and that's final."

Agnes crinkled her forehead. *What is he talking about? Real estate?* "Colonel, I called to say that I—"

"*Tut tut.* None of that. I know you think you have the last word on this, but that tiger is doing a service for the war effort, and I won't have you upsetting the apple cart now. You have no legal claim to—"

"I know he's helping the war effort. That's what I called to say—"

"Eminent domain, I say! I'm claiming eminent domain! And, I'm not paying you a red cent, either. I'll draft the beast into the military as a private if I have to."

Agnes paused and crinkled her brow. "How can you claim eminent domain on a tiger? Isn't that a property thing? Besides, I didn't say..." The colonel's bumbled words began to make sense. *Oh, I get it. Draft Shere Khan into the military?* They were both talking at cross-purposes about the same thing. "Are Vincent and Katherine there yet? Have you talked to them?"

"I haven't seen them. And, if I do, I'll tell them the same thing. Shere Khan isn't going anywhere. You have no legal title to him and the US government claims national rights to... something! He's staying right where he is for the duration of the war, helping us sell war bonds. And, that's final!" Agnes could almost see his set jaw, his ears turning red, and the stub of his cigar clenched in his teeth tight enough to bite through.

She laughed. "Colonel. My dear colonel. That's why I called. To ask you to stop Vincent and Katherine at the gate. I don't want Shere Khan to go, either. He needs to stay right where he is for as long as you'll have him. Maybe when the war is over, I can find a place for him, but we'll worry about that another day." She sucked in her breath. "But, you've got to call the gate and stop Vincent and Katherine. They could be there any minute. They're going to take him to the train station in Santa Rosa. You have to hurry. It might be too late, already."

The colonel chuckled. "Well, I'll be. Now, don't you worry your pretty little head. I've already left orders at the gate that Vincent and Katherine aren't allowed on the base today, for any reason. That'll stop them, all right."

"Maybe you could leave word to have them call me when they get there? I need to tell them I've changed my mind, and they have my blessing if they want to go on to San Francisco and get married."

"Married, you say? Well, isn't that nice. Why, I remember when Edith and I were married. We were in a different war, then, remember? 1918. A couple of crazy kids in love."

Yes, she remembered. She touched the silver chopsticks in the back of her bun, her husband's gift to her when he went off to war in 1918, and never returned.

Memories flushed her cheeks. "Yes, I'm pleased myself. Katherine deserves a nice man and Vincent seems to love the socks off her, so that's good."

"Well, now, I'll call the gate and leave your message. I plan to pay a visit to our tiger this afternoon and see how he and the lad are doing. Any message you want me to give young Charles?"

"Just tell him, he was right about Shere Khan, and I was wrong. He'll get a kick out of that, because he knows I'm never wrong about anything. Take care, colonel. Give Edith my love."

Agnes hung up the phone and glanced at the clock. So far, other than occasional headaches, none of Dr. Thigpen's dire warnings about possible withdrawal side-effects had occurred. She'd had no fainting spells and apparently no delusions since she stopped taking the doctor's pills. She chuckled. At least, she hadn't tried to murder anyone lately. So far, so good, but still a few days to stay away from ladders and city hall.

She twisted her engagement ring. "I must call Godfrey and tell him the news. He'll be so pleased that Shere Khan is staying at the military base." Unfortunately, she'd have to listen to his 'I told you so's.' He would take great delight in pointing out that everyone was right and she was wrong. She deserved any chastisement he wished to dish out.

Chapter Thirty-Three

hen next they talked, Colonel Farthingworth shared with Agnes his surprise that when he checked with the guards at the gate, they reported that Katherine and Vincent never appeared to claim the tiger. Apparently, the simultaneous decision to leave Shere Khan at the military base struck Agnes and Colonel Farthingworth, as well as Katherine and Vincent. Shere Khan's morning nap went undisturbed until Charles awoke him for his 11:00 A.M. walk around the base. How surprised Charles must have been when Vincent and Katherine failed to appear at 7:00 A.M., as he had expected.

A number of hours later, Vincent pulled into the Stargate Motel near the outskirts of San Francisco and rented two adjoining rooms. He carried Katherine's suitcase into her room and laid it on the end of the bed. "Are you sure you want to go through with this? My appointment with Dr. Schatzsman is at 4:30 this afternoon." He glanced at his watch. "It's a little after 11:00 A.M. We could get some lunch before you start putting on your costume."

Katherine set her handbag on the dresser and glanced in the mirror. "Probably a good idea. I can't very well go to lunch after I put on my stage make-up."

Vincent nodded. "Then let's go. I saw a coffee shop a few blocks back. We can have lunch, take a little walk on the beach and be back by 2:00 P.M. Is that enough time to get into character before our appointment?"

"I think so."

"Are you sure you can pull this off?"

"I'm going to apply a temporary color rinse and put Marsel finger waves in my hair like the older ladies still wear. I sneaked out Grandma's best *Sunday Go To Meeting* dress. With the right make up, I'll look years older and with padding in her dress, he'll never recognize me. Don't worry. I can do this."

"Then let's go and have a good time before the games begin." Vincent took Katherine's hand and led her back to his Ford pickup truck.

Agnes paced the living room, though she wasn't sure why she was so anxious. Perhaps she was waiting for the kids to call from the military base when they arrived at the gate and learned they couldn't take the tiger. Surely, they *would* call if they had any reason to doubt that she had changed her mind and agreed to let Shere Khan stay. Would the kids let her know if they planned to continue on to San Francisco, even after the change of plans? Probably not, if they wanted to keep their elopement a secret. Her smile faded when she realized she would likely still be charged for Shere Khan's shipping passage even when they didn't show up. Perhaps she should call and inform the station of the change in plans. She turned at the fireplace and paced back toward the kitchen.

She flumped down on the sofa and drummed her fingers on the newspaper Vincent left on the coffee table the night before. *What?* Her gaze fell on a circled ad in the want ads and read aloud, "The Plockhorst Good Shepherd painting. 24" X36" Vintage. $200. Willard Shultz. 7221 Geary Street, SF. Call MU2-4220 for appointment."

She grabbed the newspaper with a shaking hand and read the ad again. She lowered the paper and gazed across the room, her thoughts in a muddle. Gradually, it began to make sense. *Willard Shultz. Willard*

Schatzsman! The church's stolen painting. The rotten doctor was trying to pawn it off under a false name. She stood and strode toward the kitchen. The kids had hoodwinked her. They weren't going to San Francisco to elope. They were going to confront Schatzsman to get the painting back! She clenched her fists, "Oh my stars and little fishes!"

It wasn't the risk they were taking that made her so mad. They were going without her. She hurried to the telephone and dialed Godfrey's number. "Hello?"

"Godfrey. How's your ankle? Do you think you can drive yet? Do you want to go to San Francisco with me this afternoon? How about money? Got any money?"

"*Uh*... Fine... Probably... Maybe... Yes... more or less in that order. Why do you ask? You're wearing me out with all these excursions. You're not taking those pills again, are you? What's got you so *het up* this time?"

In about sixty seconds, Agnes told him she changed her mind about Shere Khan, the San Francisco Examiner ad on her coffee table, and her theory of the kids' sting operation. "We have to get down there right away. I know they're going to confront him. There's no telling what he'll do when he sees Katherine."

"*Wow!* Shouldn't you call Chief Waddlemucker and tell him what you told me?"

"There's no time. We have to go. I'll have Mavis watch Maddie and see if I can borrow some of her gas ration coupons. As vice president of The First Church of the Evening Star and Everlasting Light Ladies' Missionary Society, she's as mad about the theft of the Good Shepherd painting as I am. She'll want to help us get it back. If you think you can drive to the city, be ready to go in half an hour. If not, I'll have to go by myself."

"No squash-blossom. Don't even think about going alone. We can take my car. It has better tires than yours. I'll run to the gas station and fill up the gas tank. We'll probably need Mavis's gas ration coupons on the way back. I'll pick you up in about half an hour. Bye!" He hung up the phone.

"Ling-Ling! You're on your own today. Mama's going to San Francisco to catch a scalawag who stole our Good Shepherd painting."

Following a good lunch and an invigorating walk on the beach, Vincent returned Katherine to her motel room. Katherine removed paraphernalia from her overnight case needed to transform her lithe beauty into an elegant but stout older woman. Metal wave clamps, Bobbie pins, a jar of Nestle Superset wave lotion, jars of rouge, a bit of gum paste, eyebrow pencils, powders, lipstick, and a bottle of hair dye lined the dresser. "Why don't you go take a nap, Vincent? I'll need to use the shower to dye my hair. You'll be underfoot here if you stay here. Come back in an hour."

"I might drive back to that fruit stand we passed a couple blocks away and pick up a bag of oranges. I'll see you later."

"Great. If they have any avocados, pick up a couple for Grandma. She hasn't found any at Wilkey's Market for a while."

"Will do." Vincent left and pulled the door closed behind him.

Over the next hour, Katherine changed the color of her hair, cleverly plucked and reshaped her eyebrows, gum paste beneath her eyes make them look puffy. She added highlights and color to her forehead and eyebrow pencil around her mouth to resemble wrinkles, powered and puffed her cheeks to heighten her cheekbones and applied a light pink lipstick in the popular 1920s style called a *cupid's bow*, still favored by older women, An hour later, Vincent returned, carrying a bag of oranges. When Katherine opened the door, he glanced toward the room next door. "Oh, I'm sorry. I must have the wrong..." His eyes opened wide. "Katherine? Oh, my gosh! Is that you?"

Katherine giggled. "Wait until I'm wearing Grandma's dress with the bosom stuffed. I told you Dr. Schatzsman wouldn't recognize me."

Chapter Thirty-Four

"I've just been the victim of highway robbery." Godfrey

On the highway between Newbury and Santa Rosa, Godfrey's little black car traveled at the break-neck speed limit of thirty-five miles per hour. Agnes glanced at her wristwatch. *12:45 P.M.* "Can't you drive any faster? What if we don't get there in time?"

"I'm pushing the speed limit as it is. We'll get there a lot faster if we don't have to stop for a speeding ticket or a blown tire."

Agnes sat back. "You're right. I'm just so worried about the kids. What if they confront the doctor and he...he... I don't know what, but that man is capable of anything! The slime ball!"

Godfrey's gaze flicked toward Agnes and then back to the road. "What, exactly, is your plan when we get to San Francisco? You really don't know if the kids intend to go to the address in the paper. If they do, likely they'll have already been and gone by the time we get there. Thirdly, whether they do or don't, what are we going to do when *we* get there? If Dr. Schatzsman is there, and that's only a possibility, once he sees you, he'll slam the door in your face. We'll be standing on the doorstep looking like a couple of fools making wild accusations."

Agnes crossed her arms and stared out the side window. Godfrey was right. What good would it do to show up at the address? She hadn't given the situation much thought. Perhaps she wasn't free from the effect of the amphetamines, after all. Dragging Godfrey off at the drop of a hat, on the basis of a newspaper ad and some coincidental circumstances, wasn't very sensible. Once again, she had acted in much the same impulsive manner as during the past few weeks.

Agnes's neck warmed. She picked at the cuticle on her left thumb. "*Um*... I... I guess I was rather impulsive." Her head jerked toward Godfrey. "If you think I'm wrong, how come you go along with everything? Why don't you make me stop and think before I get into trouble?"

"Oh. So, now it's my fault? You drag me out of bed and tell me I have half an hour to come on a hair-brained mission? Should I ignore you and let you jump into the lion's den alone? What kind of a help-mate would I be if I didn't protect you from your own stupidity?"

"My what? Stupidity? Is that what you think of me?"

Godfrey pulled the car to the side of the road, stomped on the clutch, shoved the gear shift into neutral, and yanked on the emergency brake. The motor hummed. He lowered his head and closed his eyes. "I shouldn't have used that word. But, let's get one thing straight. I love you and will protect you as long as there's breath in my body. If you need my support, even if I don't completely agree, I'm there for you. I do, however, expect you to meet me with the same level of consideration. I'm not a fool, Agnes. I've spent twenty-seven years working with the government on dangerous and sometimes covert missions. I may be getting on in years, but I still have a good mind and common sense. Use it."

Agnes gulped. "You're right. I've been impulsive and made some foolish mistakes. I can't entirely blame the drugs, but I'm sure they affected my judgment and some of my decisions." Her eyes pricked with tears. "Maybe my head isn't entirely clear yet. But, either Vincent or Katherine circled the newspaper ad. I'm convinced Dr. Schatzsman placed the ad using a false name and the kids are headed to San Francisco. How could I not think they plan to confront him? Then, I discovered my best Sunday dress missing from my closet. It's just like Katherine to think she could disguise herself so he won't recognize her. I'm afraid for their safety. Is that so hair-brained?"

"Maybe not. But, Vincent is a trained FBI agent. He's not going to let Katherine do anything foolish. Maybe you were right when you first thought they were eloping. Maybe Vincent circled the ad because he thought it was a coincidence that it was the same painting you lost."

"I suppose you think Katherine took my dress to wear at her wedding? You might as well try to convince me that one day we'll fly a rocket ship to the moon."

Godfrey's face pinked up. "You're probably right, sugar-plum." He glanced over his shoulder, released the emergency brake, shifted into first gear, and pulled the car back onto the road. "We'll see. We'll go to the address, knock on the door and see who opens it. Perhaps when we get to the city, we should call the local police department and report our suspicions."

"You know best. I place myself entirely in your capable hands." Agnes leaned over and planted a kiss on Godfrey's cheek.

An hour later, they were on Highway 101, a modern, two-lane road, passing fields of apple trees on the left and right, occasional fruit stands and rolling hills. Rows and rows of chicken houses lined the highway. Near the town of Petaluma, a sign read, *Welcome to Petaluma – Home of 4000 Egg Farms*. The road ran through the center of town and proceeded toward San Rafael.

The terrain rose and fell as the highway neared San Francisco. Along one particularly difficult incline, Godfrey's car faltered, lunged and bucked. Billows of steam crept along the hood of the car toward the front window. Once again, he pulled the car to a stop on the side of the road.

"What's wrong?" Agnes said, glancing at her wristwatch *2:45 P.M.*

"Stupid car's not used to being driven so far in one day. The engine's overheated. Don't worry. I came prepared. Thought this might happen." He opened the door and stepped out.

Godfrey lifted the canvas bag of water hanging over the protruding headlight. He placed his folded handkerchief over the radiator cap. As he slowly unscrewed it, a rush of steam gushed around the edges. With a final quick twist, steam and hot water shot into the air. Godfrey unscrewed the stopper on the bag and gradually poured a bit of water from the bag into the radiator. As the steam subsided, he emptied the remainder of the water and replaced the radiator cap. "That should do it," he called, hanging the bag over the headlight and climbing into the car. "See? That didn't take long. We should make San Francisco within an hour with no further trouble."

"From your lips to God's ears. Now, when you pass the next gas station, if you'll please stop, I could use a *rest*. I feel somewhat sick to my stomach."

"It's probably all this driving. I should top off the gas tank and refill the water bag, anyway. Gas is likely cheaper here than in the city. Here's one, now." He pulled into a Flying Red Horse gas station and stopped beside a red gas pump with a white glass ball on top depicting a red flying horse. Agnes got out of the car and hurried to the rest room on the side of the building.

A few minutes later, scowling, Godfrey slid into the driver's seat, slammed the car door, and pulled back onto the road. Agnes patted her neckline with her handkerchief. "What's wrong? You look like you swallowed a bug." She touched the handkerchief to her forehead and tucked it back into the neck of her dress.

"It's nothing, really. I'm just annoyed. I've been the victim of highway robbery. I paid twenty cents a gallon for the gas, plus a ration ticket. Can you imagine? At that rate, if a fellow lived around here, he could never afford a car. He'd have to hitch-hike to work."

Agnes patted his arm. "Never mind. We knew things would cost more today. Just consider it the price we have to pay to bring the doctor to justice."

"*Humph!* So you say. If you ask me, which nobody did, we're on a wild goose chase."

Agnes clutched her stomach. "Then, it's a good thing nobody asked…Godfrey! Pull over. I'm going to be sick." Agnes grabbed her handkerchief and put it over her mouth. Godfrey brought the car to a stop on the shoulder, just in time for Agnes to throw open the door, lean her head out and retch into the dirt.

"My dear!" Godfrey retrieved the radiator water bag from the headlight and carried it over to where Agnes sat with her head in her hands. He kicked dirt over the vomitus and handed the bag to Agnes. "Here, take a drink. This should help."

After rinsing her mouth, and wiping her face and hands with Godfrey's handkerchief, she leaned back and closed her eyes. "Thank you."

"Are you sure this is a good idea? There's really no reason we have to go on. We could get something to eat and head on home."

"I'm fine. I never have been a very good traveler. I'm not the least bit hungry, but maybe a glass of iced tea would be nice."

Godfrey glanced at his wristwatch. "It's after two o'clock and neither of us have had lunch. I think we should stop and get a sandwich."

Agnes stared at the vast blocks of houses and warehouses in sight. How could people live, boxed in on all sides like rabbits in a hutch, bound by fences and walls and postage stamp sized front yards? Even the air smelled of smog, car fumes, and the faint scent of vomit she'd been unable to wipe from the hem of her dress. She put her hand to her forehead.

Godfrey found a diner, stopped in the parking lot, and turned off the engine. "This looks like a nice place. We'll stop here. A cup of tea will do you a world of good."

Chapter Thirty-Five

"I studied drama in college." Katherine

Somewhere in a small room in a second-rate motel, Katherine completed her transformation from being an attractive young woman to a stout, haughty-looking older woman. She stuffed the bust of Grandmother's dress with the hand towels from the motel bathroom. With a glance into the pitted mirror over the bathroom sink and a final pat to the Marcel finger waves in her hair, she turned to face Vincent, sitting in the single straight back chair beside the bed. "Well, I guess I'm ready. What do you think?"

"You look like a librarian. Have you given any thought to how we're going to play this?"

"What, exactly did you tell the doctor when you called about the painting? I guess we start there."

"I said my mother and I saw his ad and were interested in buying the Plockhorst painting. He said to drop by about 4:00 P.M. and he'd show it to us. Problem is, once we verify it's the church ladies' painting, then, what do we do?"

"You'll have to make a citizen's arrest, or we could go straight to the police department and report him as the thief. Did you bring your pistol?"

Vincent patted his chest pocket. "Hopefully, I won't have to use it. Are you ready?"

"Let's do it."

Vincent drove across town and slowed when they approached the address on Geary Street. "There it is. Now, to find a place to park." He drove another block and circled back.

"There. That car is pulling out. Park there." Katherine pointed to a black Hudson pulling away from the curb.

Vincent parked about a half block from Schatzsman's house and circled the car to open Katherine's door. They read the house numbers as they passed each house until they came to the one listed in the ad. "Are you ready, Mrs. Peckenpaw?"

Katherine's mouth twitched. "Don't make me laugh. I'll crack my wrinkles." She forced her face to be expressionless. She pulled the powder compact from her purse, snapped it open and peered into the mirror to check her cheeks where the painted lines around her mouth resembled wrinkles. "Still good. Ready?"

They climbed the steps and rang the doorbell. "Here goes nothing," Vincent whispered.

The door opened and as expected, Dr. Schatzsman stood on the stoop. "Come in. I've been expecting you…Mr. Peckenpaw?" With a frown, his gaze moved from Katherine to Vincent.

Vincent nodded and shook the doctor's hand. "May I present my mother, Abigail Peckenpaw."

"Ma'am. Pleased to meet you." He reached for Katherine's hand. She turned her head as though not seeing his outstretched hand or deigned not to touch it.

"Charmed, I'm sure." She lifted her nose in a manner suggestive of a snobby society woman.

Dr. Schatzsman frowned and pointed to a staircase. "If you'll follow me, my artwork is upstairs in my studio." He led the way up two flights and opened a door into a room where artwork filled three walls. A table sat in the middle of the room, with a sofa and several soft chairs on each side. At the end of the room, floor to ceiling bookshelves stood on each side of the fireplace.

"Lovely library. You're an art aficionado, I see. Is that a Salvador Dali?" Katherine gazed at the muted colors on a painting that appeared to be in the style of the noted artist.

"It is. One of his more recent works, and my latest acquisition."

She raised her voice and put on an affected New York accent, "Intriguing. How did you come to acquire such a well-known, yet crude, painting?" She turned toward him, and then back to the Dali painting, her nose tilted upward, as though gazing at a kindergartner's stick-figure drawing.

Dr. Schatzsman's face flushed. "The price was not beyond the reach of a dedicated collector." He raised an eyebrow. "Excuse me, but you look so familiar. Have we met before?"

Katherine shrugged and extended her gloved hand, fingers tipped, as though expecting him to kiss her hand. "My late husband was Wilbur Peckenpaw, of the New York Peckenpaws. The sheet metal king? I'm sure you've heard of him. We may have met at a social event in New York. When were you last in New York?"

The doctor shook his head. He took her outstretched hand, gave it a gentle squeeze and dropped it like a hot coal. "I haven't been in New York for many years, but I still think we've met somewhere... perhaps here in San Francisco?"

"It's possible. My son and I..." She leaned her head toward Vincent, "... are visiting Roger Latham and his family here in the city for a few days." At the doctor's blank stare, she added. "Oh, surely you know Roger. He and I went to school together years ago. Surely, you know the San Francisco mayor?"

"I don't believe I've had the pleasure of..." The doctor appeared confused.

"Well, that's neither here nor there," Katherine said. "We came to see a painting? A Plockhorst? A minor work, of course, but we had a copy hanging in my son's nursery ever so many years ago. I thought it would be quaint to put a copy in my late husband's study." She gazed at the paintings on the wall, seemingly as unimpressed by the collection as if she lived and slept in the lobby of the Metropolitan Museum of Art located in New York's Central Park.

"Of course. Of course. Wait right here. It's in my office. I'll be right back." The doctor stepped into the next room, closing the door behind him.

Vincent whispered in Katherine's ear. "Good heavens, Katherine. I had no idea you could put on such an act."

"I thought you knew I studied drama in college."

"You've almost convinced me you're a New York society snob. Now get ready. Can you keep up the ..." Dr. Schatzsman came through the door with a painting turned toward his body. A wire stretched across the top of the frame and a small square paper was attached to the lower right hand corner. He laid the painting face up on the table before Katherine could read the writing on the small scrap of paper.

Katherine gazed at the gentle face of the Savior, suffused with kindness as He cradled a lamb in the crook of His arm. His face was that of a gentle shepherd lovingly tending His flock. The sheep surrounded Him, as though drawing comfort from His nearness and protection, gazed into His face. The painting suggested the Savior would provide the same love and protection to the viewer.

Katherine ran her gloved finger over the frame. "It's beautiful. Exactly as I hoped. May I see how it's mounted?" Her heart skipped a beat as the doctor turned the painting over, displaying the wooden frame and the small white paper in the corner. She leaned forward and read the name of the original owner and date of purchase. It was the same as the information on the bill of sale in her purse. The moment of truth! Should she pull out the bill of sale and confront him, or should she and Vincent leave and report the theft to the police? "I'm sure you have the appropriate provenance for the picture." Katherine tilted her head toward the picture. "My accountant is such a stickler about my art acquisitions."

Vincent grasped her arm. "Now, mother. It's not like we're acquiring the Salvador Dali over there. You're only buying the Plockhorst on a whim." The tone of his voice and his words suggested he was bored and humoring his mother.

"Well, say. If you're interested in the Dali," the doctor's smile brightened. "I might be persuaded to part with it for the right price."

"I don't think so," Katherine said. "I've never been fond of his particular style. My only interest today is the whimsical Plockhorst. Did you say $100? And, about its provenance?"

Schatzsman's eyebrows knit together. "I believe my ad said $200. At such a meager price, I don't believe such provenance is required. Are you interested or not?" He rolled his top lip over the bottom and then licked both lips.

Katherine pulled the bill of sale from her purse. "In that case, since I *do* have documentation of ownership, I'll take the picture back to the Newbury church where it belongs." Her hand trembled and her heart raced as she laid the paper on the table and reached for the picture. "This is the Good Shepherd lithograph stolen from our church last week." She nodded toward the far wall. "I have to wonder how many of your others were likewise stolen."

"I'm placing you under citizen's…" Vincent reached inside his coat to draw his pistol, but before he could pull it from his pocket, the library door crashed open.

The door slammed against the wall as Agnes and Godfrey stumbled in. "Here they are," she said.

As Vincent glanced toward the door, the doctor noted his distraction and leaped forward. He sent a striking blow to Vincent's chin knocking him to the floor. The pistol flew from his hand as he and the doctor tumbled to the floor. Vincent and Dr. Schatzsman rolled around on the floor, flailing, groping, and struggling, each trying to regain possession of the gun.

"What's going on in here?" Agnes's face paled. "Good grief. Godfrey! Do something. Make them stop."

"Grandma? What on earth are you…?"

Godfrey reached for the fireplace poker and raised it over the tussling men. Back and forth, up and down, the men struggled. As they twisted and turned, Godfrey aimed and swung the poker directly at the doctor's head. At that moment, Vincent flipped the doctor onto his back. The poker came down on Vincent's head. "Oh, no! What have I...?" Godfrey dropped the poker, his face as pale as buttermilk as Vincent tumbled to the floor.

Chapter Thirty-Six

"What...on...earth...have you done to your face?" Agnes

When Vincent hit the floor, Dr. Schatzsman scrambled to his knees and seized the pistol. "Back off, all of you!" He jerked the pistol toward the next room. "Drag that guy into the study." Sprinkles of perspiration dotted his forehead as he struggled to his feet. His gaze moved from face to face. A faint smile of recognition twitched his mouth. "Why, Mrs. Odboddy. As I live and breathe, what brings you to my humble abode? It wouldn't have anything to do with this sweet old lady's interest in my artwork, would it?" His grin widened as he turned toward Katherine. Agnes's entrance had finally allowed him to recognize Katherine, despite her disguise. In any event, as they said in the movies, *the jig was up,* and the devious doctor not only had the upper hand, but he held a revolver in it.

Godfrey helped Vincent to his feet. "Sorry, old man." He pulled his handkerchief from his pocket and pressed it to the lump on the back of Vincent's head. Vincent grimaced at the pressure on his head.

"I said, move it!" Dr. Schatzsman's expression confirmed he'd completely forgotten the words of his Hippocratic Oath and was prepared to do great harm if his captives didn't obey his commands.

"Better do as he says," Vincent muttered, taking Katherine's arm and moving toward the study. Agnes gripped Godfrey's arm and followed.

She paused at the door. "You won't get away with this, you cretin. The FBI is right outside. If we're not out of here within ten minutes, they have orders to come in shooting."

"Really, Grandma?" Katherine whispered. "You called them?"

"*Hush,*" Agnes muttered under her breath. "Of course not. He doesn't need to know that."

"That's a pretty story, Mrs. Odboddy… Too bad it's not true." The doctor chuckled. "You take me for some kind of fool? The FBI wouldn't let you come in here alone." He shoved Agnes into his study and pulled the door shut. A key turned in the lock.

"Grandma. What are you doing here? How did you find us?"

Agnes peered into Katherine's face. "What…on…earth… have you done to your face? And, that's my dress." She pinched at the sleeve of her best Sunday-Go-to-Meetin' dress, and then poked at the padded bosom. "And, I suppose this is some sort of commentary on my figure?"

"Ladies, please!" Godfrey grabbed Agnes's arm. "Can we discuss this later? Obviously, Katherine, your grandma saw the ad in the newspaper, figured out what you were up to, and we drove down to make sure you were okay."

"Well, didn't that work out fine? We had everything under control until you burst in. Now, look at my poor Vincent, thanks to you, Godfrey."

"I said I was sorry."

"Shut up! All of you." Vincent stepped between Katherine and Godfrey. "Listen to yourselves. It would be more productive to figure out how we get out of this mess. Godfrey, check the windows. Katherine, see if there's a telephone in here. Agnes, look for any sort of weapon we can use if we can get the door open. Now, move. All of you." He sank into a chair with his hand clutching the handkerchief to the back of his head. Despite his injury, he had taken control of the situation, declared himself the leader and set them on a plan to execute their escape. They each scurried to follow his instructions, without questions, and returned in a minute to report their findings.

"We're on the third floor and the window is painted shut. Even if we could pry it open, or break it, we're too high up," Godfrey reported.

"I doubt the ladies could..."

"There's no telephone in here," Katherine said with a sigh.

"All I could find was this lamp base. It's pretty sturdy, but it's not a match against Vincent's pistol. I suppose it was loaded..." Agnes raised her eyebrows as she held out the brass lamp, its cord dangling from her hand. "Never mind. You wouldn't have brought an empty pistol or loaded it with blanks."

"No, I wouldn't." Vincent shut his eyes, as if seeking a new plan.

Agnes went to the door and put her ear against an upper panel. "I can hear him walking around out there. Sounds like he's moving furniture. What do you suppose he's up to?"

"He's probably getting ready to make a break for it. Maybe packing some of his more valuable artwork. I wonder where he thinks he can go once we get out and report to the authorities?"

"If I'm not mistaken," Godfrey said with a shake of his head, "he doesn't plan for us to get out."

"Now, none of that," Agnes pulled one of the sterling silver chopsticks from the bun in the back of her hair. "Once he leaves, I'll pick the lock. I've done it before. I can do it again." She placed her ear to the door again. "I don't hear him. I think he's gone."

Her companions rushed over and pressed their ears against the door. "I don't hear anything, either. Go ahead, Grandma, give it a try." Katherine's make-up cracked as she smiled.

Agnes knelt beside the doorknob, poked the chopstick into the keyhole and jiggled it.

Katherine returned to the window and peered at the street, two stories below. She pulled the curtain aside and jumped up and down, waving her arms. "We're too high up. Nobody can see me. Maybe we should break the glass. Someone might look up."

"Let's give Agnes a chance to work on the door for a bit," Vincent said, stepping closer to the door.

"It should work, but it's not. The point of my chopstick is a bit too fat. I need something with a sharper point."

Godfrey yanked open the center desk drawer and pulled out a fountain pen. He removed the tip. "Give me your chopstick. I'll attach the nib to the end of it. That should do it."

"How are you going to attach it?"

Godfrey stared at the chopstick and the fountain pen nib. "I'm not sure. If we had some duct tape, we might tape it… He dug around in the desk again. "Nothing. We'll have to find something else. Everyone, look around. See what you can find with a sharp point."

Katherine opened a cupboard containing office supplies. "Maybe there's some tape in here. Wait! Look what I found." She grabbed the doctor's black leather medical bag and set it on the desk. Vincent opened the bag and pulled out vials and bottles.

"Here's some tape, but I think this might even be better." He handed Agnes a metal probe with a sharp point on the end that resembled a dentist's pick. "Try this." Agnes inserted the probe into the lock.

"*Uh oh.*" Vincent sniffed at the edge of the door.

"What is it?" Katherine moved closer.

"I smell gas. I think the son of a biscuit-eater has broken the gas line. Hurry Agnes, we don't have much time or we're in big trouble."

Katherine threw herself against Vincent's chest. He wrapped his arms around her. "Oh, Vincent, no. I can't believe he'd do that. He… he's a doctor. He's supposed to save lives. He wouldn't stoop to murder, would he?"

Chapter Thirty-Seven

"Don't be such a prude and take off your dress." Agnes

gnes paused in her efforts at the keyhole. "No sense wasting your tears. The good doctor didn't think twice about poisoning me with amphetamines. What makes you think he wouldn't resort to murder? He knows if we get out of here and report his art smuggling business, he's looking at decades in jail."

Katherine sniffed and wiped her eyes with the back of her hand, smudging the pancake make-up on her cheeks, creating a comical, almost grotesque appearance. Vincent pulled his handkerchief from his pocket and dabbed at the smudged make-up under her eyes.

Agnes inserted the metal probe back into the lock while Vincent hovered over her shoulder. He put his nose closer to the crack of the door and sniffed again. His cheeks paled. "It's getting stronger. I don't think it's safe out there now, even if you got the door open. We'll have to find another way."

"Well, I don't intend to sit here and wait…" Godfrey picked up the desk chair and flung it against the window. With a crash, shards of glass burst out and tumbled to the ground, two stories below. He went to the window. "Help! Somebody. Call the police!" A few cars passed by the house, but none appeared to have noticed either the broken glass or heard Godfrey's cries. "They can't hear me. We're going to have to go to Plan B."

Vincent unzipped his pants and slid them down his legs. "Serious times call for serious actions. Katherine? Take off your dress."

Katherine's cheeks warmed. "Really, Vincent. I realize this is a life and death situation, but we can't... I mean, my grandmother is standing right here. I love you and even though we might die, I don't think I can... I mean, this isn't..." She cast a bewildered glance toward Agnes and Godfrey. He was sliding off his trousers and Agnes was unbuttoning her dress. "Grandma! You, too? I can't believe you would..."

Grandma pulled her dress over her head and handed it to Godfrey. "Oh, *hush*. Don't be such a prude and take off your dress. Your virginity isn't at risk. Can't you see he intends to tie our clothes together to make a rope so we can climb out the window?"

"Oh!" Katherine ducked her head, unbuttoned the buttons under the arm of her dress, and slid it over her head. She handed the dress to Godfrey and stepped behind the desk. Godfrey yanked down the drapes, tied their two pairs of trousers together at the end of each drape, end to end, and added Katherine's dress to the bottom of the clothing rope. "It's still not long enough," he said, tying Agnes's dress to Katherine's. "We're going to need both of your under slips, too. Ladies? I'm sorry, but this is no time for modesty." The noticeable smell of gas crept insidiously beneath the door. "And, you'd best hurry if we're going to get out of here alive. The slightest spark and this place will blow."

Agnes peeled off her slip and stood in her brassiere and rubber corset. Two straps with metal hooks at the bottom were attached to dark stockings with patriotic holes below the knees.

Thoughts of Maddie came into Katherine's head and anxiety for her future filled her chest. Chill bumps raised on her arms, not only from the cool air in the study but from the thought that if she and Grandmother both died, not only would they be found in their underwear with two men equally undressed, but Maddie would have no one to care for her. The faint scent of gas made her nauseous. She stepped over to the window, stripped off her slip and stood in her brassiere and panties. Elastic bands on her upper thighs held up her less than perfect nylons. Her cheeks warmed when Vincent's gaze traveled from her face to her knees and back again. His cheeks pinked up and he jerked his head away. He knocked out the remaining pieces of window glass still clinging to the corners of the window frame. He pulled off his undershirt and handed it to her. "Katherine?" His voice trembled. "Put this on. You'll go first. You're the lightest. Take off your shoes. When you get down, run to the nearest house and call the police." Katherine took the shirt and slipped it over her head, covering her bosom and half-way over her panties.

Godfrey removed his undershirt revealing a clump of grey hair clustered on his barrel chest. He attached his undershirt to the end of Katherine's and Agnes's slips. "I think it will reach pretty far down, now. You may have to jump the last little ways." He tied a small loop in the end for her foot and attached the top piece of clothing to the radiator beneath the window.

Vincent placed the flat office chair pillow over the edge of the windowsill. "Up you go, Katherine. Sit on the edge and put your foot in the loop. As soon as you safely can, jump, so we can get Agnes down next."

Katherine followed his instructions and climbed out the window. What would people think, seeing a half-naked woman, dropping from a third floor window on a rag rope? She held tight to the clothing rope as the men lowered her over the edge and down the side of the building. First she was facing the wall, and then the cloth rope swung and spun her around so she faced the street. She heard material ripping when she was about seven feet above the ground. Lest the material should tear and prevent Grandmother's escape, she pulled her foot from the loop and tumbled to the ground. Pain shot through her hip as her breath was knocked from her. She glanced up in time to see Agnes's face appear in the window as Vincent pulled the clothing rope back up the wall.

Katherine struggled to her feet and limped onto the lawn, still dizzy from the gas and the fall. She knelt on the grass and took a few slow breaths to clear her lungs. Would the cloth rope hold Grandma's extra weight? What about Godfrey, clearly the heaviest among them? She had to find help. Maybe a neighbor would have a ladder. She looked up and down the street. Why weren't any cars coming? Grandma's car was parked a ways down the street but without keys, it was useless. She'd have to go to a neighbor's house and knock on the door. Maybe they'd call the cops when they saw a half-naked woman standing on the porch. It couldn't be helped. She looked back. Grandma was about nine or ten feet off the ground when her foot slipped and she tumbled the rest of the way. She lay still, not surprisingly, the breath knocked from her. Should she go back and check on Grandma, or go on and get help?

Katherine ran down the street to the nearest house, took the porch steps two at a time and pounded on the door. "Help me! Somebody! Can you hear me? We need help. Call the police. Please open the door. Do you have a ladder?" She heard voices inside. Maybe a radio? She knocked again, but no one came to the door. Maybe she had frightened them by screaming. Hopefully, they'd call the police.

She hurried to the next house, trying to calm her nerves. *Don't scream. Just knock.*

She pounded on the door. Footsteps approached. "Who's there?" The door opened slightly and an elderly woman's face appeared in the crack. She gasped and put her hand over her mouth when she saw the state of Katherine's undress and the smeared make-up on her face.

"Don't be frightened. I need help. Would you please call the police and ask them to come to 7221 Geary Street?"

"My dear. What has happened?" The door opened farther. "Have you been assaulted? You're nearly buck-naked." The woman's gaze moved from Katherine's head to her feet. She must have decided that a nearly-naked elderly-looking woman with a glob of smeared lipstick needed help more than the possibility she was a threat. "Come in here. I'll get you a robe."

"Thank you." Katherine stepped through the front door. A quick glance around the room revealed a comfortable living room that resembled their own home. A canary perched in a golden cage beside the fireplace. "I appreciate the robe. My friends are three doors down and they're trapped on the third floor. I really need…" At that point, her nerves and strength at an end, she burst into tears and collapsed on the sofa beside a partially crocheted sock connected to a ball of yarn.

The woman hurried to the kitchen phone and dialed the operator. Once connected to the police, she gave the address and asked for assistance. She retrieved a bathrobe from her bedroom and helped Katherine don the garment. "Why, you're not an old woman, are you? What have you got all over your face?" Indeed, after climbing down the clothing rope and falling on the grass, Katherine's make up was stained and smeared, giving her a grotesque appearance.

"I don't have time to explain. It's stage make-up, of course. But, my grandmother's in trouble and I must go back and help her. You wouldn't have another robe, would you?" Her cheeks flushed. "I know you must think I'm crazy. I'll come back and explain everything as soon as my friends are safe."

The Good Samaritan pulled a blanket from the back of the couch. "Take this. Bring it back when you can. I can't wait to hear your story. Go on. I'll see if I can get my gentleman neighbor to come and help. Three doors down, you say?"

As the canary burst into song, Katherine nodded, grabbed the blanket and rushed out the door. The bird's song assured her that God was still in his Heaven, and canaries still had the ability to make lilting music in spite of the circumstances.

By the time Katherine returned to Dr. Schatzsman's house, Grandmother was sitting on the lawn, her head in her hands, but otherwise none the worse from her fall. Vincent stood beside her and Godfrey's leg hung over the window sill. Another few minutes and they'd all be free. Embarrassed and humiliated, to be sure, but safe.

Katherine rushed up to Grandmother. "Are you okay? Are you hurt?" She wrapped the blanket around her shoulders and put her arm around her grandmother's waist. "Can you stand? We really should get farther from the house. Something could still…"

Vincent jerked his head toward the street. "Take her back to the car. I'll try to help Godfrey. I doubt the rope will hold his weight."

With no one above in the window to lower him, Godfrey had to go hand over hand down the clothing rope. It was no surprise that about half-way down, the clothing ripped apart and he fell. Vincent tried to break his fall and both of them went to the ground. Vincent got to his feet. "Can you stand?" He lifted Godfrey to his knees and then upright and the two of them staggered toward the street, shivering from the chilly San Francisco air.

Katherine had just opened her car door and helped Grandmother into the passenger seat when an explosion rocked Dr. Schatzsman's house, sending building material and shattered glass shooting across the yard and into the air. The concussion of the blast knocked Vincent and Godfrey off their feet and sent them sprawling onto the sidewalk.

"Oh my God! Vincent! Godfrey!" Katherine dashed back to where they lay. A siren wailed in the distance, and then grew louder as it neared the house. Katherine knelt beside Vincent and drew his head into her lap. Only minutes before, the street was bare of anyone who might help. Now, it was filled with curious neighbors. The elderly woman who gave Katherine the robe joined the crowd. Before long, several police cars arrived. The officers scurried around, attempting to keep people away from the house, now ablaze. Flames leaped from every section of the structure. Chunks of wall crumbled and the occasional crackle of breaking glass shattered as the silent crowd watched the blazing structure. Black smoke billowed up, caught in the wind, and drifted toward the Golden Gate Bridge.

Katherine gazed at the conflagration. Her cold cheeks tingled. If they had not made their escape down the clothing rope, they would have died in the explosion, as Dr. Schatzsman intended. How could such evil exist in a man trained to honor and protect human life?

She brushed shards of broken glass from Vincent's hair and kissed his forehead. Another siren wailed and a fire truck screeched to a halt at the curb. Firemen jumped off the vehicle, pulled hoses, twisted dials, and removed gear from cubicles and cubbies. Within a minute, water spewed toward the structure, as ineffective as spitting into the flames. Another fire truck arrived, and then another. Realizing the futility of saving the burning building, they turned their hoses onto the adjoining homes to keep the fire from spreading.

Agnes knelt beside Godfrey. She removed the blanket from her shoulders and spread it over Godfrey's shivering torso. "You need this more than I do. Are you okay?"

"I'm fine. The fall didn't help my ankle any, but I'll survive," he said, grimacing as he twisted his foot from side to side. He handed the blanket back to Agnes. "You keep that blanket. I can't have my lady standing in her *altogether* on a street corner. What will people say?"

When examined by an ambulance attendant, who provided blankets all around, they were found to be in satisfactory condition. The attendant advised Agnes to seek additional care from her own physician for the scrapes and contusions on her hip. "Isn't that a joke," she said, her eyes flashing. "My personal physician is the one who turned on the gas, set the house on fire, and tried to kill us." Katherine squeezed her grandmother's hand as they watched the three-story building burn to a pile of smoldering rubble.

Chapter Thirty-Eight

"My dear, stripes becomes you." Godfrey

gnes looked up as a San Francisco policeman approached with a notebook in his hand. His scornful gaze traveled between Godfrey, Vincent, and Agnes sitting on the curb with blankets around their shoulders. "For the love of Pete, what happened? You folks having some sort of orgy in there, and set the house ablaze?"

"It's not what it looks like, officer." Vincent stood and offered his hand. "Vincent Buckwalder. I'm with the FBI." He moved his hand beneath his blanket and patted his boxer shorts. "Unfortunately, I seem to have misplaced my identification." He gestured toward his companions. "We were engaged in an undercover operation, and the suspect got the upper hand, locked us in his study, and turned on the gas..."

The officer held up his hand. "Stop! Before we go any further... If this was an FBI affair, I'm not the guy to talk to. You'll have to report to my commanding officer. He's in charge of anything involved with the FBI." He turned to his partner. "Take these folks down to headquarters. Find them something to wear and take them to Chief Chatworthy. I'll stay here until the fire is under control."

"Yes, sir." The officer motioned toward one of the police cars. "If you'll follow me..."

Vincent helped Godfrey up from the ground and Agnes from the curb. "Can you walk?"

"I think so." Agnes took Godfrey's arm and they hobbled after the officer toward the street.

An hour later, wearing black and white striped jumpsuits intended for inmates at the county jail, Godfrey, Vincent, and Agnes were seated in an interview room at the San Francisco Police Department headquarters. Rosy-cheeked, Katherine joined the others in the interrogation room.

"We're all here. What took you so long?" Agnes patted the chair next to her.

"I had to wait for someone to bring me a washcloth and soap so I could get all this heavy stage make-up off my face." She gestured to her striped jumpsuit. "And this is the best they could give me to wear."

"My dear," Godfrey joked as he pulled out a chair. "Stripes become you."

"Indeed," Agnes added. "I never favored black and white stripes, myself, but on you, they look good."

"Oh, stop! You guys. This is no laughing matter." Katherine hid her face in her hands.

"I suppose you want coffee?" Agnes poured Katherine a cup from the carafe provided by the staff. She gazed into the large mirror and straightened the chopsticks in her bun. "I didn't have a comb. This is the best I could do under the circumstances."

Godfrey reached across the table and squeezed her hand. "You look fine, my love."

Agnes nodded toward the mirror. "I'll bet they're watching us from the next room. At least that's what they do in the detective movies. That's not a regular mirror, you know. It's a window. They could have a crowd back there watching us, eating popcorn, and laughing their heads off." She gazed around the room, empty except for the scratched table and metal chairs. Just the sort of dismal room one would expect to squeeze confessions from the dregs of society. The door opened and an officer stepped in with a notebook under his arm.

"I'm Chief Chatworthy. I see that you've had an opportunity to freshen up and we've found you something to wear. I'm sorry we don't have anything better to offer." His face flushed. "Hope you can get home okay without these clothes causing you trouble."

Vincent spoke up. "This is fine. We appreciate the clothing and hospitality."

The chief sat. "I heard about your ordeal. So, let's get right to it and see if we can figure out what happened."

Godfrey forced a smile. "We're all happy to be here. An hour ago, I wasn't so sure we'd be having this conversation."

The chief picked up his pen. "*Humm ...* So, who wants to start? Why were you in that house, and exactly what happened?"

Over the next fifteen minutes, between Vincent and Godfrey and a few additional details from Katherine, the officer heard the whole story of Dr. Schatzsman stealing the Good Shepherd painting, his ad in the San Francisco examiner, Katherine and Vincent's charade as would-be buyers and their attempt to purchase the stolen painting. They finished their tale with only a few of Agnes and Godfrey's untimely interventions.

The chief's face paled when they told how they were locked in the office at pistol point with the gas creeping under the door. He shook his head. "You're all lucky to be alive. With the gas filling the rooms, any spark could have set off an explosion. Even a phone call could have..." Vincent and Godfrey exchanging quick glances caught his eye. "What?"

"I heard a phone ring just as I dropped onto the lawn and Vincent pulled me toward the street." Godfrey glanced at Agnes. "That must be what caused the spark that made it blow!"

"I heard it too!" Vincent said. "Do you think the doctor called, hoping to set off the explosion?"

Agnes's open hand smacked the table. "Dad blame it! I wouldn't put it past him. Once he was safely away, he probably figured that would finish us off."

The chief rapped for attention. "Wait now. You're saying the gas leak wasn't an accident? That's a pretty serious claim. You're suggesting this was attempted murder? We don't take such accusations lightly."

Godfrey tugged at the neck of his jumpsuit. "It was no accident. Even if the doctor didn't make that phone call, I'd say his intent was pretty clear when he locked us in a room at gunpoint and turned on the gas. Just how seriously should we take it?"

The officer nodded. "I concede your point. I'll have you sign a formal complaint and we'll bring the doctor in for questioning." He slid his chair back. "Well, if there's nothing else you want to add, that's all we'll need today. An officer will drive you back to your cars and you can be on your way. Your local police department can follow up with any more needed information. Chief Waddlemucker, right?" He scribbled the name on his report, nodded to the ladies, and left the room.

"Well," Vincent said. "Doesn't sound like he's terribly interested. I have a hunch the good doctor is on his way to Mexico by now, anyway." He glanced at the wall clock. "We better get going. It's going to take several hours to get home."

Agnes stood and straightened the legs on her jumpsuit. "You're assuming we can get back to Newbury. Even if the cars weren't damaged by the fire, we have no car keys, no driver's licenses, and no money or ration tickets for gas."

"We stopped for gas right outside of San Francisco," Godfrey said. "My car has plenty of gas. How's yours, Vincent?"

"I'll likely need to borrow gas money to get us home. I was planning to fill up before we left town." He grasped Katherine's hand. "What about our motel rooms. Are we still spending the night here?"

"I don't want to stay in San Francisco any longer than necessary, since I have nothing to wear except striped prison pajamas. I just want to go home."

"Then, I assume the idea of getting married is off the table too, right?" Vincent chuckled.

Katherine shook her head. "I never planned to wear black and white stripes to my wedding, but, it would be quite a story to tell our grandchildren, wouldn't it?"

Chapter Thirty-Nine

"What are you wearing jail clothes?" Emily Tinesdale

As promised, Chief Chatworthy provided an officer to drive Agnes and company back to Geary Street to their cars. Due to fire hoses and apparatus strewn across the street, the police car stopped several house-lengths away from the burnt remains of the mansion. A fine layer of ash covered the top of Godfrey's car, parked closest to the front of the decimated building. Only one fire truck and crew remained, tramping back and forth across the damp pavement, winding hoses and removing pieces of rubble blown from the fire into the street. The smell of burning wood still hung in the air. A blackened fireplace jutted from the ragged half-wall still standing. Steam rose from the soaked ashes and an electrical wire hung haphazardly near what remained of the brick steps on the front porch.

"Oh my!" Agnes opened the door of the police car and stepped onto the sidewalk. "To think how close we came to …"

Katherine stepped out behind her. "Don't think about that, Grandma. We're all safe. We'll be in our own beds tonight." She stared for a moment at the wreckage and then reached back into the police car to retrieve the blanket and bathrobe she'd borrowed. "I have to return these things to the lady down the street. You don't have to wait. Why don't you and Godfrey get started for home? We'll be along later." She nodded down the street toward Vincent's car. She leaned back into the car. "Thank you, officer, for the ride."

"You folks take it easy, now." The officer removed a five dollar bill from his wallet. "You might need this on the way home."

Katherine took the bill. "Why, thank you. I wasn't sure what we were going to do. Give me your address. We'll pay you back."

"No need. Help someone else when you get a chance." He waved and drove away.

While Godfrey and Vincent worked under the hood to get the cars started without keys, Katherine walked down the block to the Victorian mansion carrying the bathrobe and blanket she borrowed from the neighbor. Only a few hours before, in desperation, she had raced up these same steps and pounded on the door. She realized that she didn't know the kind woman's name, who, without question, had taken her in, nearly hysterical, and clad only in her underwear. What a remarkable woman, to have such compassion for a stranger in such a state. Now, though still inappropriately clad in a prisoner's jumpsuit, she knocked on the door and stood back. She could hear the canary twittering inside. Her gaze moved toward the lovely wicker swing on the porch and the flower bowls overflowing with petunias and marigolds hanging from the ceiling, none of which she'd noticed earlier that day.

The door creaked open and her Good Samaritan peeked out. "Hello? Oh, it's you. My stars, you're lovely. I hardly recognized you. At least you're fully dressed, though it's not much of an improvement. Come in, come in. I've been so worried about you. Why are you wearing jail clothes? You haven't escaped from jail this time, have you?"

Katherine glanced down at her black and white striped jumpsuit. "No. We filled out a report at the police department. It's the only clothing they had, but at least it's clothes." She held out the bathrobe and the blanket. "I wanted to thank you for your kindness." She stepped through the door. "Considering the state I was in earlier, not many people would have helped me. For that matter, I guess I'm still not fit to be seen in public."

"Oh, *pshaw*! No trouble at all. Won't you sit down? It won't take a minute to put the kettle on to boil and make us a nice cup of tea. I want to hear all about...whatever happened down there." She jerked her head toward the smoldering ruins down the street.

"I really don't have time for tea, but I did promise to come back and tell you..." It occurred to Katherine that perhaps she shouldn't go into too many details with the doctor still on the loose. She didn't wish to frighten the woman. "By the way, my name is Katherine Odboddy." She put out her hand and they shook hands.

"I'm Emily Tinesdale. Surely, you can sit for a minute. I have so few guests these days."

Katherine sat. "Okay, for a minute. My grandmother was grateful for the blanket. You see, we were trapped on the third floor when the fire started and we had to tie our clothing together to make a rope so we could climb out the window." That was fairly close to the truth, without going into details about Dr. Schatzsman locking them in the office. Best leave those details for another day. She gazed at the canary, gurgling by the fireplace.

"Oh, my dear! How terrible for you. Now I understand why you were nearly naked as a jaybird when you came to my door." Mrs. Tinesdale shook her head. "And, that divine house up in smoke. *Tsk tsk!* I suppose all that lovely art work was lost, too?"

Katherine's head snapped back at the mention of the art work. "Art work? You've been in the house and seen it?"

"All Mrs. Pustlebuster's beautiful paintings? Of course. We visit back and forth from time to time. She runs that delightful art studio downtown. Folks say some of those pictures are worth oodles of money, but I never cared for that crazy modern artwork. Picassy and Dolly and such." She gestured toward a pastoral painting over the fireplace. "I much prefer more realistic scenes, like that one. I purchased it at her studio last year when she held her grand opening."

"Let me get this straight. You said the house belongs to Mrs. Pustlebuster? Not Dr. Schatzsman?"

"Who? Oh, you must mean that man who comes for a few days every month or so and brings in those wooden crates? I assumed he was some sort of buyer, delivering art work from overseas."

Wouldn't Grandma be shocked when she heard that City Councilman Horatio Pustlebuster and Dr. Schatzsman were in cahoots, selling stolen art work in a San Francisco art gallery? On the other hand, any man who would insist on the destruction of an innocent animal like Shere Khan certainly wouldn't hesitate to sell a few stolen paintings. Katherine stood. "I really must go. My fiancé is waiting in the car. But, thank you again for your kindness." Mrs. Tinesdales's canary burst into song as she backed toward the door, turned the knob and scurried down the steps. His shrill melody followed Katherine down the sidewalk to where Vincent waited in his car.

Chapter Forty

"Home again, home again, jiggity-jig!" Godfrey

On the long drive back to Newbury, the conversation in Godfrey's car concerned Dr. Schatzsman's art theft and the disturbing day's events. Much praise was afforded to Godfrey for attacking the doctor when he and Vincent scuffled for the pistol. Striking Vincent with the poker by mistake was not mentioned in Agnes's praise. Bursting into the house during Vincent's citizen's arrest was lightly skipped over, as well, while Dr. Schatzsman's evil intent to commit murder was expounded upon with gusto. Agnes proclaimed if her chopsticks had a sharper point, she could have picked the lock and they could have escaped long before gas filled the house, and they would never have had to go through the window in the first place. Godfrey was certain that his decision to break the window was the deciding factor in saving their lives. He opined that his plan to use the drapes and their clothing to make a rope to climb from the window was surely the difference between their lives and death. Agnes agreed.

With such a vigorous and exhilarating conversation, it seemed no time at all between San Francisco and Newbury and by 10:15 P.M., Godfrey pulled up in front of Agnes's house. "Home again, home again, jiggity-jig!" Godfrey chuckled and reached for Agnes's hand. "I expect you're glad to be home, my love." He drew her hand to his lips. "One of these days I won't have to say good-by at the curb."

"It has been quite a day, to be sure."

Godfrey got out of his car, walked around, and opened Agnes's door. He walked her to the front porch, pulled her into his arms, and kissed her cheek. "So with a kiss, I'll say good-night. I do think you look fetching in stripes."

Agnes giggled. "Tomorrow? I'm making ox-tail stew for dinner, if you'd like to join us."

"I'll be here with bells on." Godfrey returned to his car and waited until Agnes was safely inside the front door with the lights turned on. She turned to wave through the window as he drove away.

As Vincent's car reached the outskirts of Santa Rosa, there was a good deal of chatter regarding Dr. Schatzsman's art theft and his evil intent to commit murder. To his amazement, Katherine informed him what she learned about Horatio Pustlebuster and his wife's involvement with the art-theft ring. She was convinced her ruse as an elderly socialite would have succeeded in capturing the doctor red-handed if Grandmother and Godfrey had stayed in Newbury where they belonged. They both felt Godfrey's untimely interference and clubbing Vincent with a fireplace poker was the only reason Schatzsman got control of the pistol and, subsequently, imprisoned them in the doctor's study. Katherine avowed that Grandmother's attempt to pick the lock with her chopstick was a fool's errand. Vincent opined that *his* plan to use the drapes and their clothing to make a rope to climb from the window was surely the only thing that saved their lives. Katherine agreed.

At 10:55, Vincent pulled in front of Katherine's house. For the next thirty minutes, his car sat at the curb and the windows steamed up like the front window in a Chinese laundry. At last, Vincent exited the car, escorted Katherine to the front door and pulled her into his arms. "Good night, my love. One of these days I won't have to leave you at the front door."

Katherine's face warmed. "Will you speak to Chief Waddlemucker tomorrow?"

"First thing. He needs to know the connection between Pustlebuster and Schatzsman and what happened in San Francisco. I'm not sure Chief Chatworthy will follow up unless Waddlemucker contacts him. I'll see you tomorrow."

"Can't be soon enough. I'll expect you for dinner tomorrow night for a full report. Grandma's making ox-tail stew."

With a final kiss, Vincent returned to his car, and when Katherine was safely inside, he drove away.

No sooner had she stepped inside and tossed her coat onto the coat rack, when Grandmother came into the living room. "Thank goodness we're home and this day is over at last," she said.

Katherine dropped onto the sofa and leaned her head back against the cushions. "I feel like I've been awake for days." She closed her eyes and sighed. "Guess what Mrs. Tinesdale, the lady who loaned us the bathrobe, said? Dr. Schatzsman doesn't own the house that burned."

"He doesn't? Whose house is it?"

"Horatio Pustlebuster. He and his wife are in cahoots with Schatzsman."

"Say, what?" Grandma slumped into the sofa chair beside the fireplace.

"Apparently, Horatio stole the paintings and his wife sold them at her art studio in down town San Francisco."

"You mean I was wrong about Schatzsman? Horatio was the thief? But, as you said, they were both involved with selling the stolen art work in San Francisco. Any dirt-bag capable of the shenanigans here in Newbury, wouldn't think twice about stealing and selling the art work. I wonder what Pustlebuster will do when he hears Schatzsman burned down his house?"

"Schatzsman is probably long gone," Grandmother said, "and Pustlebuster is none the wiser about what happened. How long do you suppose it will take to nab Schatzsman?"

"They'll likely pick him up at the Mexican border hiding inside a taco truck. Pustlebuster and his wife are in for a big surprise when they're arrested for art theft." Katherine moved the San Francisco Examiner newspaper and put her feet up on the coffee table.

"By the way, Katherine, this morning when I spoke to Colonel Farthingworth, he said you and Vincent never showed up at the military base to fetch Shere Khan. As it happens, I'd already changed my mind about letting him go, but I was curious what happened." Agnes pushed Katherine's feet off the coffee table.

Katherine's eyes sparkled. "Was that just this morning? It feels like a hundred years ago. We decided you were wrong and we couldn't go along with you. It wasn't right to send Shere Khan to Oregon when he was perfectly situated at the military base. We figured we'd deal with you when we got back. So, Vincent turned the truck around and we headed for San Francisco to get the painting back. There was no way I could let that poor tiger live in a tiny cage. He's a spoiled, pampered pet. He'd never survive."

"You're probably right. If it wasn't for those pills that Dr. Schatzsman gave me, I'd have never thought it was a good idea. When I came to my senses and contacted Colonel Farthingworth this morning, he said he'd decided to challenge my decision, as well. He wasn't about to release the tiger, either."

"It seems we all came to the same conclusion about the same time," Katherine said.

"*Humph!*" Agnes paced the living room. "But, going after the painting without me … As soon as I saw that ad circled in the Examiner … I knew what you were up to."

"So, naturally, you thought it was a good idea to interfere and follow us down there?"

Grandmother's face flushed. "I suppose… We only came because…because I was…*um*…afraid for your safety."

Katherine leaned forward. "Fat lot of good it did for you and Godfrey to burst in. We had everything under control until…until…" She paused and shook her head. "Maybe it's best if we don't talk anymore about it. Sometimes it's best not to…"

Katherine knew Grandmother would sooner pass a kidney stone than admit the real reason she went to San Francisco. She couldn't allow anyone else to get the credit for bringing down the doctor when her previous efforts failed. And, she certainly didn't want to admit that Godfrey's and her interference caused their capture.

Katherine slid off the sofa and headed for the kitchen. "I'm starving. Do you want a sandwich?" She pulled bread from the breadbox, opened the icebox, and retrieved the liverwurst.

Grandmother took the liverwurst from Katherine. "Run on over to Mavis's and bring Maddie home. I'll put the kettle on for tea and have sandwiches ready by the time you get back."

A few minutes later, sitting at the kitchen table with a sandwich in her hand, Maddie asked, "When are we going to visit Shere Khan? I miss him."

Katherine and Grandmother exchanged a quick glance. "You know, that's a good idea," Grandma said. "I'll call Colonel Farthingworth in the morning and get permission to visit as soon as possible. You know, Shere Khan is very happy on the base with Charles," she said as she smiled at the child.

"Katherine? I have an idea." Maddie took a swallow of milk. "When you and Vincent get married, Shere Khan can carry your rings down the aisle." She giggled into her sleeve. "Wouldn't that be funny?"

Katherine put her hand to her cheek. "Why, Maddie. What an idea. What makes you think we're going to get married? Grandma's the one wearing an engagement ring, not me. Why don't we let Shere Khan carry the rings at her wedding?" She glanced at Grandmother with a smirk.

"Grandma, when are you and Godfrey getting married?" Maddie asked.

Grandmother twisted Godfrey's ring. "That's a decision that needs further discussion. We should get Katherine married first, and then we'll talk about me, okay?"

Chapter Forty-One

"Oh, dear Lord, what has my meddling wrought?" Agnes

Agnes slept late the following morning. Every bone in her body ached as she sat up and glanced at the clock. 7:45 A.M. No small wonder after yesterday's fiasco.

Ling-Ling jumped onto the bed, purring like a lawnmower. She pawed at the covers as if to say, *Get your lazy bones out of bed. Katherine won't feed me. I could waste away from starvation.*

Agnes swiped her hand down Ling-Ling's silver back, slipped out from under the covers, and dressed. She stood in front of the bathroom mirror and wound her hair into a bun. Satisfied she had done all that was possible to make herself presentable for the day, she gave her hair a final pat, shoved the silver chopsticks firmly into her bun, and headed for the kitchen. Ling-Ling pranced beside her on chocolate-colored paws, anxiously awaiting her breakfast.

Maddie and Katherine sat at the kitchen table eating oatmeal. "Good-morning, Grandma. How do you feel this morning?"

"Like I've been run over by a train, otherwise fine. You?"

"I'll survive." Katherine grinned, stood and hurried to the bathroom to finish combing her hair.

"Maddie? What shall we do today? Agnes poured a cup of coffee and sat at the table.

"Could we go and visit Charles and Shere Khan?"

"*Um* ... I don't know. I have some business to sort out. Maybe, this afternoon."

"Okay." She ran to the bathroom. "Katherine. Grandma says

maybe we can visit Shere Khan today."

Agnes glanced at the kitchen clock. 8:05 A.M. Perhaps the chief would be in his office by now. If he hadn't heard from the chief at the San Francisco Police Department, it was time he learned about the attempt on their lives. She dialed the police department and listened while it rang. "Hello? Connect me with Chief Waddlemucker, please." The operator connected the call.

"Hello? Chief? Mrs. Odboddy here. I need to see you immediately. Can you stop by? I've got Maddie today, so I can't come to the office… Yes… As soon as possible, please. It's very important. Okay. See you soon." She hung up the phone.

Katherine came into the kitchen, dressed for work. "I'm leaving. Will you be okay? I could call Myrtle and stay home today."

"No. You go on to work. You have appointments. Maddie and I will be fine. The chief is coming by in a little while. I'll call you later and let you know if anything's changed."

"Okay." Katherine kissed Maddie and went out the front door. Within a minute, her car pulled away.

Maddie returned to her room to play with her dolls, Agnes warmed her cup of coffee, and sat at the table to read the morning newspaper.

Bing Bong!

Was that the chief already? He must have jumped into his car and driven right over.

Agnes hurried to open the door. "Come on in…*Pustlebuster?*" The hair on the back of her neck stood on end. What could he want?

Considering yesterday's events and his involvement with Schatzsman, showing up this early didn't bode well for her future health. Maddie was safe in her room with the door shut. Best keep their voices low so the child wouldn't come into the living room.

"Mrs. Odboddy. So nice to see you again. Sorry I didn't call. I was in the neighborhood." The tall man with slicked back red hair stepped inside and took off his hat. He shoved the door shut before Agnes could make a move to stop him.

I'll just lolly-coddle him until Chief Waddlemucker gets here. "Mr. Pustlebuster, whatever are you doing here? I thought our business was settled when we took Shere Khan out of the county." She inched her way across the living room toward the fireplace where the pokers stood on the hearth. If he tried any funny business, she could always grab one to defend herself.

Pustlebuster bent his long legs and sat on the edge of the sofa. "I'm sure you meant to ask me to sit down. We need to talk."

Agnes sat on the sofa chair beside the fireplace. "Of course. What's on your mind? You won't mind if I don't offer you tea."

Pustlebuster sniffed, ignoring the insult. "I've had some dreadful news. I learned you and your friends were in my house in San Francisco when it *accidently* caught fire. I came to express my deepest and most heartfelt apology for what happened. I was pleased to hear you got out without injury." Mr. Pustlebuster tented his long, skinny fingers and moved them together and apart like a spider dancing against a mirror.

Agnes tossed her head. "Oh, weren't we the lucky ones to escape the locked room. I'm sure it must have been horrifying, learning about the loss of your home and all that artwork. Dr. Schatzsman must be prostrate with grief at his role in the explosion. I do hope you were insured." Agnes inched her fingers against the crocheted edges of the doily on the arm of her chair, moving them a bit closer to the fireplace poker.

The councilman waved his hand dismissively. "I was insured to the max. No harm done. Losing my personal collection of a few minor works was incidental. I feel terrible you folks were inconvenienced in any way due to the accident."

"Accident?" Agnes looked up at the councilman. "Is that what Dr. Schatzsman told you? That it was an accident?"

Mr. Pustlebuster's eyelids crumpled into a fixed glare. "You know what? This unpleasantness between us has got to stop. I figure we're about even. Your attempt to murder me at city hall trumps an accidental fire in San Francisco, don't you think?"

Agnes's mouth dropped open. City hall? Attempted murder? How could he possibly know about her delusional ideation to kill him several weeks back? Who knew? Dr. Thigpen in Boyles Springs had some inkling of her murderous fantasies, but no details. Dr. Schatzsman found her pistol at city hall, but couldn't have known why she brought it. The only person she'd confided the whole sordid details, was Chief Waddlemucker... Had he betrayed her confidence?

Warmth crept up her neck and burned into her cheeks. "What a peculiar thing to say. What do you mean? I attempted to murder you at city hall? What a ridiculous accusation." Agnes's heart thumped against her chest. She clasped her hands to keep them from trembling.

"Now, Agnes, don't play coy with me. When I found your pistol in the rubble, I wondered why you brought it to city hall. As president of the city council, I have access to police department records, so I checked the files. What a surprise to find your confession on Chief Waddlemucker's report. It was most enlightening." His gaze lowered and his mouth pulled into a hard line. "You're not going to deny the details of his report, are you?"

The tingles on the back of Agnes's neck raced up the back of her head and settled in a shooting pain across her forehead. All this time, she'd thought Schatzsman had found her pistol, but it was Pustlebuster who spirited it away. She swallowed a lump in her throat. "Then, why did Dr. Schatzsman leave my pistol in the theater alley? Why implicate me in the assault on the guard?"

Pustlebuster's laugh chilled her bones. "Don't be silly. Our good doctor had nothing to do with the theft of the Reep lithograph. I was the one at the theater and left the pistol in the alley to discredit your accusations against Schatzsman. Couldn't have my partner arrested when we'd begun to work so well together, now, could I?"

Agnes's heart raced. All this time, she'd thought… "Why are you telling me this?"

"I want to call a truce, Agnes. I have something on you, and you have something on me. You recant your story about Schatzsman locking you in the study yesterday. Admit it was an accident. In return, I won't take Chief Waddlemucker's report of your attempted murder confession to the *Newbury Gazette*. Imagine what a stir that would make. That sounds fair, doesn't it?"

Agnes stood and paced the living room. While she debated with the old reprobate, her mind raced. He had possession of some damning information. Not that she had such a stellar reputation, but telling the story of her attempted murder plot in the newspaper could do great harm to her and Katherine's reputation. The chief could be forced to file *conspiracy to commit murder* charges against her. But, her lapse of judgment had nothing to do with Katherine or Godfrey or Vincent. "I wasn't alone in the library," she said. "As an FBI agent, Vincent would never go along with such an arrangement."

"I've heard that children can be involved in all kinds of fatal accidents, and you've got such a sweet little girl. I'm sure you can help your friends realize the wisdom of our arrangement."

Agnes's heart seized. He was threatening Maddie. Perhaps such a threat could keep Vincent and Godfrey and Katherine from telling the truth about the San Francisco fire, but it didn't change the evidence concerning the stolen art work finding its way into Mrs. Pustlebuster's San Francisco art gallery. "You're asking the impossible. You and Dr. Schatzsman are robbing houses and selling the art work in San Francisco. I don't have any control over that investigation."

"How you talk against the doctor and me. We're pillars of the community, men of sterling reputations. Any further ridiculous charges such as that must stop, if you know what's good for your little family. You're probably right that further procurement of art work should cease for the time being, until all this damaging gossip has ended."

Pustlebuster stood. "Well, I think we understand each other. I'll leave you with this thought. Some secrets are best left unsaid, for all concerned. Don't you agree?"

The trembling in Agnes's knees left her almost unable to bear her weight. She opened her mouth, but said nothing. There was nothing to say. She was caught, like a rat in a trap, and there was no escape. Any further talk on her part could result in her own misfortune or threaten Maddie's safety.

How she wished she had one of those bugging thing-a-ma-jigs installed in the living room, like in the Ellery Queen movies. Pustlebuster admitted the burglaries, finding her pistol, and framing her for the attack on the night watchman. He even admitted knowing the doctor tried to kill them in the fire. But, if he produced the report of her delusional attempt on his life, who would be believed? A confessed murderer or two pillars of society?

A shadow near the kitchen door caught her gaze. Had Maddie come out of her room?

Pustlebuster reached for the doorknob. "I don't think there's any more to discuss, so I'll be taking my—"

"Not so fast, Pustlebuster."

Agnes's head whipped around. *Chief Waddlemucker?* Never in her seventy-something years had Agnes been so pleased to have a man sneak up behind her with a pistol. If the chief overheard the councilman's confession, it was even better than an Ellery Queen bugging device.

Chief Waddlemucker stepped into the living room, both hands wrapped around his silver-plated pearl-handled revolver. He released one hand from the pistol and pulled handcuffs from his back pocket.

Ling-Ling slipped from the kitchen, wove through his legs and leaped onto the sofa. *Meow!*

The chief's head flew back, his eyes closed, and his body contorted. He dropped the handcuffs, raised his hand to his nose...and sneezed! Taking advantage of the chief's momentary lapse, Pustlebuster sprang across the room, knocked the gun from Waddlemucker's hand and plowed his head into the official's protuberant belly. They tumbled to the floor and Ling-Ling streaked from the living room. Her furry little feet thudded down the hall and into the garage.

Shocked by the sudden attack, Agnes stood riveted to the floor as the men scrabbled for the gun. Remembering how her chopstick had saved her once before in a similar situation, she pulled it from the back of her hair and plunged it into Pustlebuster's thigh. He howled and clutched his leg. The chief retrieved his pistol and scooted away from his attacker. "Hold it right there!" He struggled to his feet, retrieved his handcuffs from the floor, and slipped them onto Pustlebuster's wrists. "Now, sit your rump-ass back down while we sort this out."

Pustlebuster dropped onto the sofa with a mumbled curse.

"Are you okay, Chief?" Agnes placed a shaking hand on his shoulder.

"Better than a minute ago when your cat nearly put a permanent kink in my career. That was quick thinking on your part, by the way. Thanks."

"Were you in the kitchen all this time, listening? How much did you hear?" Agnes crossed her fingers behind her back and held her breath.

"I came in around the part where he left your pistol at the theater, so pretty much everything—certainly enough to put this scumbag away for five-to-ten."

Pustlebuster slumped on the sofa, his complexion now tinged an unhealthy green.

"How did you get in the house, Chief?" Agnes straightened his rumpled collar.

"I heard from the San Francisco detective. He mentioned Pustlebuster's involvement in the art thefts. When I drove up and saw his car out front, figured I'd better go around back. I saw Maddie through her bedroom window reading to the cat, so I motioned for her to open the back door. I sent her over to your next door neighbor."

"It's a good thing she was home today. I guess things always work out for the best."

"Speaking of things working out, you know that Good Shepherd painting you were so worried about? The one stolen from the church?"

Agnes sighed. "Yes. I'm afraid it was destroyed in yesterday's fire."

Chief Waddlemucker chuckled. "Well, not so fast. The San Francisco P.D. put out an All-Points-Bulletin as soon as you guys filed your report about the fire. Schatzsman was stopped at the Mexico border a few hours later. Guess what he had in the back seat of his car? The Good Shepherd painting, a *Picasser* and a *Salvadory Dolly,* and a couple others. I guess he took along a few of his favorite paintings figuring he could sell them in Mexico to finance his get-away."

"Chief! I could almost kiss you. That's the best news I've heard all day. You have to admit, without my help, you'd have never caught these scum-buckets."

"You're right. If you ever stop pointing out the bad guys, I might as well retire. Now, help me get this hockey-puck off your couch and into my vehicle. I'll be half the day filling out paperwork. What are you planning to do now?"

The screech of tires took Agnes to the front window. She pulled back the curtain as Katherine leaped from her car and rushed into the house. "Grandma? Are you okay?"

"What are you doing back? You just left a few minutes ago."

"Mavis called with some story about Chief Waddlemucker being in the backyard with a gun. She gazed between Mr. Pustlebuster on the sofa and the chief. "Care to explain this?"

"Time for me to take our friend to the hoosegow. On your feet, buster. *Heh Heh!* Get it? Pustlebuster!" The chief pulled Pustlebuster to his feet and out the door.

While Agnes made a fresh pot of coffee, Katherine fetched Maddie from Mavis's house. Maddie returned carrying a black and white kitten. "Can we keep him, Grandma? Mrs. Wilkey's son brought him home from his trip to Oregon. She gave him to Mavis but she said I could have him if it was okay with you. I named him Sasha. If Katherine says it's okay, can we keep him?"

"I don't know. What will Ling-Ling think about a little intruder in her world?"

Katherine made a bed for the kitten near the stove where he promptly curled up and went to sleep, his tail curled around his nose. "*Aww*. Look how cute he is. Why, look how many toes he has on each foot." She stroked the tiny white paw and pinched his foot to extend his claws.

Agnes poured two mugs with coffee and sat at the table. Maddie kept an eye on the sleeping kitten while Agnes and Katherine discussed the excitement with Pustlebuster and Chief Waddlemucker.

"With everything settled, we can finally breathe again," Katherine said. "Grandma and Godfrey are engaged. The Good Shepherd picture will soon be back where it belongs and the thieves in jail. And best of all, Shere Khan has a fine caretaker and is able to entertain folks to his heart's content."

Maddie scrunched up her face. "I miss Shere Khan. We haven't seen him for ever so long. Grandma said we could visit him today. Maybe we can take a picnic and stop at the ocean and see the seals."

Katherine and Agnes exchanged a quick glance. Agnes's face lit up with a delighted smile. "You know? That's exactly what I had in mind. I can't think of a better way to celebrate our good fortune. I'll call Colonel Farthingworth and tell him we're coming for a visit. Maybe Godfrey would like to come along." Agnes stood and reached for the telephone. "And, when I see Shere Khan, I'm going to give him the biggest kiss he's ever had...right on the end of his furry orange nose."

About Elaine Faber

Elaine Faber lives in Elk Grove, CA, with her husband and a feline companion. She is a member of Sisters in Crime (SIC), Cat Writers Association (CWA), and Northern California Publishers and Authors (NCPA). Elaine volunteers with the American Cancer Society. She has published nine cozy mystery novels, and an anthology of cat stories. Her short stories are also published in 21 independent anthologies.

Black Cat's Legacy ~ Thumper meets Kimberlee and with the aid of his ancestors' memories, helps her pursue her father's cold case murder. http://tinyurl.com/lrvevgm

Black Cat and the Lethal Lawyer ~ Thumper (Black Cat) goes to Texas and confronts an embezzling attorney and thwarts an attempted murder plot. http://tinyurl.com/q3qrgyu

Black Cat and the Accidental Angel ~ Black Cat and his companion are left behind following an MVA and find new adventures on an emu farm. http://tinyurl.com/y4eohe5n

Black Cat and the Clue in Dewey's Diary ~ Kimberlee follows clues to stolen gold coins in Austria, as Black Cat faces intrigue in home town Fern Lake. http://tinyurl.com/vgyp89s

Mrs. Odboddy—Hometown Patriot ~ Eccentric Mrs. Odboddy is determined to expose Nazi spies and conspiracies on every hand. http://tinyurl.com/hdbvzsv

Mrs. Odboddy—Undercover Courier ~ Mrs. Odboddy prevents Nazi spies from stealing the 'secret documents' she is carrying by train to President Roosevelt. http://tinyurl.com/jn5bzwb

Mrs. Odboddy—And Then There was a Tiger ~ Falsely accused, Agnes seeks the missing war bond money and befriends a displaced carnival tiger. https://tinyurl.com/yx72fcpx

The Spirit Woman of Lockleer Mountain ~ Is the woman in the woods a missing neighbor, or is she the local Native American's Spirit Woman? http://tinyurl.com/y7rp7f3x

All Things Cat ~ Twenty-one short stories about, or written by cats from all walks of life. http://tinyurl.com/y9p9htak

Mrs. Odboddy's Desperate Doings ~ Determined to expose an art thief, Agnes also vows to find a safe and permanent home for Shere Khan, the displaced tiger.

Elaine's Website http://www.mindcandymysteries.com

Historical Facts Used in This Novel

EDWARD REEP

Edward Reep, a California resident and water color artist, became a photographer and combat artist for the United States Army during WWII. Widely publicized in newspapers and magazines, Reep's poignant war-time depictions made him popular with the public before and after the war. He was awarded a Guggenheim Fellowship to help finance his pursuit of art due to his outstanding contributions to war art.

JAPANESE SUBMARINES

In 1942, the Japanese navy dispatched submarines to the USA along the western coastline from Oregon to the Aleutians. Along with several other incidents, they successfully shelled a lighthouse near Vancouver Island, WA, and torpedoed and shelled a freighter off Cape Flattery, WA. The freighter was towed to safety with no loss of life. Though a factual event, the date and location was altered somewhat in our story for purposes of involving Agnes and fictionalizing the event.

OREGON HUNTING PRESERVE

During WWII, hunting of wild boar, elk, deer, bear, cougars, and other animals was legal in season with appropriate permits in Oregon. The concept of the Zeigerman Hunting Preserve with the implied suggestion that the zoo animals were then 'hunted' is fiction and in no way suggests such an event occurred.

ZOO EUTHANAZIA

During WWII many USA zoos closed due to personnel shortages but mostly due to the lack of adequate food supply needed to sustain the animals. Poor nutrition led to the death of many large animals and many more were euthanized due to the inability to properly care for and feed them. In no circumstance would an existing zoo take on a displaced carnival tiger. In such a case, the animal would likely have been euthanized. Shere Khan's plight in this novel is, therefore, based in fact.

THE GOOD SHEPHERD PAINTING

Bernhard Plockhorst is most famous for the painting of The Good Shepherd shown with a staff in one hand and a lamb in the other. He also painted the famous picture of the guardian angel watching over two children as they traversed along a dangerous cliff. His image of the face of Christ is the most accepted rendering of Christ's likeness in the Christian Church. Plockhorst was from Germany, famous during the latter part of the 1800. Copies of his paintings are in practically every Christian church and many USA homes.

AMPHETAMINES

Though home front USA citizens knew little about amphetamines during the 1940's, Hitler widely distributed Benzedrine and Pervitin to Germany's battlefield soldiers to enhance stamina, endurance, and performance. Likely many of the atrocities of war were committed due to the effects of enhanced drug use. Wide effects from amphetamines vary, but well could include the symptoms Agnes suffered from their use.

Also by Elaine Faber

Mrs. Odboddy: Hometown Patriot

Elaine Faber

Mrs. Odboddy Hometown Patriot

A WWII tale of chicks and chicanery, suspicion and spies.

Since the onset of WWII, Agnes Agatha Odboddy, hometown patriot and self-appointed scourge of the underworld, suspects conspiracies around every corner…stolen ration books, German spies running amuck, and a possible Japanese invasion off the California coast. This seventy-year-old, model citizen would set the world aright if she could get Chief Waddlemucker to pay attention to the town's nefarious deeds on any given Meatless Monday.

Mrs. Odboddy vows to bring the villains, both foreign and domestic, to justice, all while keeping chickens in her bathroom, working at the Ration Stamp Office, and knitting argyles for the boys on the front lines.

Imagine the chaos when Agnes's long-lost WWI lover returns, hoping to find a million dollars in missing Hawaiian money and rekindle their ancient romance. In the thrilling conclusion, Agnes's predictions become all too real when Mrs. Roosevelt unexpectedly comes to town to attend a funeral and Agnes must prove that she is, indeed, a warrior on the home front.

Mrs. Odboddy: Undercover Courier

Asked to accompany Mrs. Roosevelt on her Pacific Island tour, Agnes and Katherine travel by train to Washington, D.C. Agnes carries a package for Colonel Farthingworth to President Roosevelt.

Convinced the package contains secret war documents, Agnes expects Nazi spies to try and derail her mission.

She meets Irving, whose wife mysteriously disappears from the train; Nanny, the unfeeling caregiver to little Madeline; two soldiers bound for training as Tuskegee airmen; and Charles, the shell-shocked veteran, who lends an unexpected helping hand. Who will Agnes trust? Who is the Nazi spy?

When enemy forces make a final attempt to steal the package in Washington, D.C., Agnes must accept her own vulnerability as a warrior on the home front.

Can Agnes overcome multiple obstacles, deliver the package to the President, and still meet Mrs. Roosevelt's plane before she leaves for the Pacific Islands?

Mrs. Odboddy: Undercover Courier is a hysterical frolic on a train across the United States during WWII, as Agnes embarks on this critical mission.

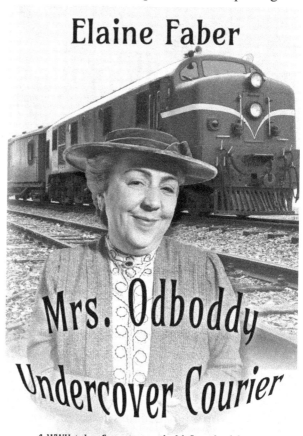

Elaine Faber

Mrs. Odboddy Undercover Courier

A WWII tale of mystery, mischief, and mishaps.

Mrs. Odboddy: And Then There Was a Tiger

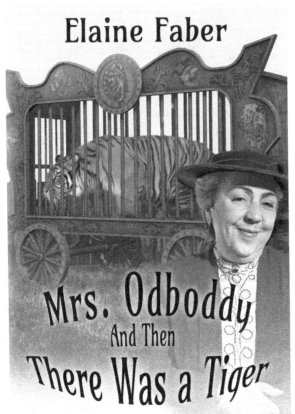

Elaine Faber

Mrs. Odboddy
And Then
There Was a Tiger

A WWII tale of conflict and carnivals, turmoil and tigers.

While the 'tiger of war' rages across the Pacific during WWII, eccentric, elderly Agnes Odboddy, 'fights the war from the home front'. Her patriotic duties are interrupted when she is accused of the Wilkey's Market burglary.

A traveling carnival with a live tiger joins the parishioner's harvest fair at The First Church of the Evening Star and Everlasting Light. Accused again when counterfeit bills are discovered at the carnival, and when the war bond money goes missing, Agnes sets out to restore her reputation and locate the money. Her attempts lead her into harm's way when she discovers a friend's betrayal and even more about carnival life than she bargained for.

Granddaughter Katherine's turbulent love triangle with a doctor and an FBI agent rivals Agnes's own on-again, off-again relationship with Godfrey.

In Faber's latest novel, your favorite quirky character, Mrs. Odboddy, prevails against injustice and faces unexpected challenges…and then There Was a Tiger!

Black Cat's Legacy

Elaine Faber

Black Cat's Legacy

A tale of intrigue and murder with a touch of whimsy.

Thumper, the resident Fern Lake black cat, knows where the bodies are buried and it's up to Kimberlee to decode the clues.

Kimberlee's arrival at the Fern Lake lodge triggers the Black Cat's Legacy. With the aid of his ancestors' memories, it's Thumper's duty to guide Kimberlee to clues that can help solve her father's cold case murder. She joins forces with a local homicide detective and an author, also researching the murder for his next thriller novel. As the investigation ensues, Kimberlee learns more than she wants to know about her father. The murder suspects multiply, some dead and some still very much alive, but someone at the lodge will stop at nothing to hide the Fern Lake mysteries.

Black Cat and the Lethal Lawyer

With the promise to name a beneficiary to her multi-million dollar horse ranch, Kimberlee's grandmother entices her and her family to Texas. But things are not as they appear and Thumper, the black cat with superior intellect, uncovers the appalling reason for the invitation. Kimberlee and Brett discover a fake Children's Benefit Program and the possible false identity of the stable master. To make matters worse, Thumper overhears a murder plot, and he and his newly found soul-mate, Noe-Noe, must do battle with a killer to save Grandmother's life.

The further Kimberlee and her family delve into things, the deeper they are thrust into a web of embezzlement, greed, vicious lies and murder. With the aid of his ancestors' memories, Thumper unravels some dark mysteries. Is it best to reveal the past or should some secrets never be told?

Elaine Faber

Black Cat and the Lethal Lawyer

A tale of betrayal and greed with a splash of fantasy.

Black Cat and the Accidental Angel

Elaine Faber

Black Cat
and the
Accidental Angel

A tale of memories lost and love found with a touch of the divine.

When the family SUV flips and Kimberlee is rushed to the hospital, Black Cat (Thumper) and his soulmate are left behind. Black Cat loses all memory of his former life and the identity of the lovely feline companion by his side. "Call me Angel. I'm here to take care of you." Her words set them on a long journey toward home, and life brings them face to face with episodes of joy and sorrow.

The two cats are taken in by John and his young daughter, Cindy, facing foreclosure of the family vineyard and emu farm. In addition, someone is playing increasingly dangerous pranks that threaten Cindy's safety. Angel makes it her mission to help their new family. She puts her life at risk to protect the child, and Black Cat learns there are more important things than knowing your real name.

Elaine Faber's e-books are available on Amazon for $3.99. Print books. $16.00.

Black Cat and the Secret in Dewey's Diary

Elaine Faber

Black Cat
and the
Secret in Dewey's Diary

A tale of history, mystery, riddles, and gold.

In this dual tale of mystery, lost treasure, and riddles, while Black Cat narrates the exciting events in Fern Lake, Kimberlee discovers a cryptic clue in a diary about a hidden treasure, and heads to Austria to solve the puzzle.

When Kimberlee and Dorian arrive in Austria, they attract the attention of a stalker determined to steal the diary in hopes the clues will lead him to the treasure first. On a collision course, it is inevitable that Kimberlee and the stalker meet in Hopfgarten.

Black Cat and Angel's lives are endangered with the arrival of Kimberlee's grandmother in Fern Lake, and the return of a man presumed dead for twenty-five years. With both arrivals, emotional and financial difficulties loom for Kimberlee's family. Since their return to Fern Lake, Angel seems reluctant or unable to adjust to her new home. Does she regret leaving Texas and Grandmother? And, when the opportunity arises, will she decide to leave Black Cat and Fern Lake.

All Things Cat

"A story isn't a story if there isn't a cat in it." Elaine Faber

All Things Cat is a selection of Elaine Faber's short stories about cats. Their stories take place both past and present in diverse surroundings: Salem, Massachusetts; a pirate ship off the coast of Maine; a haunted hotel in the Sierra Mountains; Roswell, New Mexico; the oval office in Washington, D.C., to name but a few locations.

The felines interact with extraordinary and remarkable characters including witches, leprechauns, a sewer truck driver, a hen-pecked husband driven to plot murder, and animal characters present at the birth of the Christ Child.

Some stories are self-narrated by a cat sharing most unusual circumstances—abandoned by his master, as the prize in an Old West poker game, routing a burglar in a WWII meat market, overcoming self-doubts about his hunting/stalking abilities, and adopting the First Family in the White House.

All Things Cat will delight the reader and provide a sneak peek into the heart and mind of cats from all walks of life. Elaine has brought both wit and tenderness to this charming collection of short cat stories. Several stories are excerpts from Elaine's full length cozy Black Cat Mysteries series and WWII novel, Mrs. Odboddy - Hometown Patriot.

Elaine Faber

All Things Cat

Short stories to warm the cat lover's heart.

Cover photo *Truffie* © Elaine Faber

The Spirit Woman of Lockleer Mountain

There are sightings of a woman and a mountain lion near Lockleer Mountain, seen at moments of crisis. Is she the legendary Native American's Spirit Woman, sent to protect the community? Nate is convinced his sister, missing for three months, and surely suffering from amnesia, is the elusive woman. He fears she will not survive the coming winter months, living wild in the wood with a mountain lion.

While Deputy Nate Darling pursues a relationship with Lou Shoemaker, he and Sheriff Peabody pursue a drug dealer, selling to the youth at the Native American reservation. Things are even more complicated

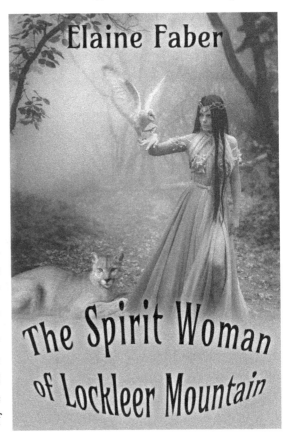

by civil unrest regarding the government's secret plans to build a mysterious facility, a big box store, and a housing tract close to Lockleer Mountain, threatening the livelihood of the local merchants.

Is there any hope that the Spirit Woman, real or imaginary, can bring harmony to the troubled community? Will Nate be able to apprehend the drug dealer, locate his missing sister, maintain his budding romance, and guarantee the financial future of Lockleer Mountain?

CPSIA information can be obtained
at www.ICGtesting.com
Printed in the USA
BVHW041350070522
636035BV00008B/1